BLOOD BROTHERS II

Reconstruction: Racism, Riots, Ratification

Ronald E Pressley and Nancy P. Holder

1122 Creations

Contents

Foreword

We have made great efforts to be historically correct in relation to all actual happenings, settings, and societal norms. If the reader detects any anachronisms, please do not allow them to ruin the story. Better yet, let us know and we may make revisions.

This novel is fiction. If readers find similarities to any persons living or dead, it is unintentional.

The story requires the use of certain dialects which we have also attempted to write in a fashion true to the period and the socio-economic level of characters. We apologize if the reader finds any of the dialogue offensive. There was no intention of disrespect, as we both hold all human life to be of value.

Introduction

The Reconstruction Period lasted little more than a decade after the Civil War, officially ending in March 1877.

Beginning with lofty intentions of reuniting the country, ensuring civil rights and opportunities to the former slaves, rebuilding the damaged South, and binding up the wounds of rebellion, it eroded into words on paper with little real-life backing.

President Lincoln's assassination and the term of President Johnson changed the focus of the administration with unfortunate results.

That the 14th and 15th Amendments to the Constitution were ratified guaranteeing citizenship to all persons born or naturalized in the United States of America and voting rights to all male citizens was a great achievement.

However, the second sentence in Section 1 of Amendment XIV received little attention or support.

> "No State shall make or enforce any laws which shall abridge the privileges or immunities of citizens of the United States; nor shall any State deprive any person of life, liberty, or property, without due process of law; nor deny any person within its jurisdiction the equal protection of the laws."

In this sequel to Blood Brothers–A Family Divided, we travel with Will Presley as he makes his way through Reconstruction, Racism, Riots, and Ratification.

> "The arc of the moral universe is long, but it bends towards justice."

Theodore Parker -1853 - 19th Century pastor

Chapter One

THE DIRTY DEED

He was not a superstitious man by nature, but somehow the nagging feeling in Will's gut was not to be ignored. The words he heard at the Surratt Boarding House continued to ring in his ears, "Them Damn Yankees are gonna pay for what they done to them people in Georgia and South Carolina. Come hell or high water, I'll make 'em pay for this."

"What do you think he means by 'makin' 'em pay for this,'?" Lenora asked.

"Don't rightly know, but I don't like tha sound of it. I've felt like for a long time tha they wuz up to something. We'll, jist keep 'er ears open an' 'er mouths shut." Will advised. "We'll find out eventually I reckon."

FORD THEATRE, April 14, 1865

Slowly creeping up the stairs to the Presidential Box in Ford's theatre, he readied his pistol. He had watched the bodyguard descend the stairs and exit the side door leading to the adjacent bar. A laugh line in the script was delivered, and the Theatre was filled with the sounds of people laughing. Booth knew his opportunity was now.

Lincoln and his wife, Mary, were laughing along with Major Henry Rathbone and his female companion, who shared the box with the President and his wife.

Lincoln Assassination

John Wilkes Booth took a deep breath, aimed the pistol, and pulled the trigger. At almost point-blank range, the force of the bullet propelled his head forward, and Abraham Lincoln was mortally wounded.

MEANWHILE, FIVE BLOCKS AWAY

"Well, that sure was a nice walk, Will," Lenora Parker spoke to her fiancé Will Presley. "It is such a beautiful Spring evening, and so relaxing."

"Yeah, Sweet Lady, it's always nice to stroll with you and hold your hand."

"Lincoln's been shot! Lincoln's been shot." An adolescent boy shouted as he ran down the street.

Grabbing his arm to stop the boy, Will demanded, "Where did it happen, and is the President still alive?"

"Down at Ford's Theatre. Don't know if he's alive or not. Saw some soldiers carrying him across the street to a house."

"Let's go over there and try to find out what's going on," Lenora suggested.

The Ford Theatre was only five blocks away from the Surratt Boarding house, where the couple had taken up residence. Lenora had a room on the second floor; Will's was on the fourth floor.

Arriving at the Ford Theatre, they encountered Judy Parker, Lenora's cousin, who worked with her at the Department of War. "What can you tell us?" Lenora quickly inquired.

"It doesn't look good for the President," she exclaimed. "Four soldiers were carrying him to that house across the street," she continued. "A young army officer and his companion who were sharing the box with the Lincolns, attempted to subdue the shooter, but the officer was stabbed in the shoulder, just before the assailant jumped down onto the stage.

"Hurriedly scaling the front of the box, and jumping, Mr. Booth (I think) landed awkwardly and injured his foot. They said he hobbled out the back door of the theater, where he was met by an associate holding a get-away horse. Before anybody could detain them, they hurried off into the night.

"A twenty-three-year-old doctor, Charles Leale, who was in the audience, rushed to assist the President. Mr. Lincoln was carried to a house just across the street by a group of soldiers and was tended by the doctor," she was sobbing.

Just after 7:00 the next morning, April 15, 1865, Lincoln succumbed.

When Will arrived for work at Fort Whipple the next morning, he heard Colonel Turner speaking to Major Williams. Turner had heard reports that an elaborate, multi-pronged scheme had been concocted to kill Lincoln, Vice-President Johnson, and Secretary of State Seward simultaneously. Thinking that they could throw the whole country into disarray by killing all three of the top men, but their plan went awry.

He droned on, "Reportedly, George Atzerodt had rented a room directly above the Vice-President. He lost his nerve and failed to act at the appointed time; so Johnson was spared and knew nothing about the plot. Lewis Powell, another co-conspirator, was supposed to slay Secretary Seward, but only wounded him. Lincoln was the only one to die." Turner was grimacing as he spoke.

Williams then spoke, "Johnson, Seward, Secretary of War Edwin Stanton, and several other cabinet members were summoned to Lincoln's bedside where they stood vigil through the night."

"Wow, that's some terrible stuff," Will exclaimed. "Whadda ye thank'll happen now?"

"They will hunt 'em all down and hang 'em, I hope," Turner retorted.

That afternoon an autopsy was performed on Lincoln, and a .44 caliber bullet fired by Booth's single-shot derringer was removed from his brain.

Two weeks later, as they sat in the parlor at Surratt House, Lenora read aloud to Will from the local newspaper, the *National Republican.* "Booth and Herold fled to a tavern in Maryland owned by Mary Surratt, who also, operated a boarding house in Washington, D.C. A doctor named Samuel A. Mudd was brought in to tend to Booth's broken ankle. After treatment, Herold took Booth and moved him to a farmhouse near Fredrick, Maryland."

"Do they think the Surratts are involved in all this?" Will wondered.

"I don't know, but Booth, Atzerodt, and Powell have all been around here a lot lately," Lenora replied.

(Booth's doctor, Mudd, was the source of what became a famous phrase, your name is Mudd.)

She continued reading, "With over 10,000 men searching, the conspirators were located two days ago hiding in a barn. When the barn was set afire by the authorities, Herold quickly surrendered.

"Booth attempted to 'shoot it out' with his opponents, but finally decided to surrender. As he walked out the front door of the collapsing barn with his hands in the air, he was shot dead by a deputy with a rifle. Herold, a half-wit, was taken into custody."

"I wonder what'll happen now here at the house," Will worried.

"Yes, me too," Lenora responded. "If the Surratts are involved in this, I don't want to live here. We had better look for another place."

"Now Lenora, let's not panic. We're gettin' married soon over where your parents live, maybe even in your family's church, Falls Church," Will was being cautious. "When we get the job in Reconstruction, we will move to wherever we're assigned. Let's just see what happens."

Mary Surratt, whose boarding house was used as a meeting place for the plotters, was convicted of conspiracy on the testimony of her Maryland tavern's manager. He testified Mary had provided him with two pistols and told him to give them to Booth when he arrived. Surratt was hanged-the first woman ever to be executed by the United States government.

The other three co-conspirators, Atzerodt, Powell, and Herold, also were executed on the gallows with Mary. Isaac and Anne Surratt continued to operate the boarding house, but John Surratt, Jr. fled to Canada and escaped judgment.

Chapter Two

A RECONSTRUCTION
ASSIGNMENT

"What are we going to do now?" Lenora asked Will.

"Well, President Lincoln's gone, and President Johnson is now 'er leader. Let's see what he has in mind. He's from Tennessee, and they got a lotta stuff tore up there, too. I thank he's gonna want it fixed back like it wuz."

"Will, didn't you serve with General Oliver Howard at Gettysburg?" Lenora asked.

"Shore did. He recommended me for a promotion and the Medal of Honor I got. He also had a unit at Antietam, but I wuz still with Burnside then."

General Oliver O. Howard was a career soldier who lost an arm in the Battle of Seven Pines in June,1862. Awarded the Medal of Honor after that battle, he was called the *Christian General,* because of his strong Christian ethics. In March,1865, he was appointed to head the Freedman's Bureau.

"Howard's the one in charge of the Freedman's Bureau. His office is in the Department of War where I work," Lenora replied.

Excitedly, Will asked, "Do you know him? Maybe you can help us get a job there."

"I don't know *him,* but my cousin Judy works for him. Congress just passed the law setting up the Freedmen's Bureau over a month ago, the 3rd of March, I think. General Howard's just now putting it all together. We have a pretty good chance. He's going to put a Regional office in Nashville. We'd probably have to move there."

Will grinned as he spoke, "You better git in touch with yer Mama and tell her ta git ready fer a weddin'."

"Are you ready for a wedding?" she smiled.

"Heck, I don't look forward to gittin' all dressed up ner nuthin', but I'm a lookin' forward ta spendin' tha rest a my life with you." Will winked at her.

"We don't have the job yet. Before we plan a wedding and moving off somewhere, let's see if we get a job," Lenora cautioned while quietly chuckling at how he always turned on the charm to make his point.

THE NEXT DAY

As soon as she got a short break at work, Lenora went looking for her cousin, Judy Parker, who was working for General Howard. Older but close in age to Lenora, Judy was a tall ash-blonde with large brown eyes. She had a ready smile and a pretty face.

"Hi Judy, I need some information. Thought maybe you could help me."

"Well, little cousin, I'll sure try," she smiled. "What can I do to help?"

"Will and I want to work in Reconstruction. I heard General Howard, your boss, was heading the Freedman's Bureau. Could you put in a good word for us or, maybe introduce us to him or something."

"Let me see what I can do. He's busy right now with Secretary Stanton, but when I find out anything, I'll yell at you."

Later in the afternoon, Judy appeared at Lenora's office door. Since the office space was shared with five other women, Judy was reluctant to share personal information.

"Lenora, can you take a break and come with me for a few minutes?"

Strolling down the hall, Judy smiled and said, "General Howard will see you in the morning. He remembers Will from Gettysburg *and* Antietam, *too.* Although the General didn't award it, he knows that Will got a medal there as well.

"Of course, you know you'll have to move somewhere down

South. What do you think Aunt Alice and Uncle Harry will say about that?"

"Don't know. We haven't told them yet. We wanted to wait and see if we could get a job first."

"I suspect you both will get a job, but it'll only last a year unless Congress extends it," Judy warned.

"The General told me he thought Will could be an assistant commissioner in charge of a department - maybe Memphis or Chattanooga. You can probably get hired as an office assistant."

"Do you think we can come back and return to our old jobs when the program ends?" Lenora worried.

"I'm certain they'll have to replace you here if you're gone for a year. There's talk going around that President Johnson will cut back in the War Department now that the war's over. Anyway, he wants you to come to his office at 7:00 A.M, tomorrow."

When Will arrived at home that afternoon, Lenora was waiting in the parlor. "We have an appointment with General Howard in the morning at 7:00. He has a full day, but will see us early, before he gets too busy."

"Great. That's super news. I hope ye thanked yer cousin."

"Of course, I thanked her. My Mama raised me right.

"What's even better is that the General remembers you as a hero. He presented you with a medal at Gettysburg and remembered that you got one at Antietam. Judy is almost certain that we both can get a job, but she said it'll only last for a year."

"Well, we'll cross that bridge when we git to it. I wonder where they'll assign us to."

"Judy thinks it'll be somewhere in Tennessee - Nashville, Memphis or Chattanooga. They plan to open offices in Knoxville and Pulaski if the program is extended. She said you might be given a job as assistant commissioner. You'd be heading an office, or at least a department."

"Wow. That'd be a good job fer us. We could do a lotta good thangs fer 'er country, 'n' try ta put thangs back like they wuz."

***

At 7:00 A.M. sharp, Will and Lenora entered the office of General Howard. "Good morning Lieutenant Presley. It's nice to see you again. I last saw you at the dedication of the Gettysburg cemetery."

"Yes Sir, it was," Will replied thinking, *'How could I ever forget one of the worst days of my life?'*

"How long will this new program last?"

"It was allowed for one year. There's no money in the Congressional budget at the present time, but there is a strong desire in Congress to get the job done."

Lenora hesitated then continued, "If we move to Tennessee or some other place, is there a chance we can get our old jobs back if it's discontinued?"

"I can't guarantee your old job back, but I can tell you that every effort will be made to find a place for you somewhere in this government. I will take care of those patriots who have been loyal to the United States of America."

Will spoke up, "Sir, I wanna contribute ta the rebuildin' er country, 'n' makin' thangs rite fer them folks who've been mistreated. I wanna raise a fam'ly in a country wher' everbody's treated equal. I thank that was Mr. Lincoln's dream, 'n' I wanna try 'n' make it happen."

"Presley, if I can find enough people like you, we *will* make it happen."

"Sir, Lenora has some office training. We're plannin' on gettin' married, and I'd like ta work with her. Would that be possible?"

"I think that can be arranged, Presley. General Fisk will be in charge of the Tennessee, Kentucky, and North Alabama region. I'll want to talk with him, but I believe you'd be a good fit to work in the Memphis office. The Regional office will be in Nashville, and we'll have another satellite office in Chattanooga."

"That sounds real good Sir," Will glanced at Lenora and smiled. "My kin folks live in North Ca'lina, so if ye open a office in Knoxville, it'd be closer ta home fer me," Will informed him.

"We'll just have to see how it goes, Presley, when and if that time comes. If Congress continues the program, then there's a chance that can happen. How quickly can you two be ready to move?"

Lenora spoke, "We have to plan a wedding first. I want to get married in my hometown of Falls Church. Then, too, we need to plan to leave our old jobs." she looked at Will for his answer.

"I would guess about a month, but we need ta talk about it before givin' ye a firm answer. Let us talk, then we'll git back with ye first of next week, General," Will replied.

"As they walked back to the wagon to return to work, Will spoke. "I know it'll be hard fer ye ta leave home, Lenora, but this is an important job we'll be a doin'. This country's got a long way ta go ta get back like it wuz, 'n' it mightn't never be tha same. But we gotta try an' fix it."

"Yes, I know Will, but I have never been so far from home I couldn't see Mama and Daddy in an hour or two. I do want to fix it, but it's just difficult to think about moving all the way to Tennessee," she wrinkled her face.

"Well, you and your Mama can start plannin' the weddin' soon as ye want to. Looks purty shore we got ourselves a job if we want it," Will was happy. "Let's go ta visit your family on Sunday and talk ta 'em 'bout it."

"Alright, but I'm certain neither one of them will be happy about the whole thing," Lenora surmised.

"Lenora, have you ever done anything your folks wuddn't happy about in your life?"

"Of course, I have. Why do you ask that?"

"Sometimes ye jist hafta go ahead 'n' do what ye thank is rite fer you. Paw used ta say, it's easier ta git forgiveness than permission.

"Tell ye what I thank we ortta do. Jist go in 'n' tell 'em what we planned 'n' be real excited about it. Betcha they won't complain too much," Will opined.

"I'll try to. I'll make sure I get the word to Daddy that we're coming on Sunday."

***

Lenora met her father when he delivered supplies on Friday. "I'm glad I caught you," she smiled, hugging her father tightly. "Will and I would like to go to church with you and Mama this Sunday, if that is alright."

Harry Parker held her face in his hands and replied, "When would it *not* be alright to have our sweet girl at home? Is this a special occasion?"

Lenora could not prevent her cheeks from turning red. As she dropped her eyes, trying not to look suspicious, she responded, "Being with my family is always special."

"I would bet that Alice will be busy tomorrow preparing our after-church feast," Harry chuckled.

"Oh, please don't go to a lot of trouble. Just being with you is enough to make me happy," Lenora said as she kissed him on the cheek.

***

Knocking on the door to Will's room early Sunday morning, Lenora asked, "Are you ready to go? It'll take us an hour to get there, and I want to go to church. The service starts at 11:00."

"Yep, I'm ready to go. Do I look proper to go to church?" Will worried.

"You'll be fine. I went to the kitchen and got us an apple and a biscuit to eat as we travel. I don't want to waste time eating breakfast," Lenora replied.

As they pulled up in front of the Parker home, Harry walked out to greet them. "Morning, Princess. You too, Presley. Y'all have a good trip over this morning?"

"Yes, Sir, we shore did Mr. Parker. Lenora got us biscuits 'n' apples. We ate breakfast as we rode." Will answered.

"Come on in the house and sit a spell. Mama's not quite ready yet. She's got a ham cooking in the oven. And she's gonna leave it cooking while we go to church."

"Well hello, Baby Girl," Alice Parker hugged Lenora. "You've been a stranger around here for a while."

"Yes Mama, we've had a lot of new things going on at work what with the Freedman's Bureau starting up and all. They're running it out of the Department of War, you know."

"Harry heard some news about that this week when he was delivering over there. Your cousin, Judy, was all excited and told him you and Will would get jobs. I think it's just wonderful that you'll help straighten out this mess we're in right now. With Mr. Lincoln being gone, I didn't know what'd happen with that," Alice was exuberant.

"That's what we came to talk to you about Mama, but can we wait until after church?" Lenora was hopeful.

As Harry walked over and hugged her, he said, "Princess, we'll talk any time you're ready, honey. Let's go to church."

After hearing Alice Parker's reaction, Will became more confident about talking with Lenora's parents about their move to Tennessee. Walking back home after church, he chatted with her father about his farm and livestock, carefully avoiding the subject of the new job. He knew that the Parker's wanted to hear from their daughter, not him.

As they sat down at the table to eat dinner, Alice Parker spoke to Lenora. "Tell us about the new jobs, Baby Girl. What will the two of you be doing?"

Hesitantly, Lenora spoke, "They want Will to be responsible for a department in a satellite office. I will work in his office as his assistant. We'll be able to work together."

"How wonderful, honey. Where will you be working?" Alice quizzed.

"We don't know for sure, yet, but they mentioned Tennessee," she whispered. "Nashville or Memphis."

"Tennessee? That's a long way from home," Alice was surprised.

Will then joined the conversation. "They have only voted for a one-year trial rite now, Mrs. Parker. If it ends in a year, we'll be comin' back here."

"Are you going to be living in a boarding house?" Harry wondered.

"That's the other thang we wanna talk about Mr. Parker," Will interjected. "We wanna go ahead an' get married before Lenora moves down there. I'll go on down an' find us a house. Lenora will stay here and' get ready for the weddin'. Will ye help her Mrs. Parker?"

"I wouldn't want her to get married *without* me helping her."

"We'll get started on it right away," Alice smiled.

"Now just hold your horses for a minute, folks. This is my Princess you're talking about here," Harry was adamant.

Will entered the conversation. "Mr. Parker, you know that Lenora 'n' me love each other, 'n' wanna spend tha rest of 'er lives tagether, 'n' our second most crucial thang is ta try 'n' fix what's been broke. '

"This job with tha Freedman's Bureau is our best chance ta do that. I hope ye know I'm a-gonna take keer of her 'n' see she stays safe. We're gonna be able ta build 'er lives tagether, raise ye some grandkids, 'n' work fer tha United States of America."

"Wow Presley, it's kind of hard to be against all that stuff you just said. You're quite the *raconteur,*" Parker smiled.

"Well, I don't rightly know what that means, but it sounds so fancy, I'll take it," Will grinned.

"It means you're a pretty convincing talker, Presley," Parker continued. "I'll miss my Princess, but for such a good cause, I guess we'll give her up for a while."

"Did you have a wedding date in mind?" Alice asked.

"It's May 28, now. I told General Howard I'd let 'im know sum'thin' by the first of tha week, and that we'd need a month to plan ta git married 'n' move. I'll tell 'im tamorrow, and plan ta go on down ta Tennessee tha first of July. If ye can be ready by tha first of August, that'd give ye about two months," Will was thinking. "I'll come home fer tha weddin', then we can start workin' purty early in August."

Alice looked at Lenora. "That should give us time to get everything together. As you know, everything inside our church was destroyed by the end of the war. That's why we have been meeting in the homes of other church members. The army used it first for a hospital and later as a stable. They did promise to repair the church, but that will take some time, so we can't have the wedding inside.

"What we can do, since the weather will be warm, is to have an outdoor ceremony on the church grounds then come back home for a nice supper."

"Oh Mama, that's a wonderful idea," Lenora said excitedly. "Getting married next to our family church will be very special."

"Of course, the time all depends on General Howard's approval, I assume," Harry interjected.

"Yep, and maybe General Fisk, too. He's tha one in charge of tha Tennessee region," Will informed them.

***

On Monday morning, Will went to see General Howard at his Department of War office. "Good morning, Sir. May I come in?"

"Of course, Presley. Do you have some news for me?" Howard asked.

"Yes Sir. Lenora 'n' me 'n' her fam'ly 'er a lookin' forward ta gittin' started with our job. I can be ready ta go on down ta Tennessee tha first of July an' git settled in. Me an' Lenora can git married 'bout tha first week of August, 'n' she can come down to start. Is that alright?" Will asked somewhat nervously.

"Yes, I think that'll work, Presley. I'll inform General Fisk of your decision. I'll have the arrangements made for your trip.

"We can put you on a Baltimore and Ohio train to Cincinnati, then on down to Louisville. You'll change trains, then go to Nashville from there. Most of the railroads in the South are inoperative now, but that'll be part of our job to get them back up 'n' running. General Fisk'll assign you a job and make travel arrangements from Nashville if need be."

"Alright, General. I'll tell Major Williams over at Fort Whipple that I'll be leavin' 'bout tha first of July," Will replied. "Thank ye, thank ye very, very, much, Sir.

Chapter Three

GRAHAM, N.C.

B ack at Roaring Fork farm in Graham County, N.C., Sally Presley, Will's mother, continued both her farming duties and her classes at the church. All four sons who remained at home worked the timber and tobacco crops.

On April 15th, 1865, Billy Bob and Pete drove onto the lot of Graham Sawmill to deliver their weekly timber load. Andy and Matt followed behind in the second wagon. The Presley boys had stayed at home during the war to handle the crops that supplied the family's means of sustenance.

"Did ye boys hear the news about Lee's surrender?" Vic Henderson inquired.

"Naw, but I bet yer afixin' ta tell us ain't ya'," Pete grinned.

Vic was a tall, slender young man with dark hair, a full beard, and a ready smile. He lost his left leg at the Battle of Antietam and now walked on a wooden peg. His grandfather, Steve, managed the sawmill.

"Yeah, last Sat'dee at Appomattox Court House in Virginia," Vic informed them.

"Is the war over already? I didn't even get ta shoot me one Yankee," Matt scowled.

"Bet Maw'll be glad it's over," Billy Bob spoke up.

"Well, it ain't all over. Sherman's still talkin' to the Rebs' southern units over in Durham. Might be a few more days afore it's finished," Vic knowingly informed them.

"Hey Billy Bob, can we stop in at tha Gen'ral Store and see Lizzie? Ain't seen her in three weeks," Matt said.

"Yep, guess we orta. Maybe she kin tell us more 'bout what's a goin' on."

"Billy Bob, if we kin stop at the *Graham Gazette*, I'll buy a paper.

Maw'll want ta read about it," Andy said.

"OK, we'll pass tha paper's office afore we git ta tha store. Hurry on in there, 'n' git yer paper," Billy Bob ordered.

Buck and Johnny, the oldest boys, had died in the Battle of Gettysburg. Will, the third-born son, had left home, and none of his family had heard from him since.

Martha, Buck's widow, and Willadeen, Johnny's widow, were still living on the farm and raising their children.

***

"Hi, Baby sista," Matt ran and hugged Lizzie. "Ain't seen ye in three weeks."

"Hey little brother, how ya been? Have ya been behaving?"

"Now that ain't a fair question. Course I'm a behavin'."

Billy Bob spoke, "Didja hear 'bout tha war bein' over?"

"Yeah, I heard Lee surrendered. Sure wish it could a happened before we lost Buck and Johnny," Lizzie sighed.

"I gotta get back ta work, boys. Tell Mama and Maggie I said hello, and Granmaw and Granpaw O'Connor are doin' good."

***

The next Saturday. April 22nd, more startling news came from Vic.

"Johnston surrendered to Sherman on Tuesday of this week. It's all over now."

On April 18th, just four days after Lincoln's assassination, Johnston signed an armistice with Sherman at a farmhouse near Durham Station.

Agreeing to, under the terms of surrender, many political conditions and military, without prior approval from Washington. Sherman was reprimanded by Grant.

The confusion was sorted out, and on April 26th, Johnston agreed to purely military terms and renounced his army and all Confederate forces in Georgia, Florida, and the Carolinas. It was the second significant surrender that month.

On April 9th, Robert E. Lee had surrendered the Army of Northern Virginia at Appomattox Court House.

***

The war was over, but it took several days for the news to filter down to all the scattered troops. On Saturday morning, April 29th, a company of Sherman's cavalry, rode into Graham.

Filling the Town Square, they were met by opposition from the Graham Militia Unit. Gunfire erupted just as the Presley wagons rolled into town to deliver the week's load of timber to the sawmill.

Hearing gunfire, Matt Presley grabbed his rifle and ran into the square. Stopping in front of Graham's General Store, he fired his musket and killed a Union soldier.

Three shots rang out, and Matt fell to the ground, mortally wounded. One bullet hit him in the right leg, one on the right side of his chest, and the third shot caught him just below his cheekbone.

Seeing her brother lying in the street, Lizzie ran out of the General store. Kneeling and lifting her brother to her chest, she held him and screamed uncontrollably.

As she did so, the captain of the Union cavalry rode up and shot her four times with his pistol.

Two Presley children lay dead in the street.

At three o'clock that afternoon, news came from Raleigh that the war had ended on Wednesday three days before.

"A rich man's war is a poor man's fight."

Chapter Four

THE NEW ADVENTURE

Boarding for his first-ever train ride, Will was a little apprehensive, but he was excited. Lenora had accompanied him to the train station and kissed him passionately just before he boarded.

"I'll miss you every single day until you return for our wedding. But I am looking forward to getting married and starting on our new adventure," she smiled wistfully at him.

"Yep, me too." For a change, Will was at a loss for words. "We'll both be busy working 'n' the time will go by purty fast I thank."

When he entered the train car, he found a seat beside the window. Looking out, he saw Lenora standing on the platform, waving at him. "My beautiful bride-to-be," he thought while trying in vain to hold back his tears. He waved until the station was out of sight.

Gazing out at the Virginia countryside, he was amazed at how quickly the scenery sped past him. Traveling at twenty miles-per-hour, it seemed fast and a little scary, but soon he settled in and enjoyed the ride. It was much smoother and more comfortable than riding a wagon or buckboard.

It was Monday, July 3,1865, and Will unexpectedly remembered that his brothers had died at Gettysburg precisely two years earlier. The memories of Buck and Johnny Presley's death and the circumstances of the Battle at Gettysburg overwhelmed him.

Will had fought for the Union army while Buck and Johnny were Confederate soldiers. These memories would continue to haunt him for the rest of his life.

He had made sure they were properly buried in the new

Gettysburg Memorial Cemetery. Still, his family back in North Carolina was unaware of the full circumstances of their deaths or where they were buried. He had left home after the war started and had not returned or been in contact with any of them.

After he was discharged from the Union army, he had worked at an army compound near Washington, D.C. Now he was beginning a job for the Freedman's Bureau attempting to rebuild the country.

At some level, he was also trying to reach atonement and the opportunity to restore his own sense of self. The horrors that he had both witnessed and took part in remained as an unspeakable burden on his shoulders. The worst part was that he could not share the whole story with anyone, not even Lenora.

While he was busy at work or planning a future with Lenora, Will could temporarily block the memories; however, the long train ride left him with more time to reflect with a mixture of sorrow, remorse, and some shame on how the past several years had changed his life forever.

The train had made three whistle stops to replenish the supply of wood and water necessary to operate the steam-powered train. Almost twenty-two hours had passed since he had boarded the train in D.C.

Now they were arriving in Charleston, West Virginia, where there was a two-hour layover. Passengers would exit here, and more would board. Will had time to wash and shave in the train station.

Re-boarding the train for the next leg of the trip, he found the dining car and had breakfast. The train departed for the two-hundred-mile trip to Cincinnati, a twelve-hour ride, which included one fuel stop.

The two-hundred-seventy-five-mile trip from Cincinnati through Louisville, then to Nashville, would take sixteen more hours. He decided to take a nap and try to rest. It was surprising how tiring a long train ride was to him.

Rest did not come easily for Will that day. When he drifted into a deep sleep, he saw himself standing on Cemetery Hill, firing his carbine at faceless Rebs.

The scene morphed abruptly into his, turning over two bodies in gray to realize they were his brothers Buck and Johnny. He could see himself crying out, "Maw, will never forgive me."

When another passenger tapped him on the shoulder, asking if he was alright, Will realized that he must have been crying out loud. There was sweat on his brow, and he felt his hands shaking.

"No, I'm fine, Mister, but thanks for askin' me. Tarred from the long trip."

When he arrived in Nashville, he would have been traveling fifty hours (two days and two hours.)

Finding a buckboard and driver outside the train station, he instructed the driver to take him to an office on Ninth Avenue.

He entered the office and was greeted by a young man dressed in civilian clothes but wearing an enlisted man's Union army cap. He smiled and said,

"Good morning, Sir, you must be Mr. Presley." He was a short man, with a small mustache, but otherwise clean-shaven, and he spoke with a curt, clipped accent like Will had heard often in the Union army. "We have been expecting you, Sir."

Will returned the smile, a little startled at being so quickly recognized.

"Happy ta be here 'n' ta make yer acquaintance. What's yer name?"

"Joseph Caldwell, Sir. I was in the Battle of Gettysburg. I'm from Maine, and served with Colonel Chamberlain's unit, Sir."

Will was impressed. "Ye boys really fought hard to hold 'Little Round Top'. That wuz a hard battle. "

"Yes, it was, Sir. We ran out of powder and were forced to fight with bayonets."

"Did you lose those two fingers in that battle?" Will wondered.

"Sure did, Sir. I was dodging a Reb's bayonet, and he caught me in my left hand. It bothered me for a while until I remembered that General Howard only had one arm."

"Yep, I asked him about that when he gave me my Medal. Said he lost it in 1862 after a battle."

"By the way, Joe, you can call me Will. I'm not a lieutenant anymore."

"Yes, Sir. I'm sorry, I meant to say Will. I will, Will," they both laughed at the joke.

"I'll tell General Fisk you're here."

General Clinton B. Fisk

General Clinton B. Fisk was the first to be appointed Assistant Commissioner of the Freedmen's Bureau in Kentucky and Tennessee. As a student at Albion College in Michigan, he briefly aspired to a career as a pastor, but changed his mind. Always a man of strong faith, he formed a close alliance with the American Missionary Association.

He was a tall, slender man with a full beard and a receding hairline, which had turned gray. He presented an intimidating countenance to Will.

"Come in Presley," General Fisk rose as he spoke. "Happy to have you with me here in Tennessee. I'm trying to staff my offices with veterans, especially decorated ones."

"Happy ta be here, Sir. Lookin' forward to fixin' thangs back like they wuz."

The General spoke slowly and thoughtfully, "I'm uncertain things will ever be as they were before, Presley, but we'll do the best we can with what we've got. How was your train ride?"

"A little more tiring than I expected, but a lot better than riding a stagecoach or wagon, I reckon," Will replied.

"It's Wednesday. You'll be here in Nashville through Friday getting oriented to the plans we've made. I'll put you on a train to Memphis Saturday morning, and you can have the weekend to get settled in and find housing at Fort Pickering. Your office is already set up and you can start to find some local employees. We'll need some people to assist you, but I prefer veterans for those jobs. Do you know any who might be interested in moving to Memphis?"

"Yes Sir. I had some men in my outfit from East Tennessee, Knoxville, and some towns close by."

"It's been my experience that you can work better with people you know. You'll need four or five people who you can count on to work with you. Can you handle that?" Fisk was testing him.

"Yes Sir. I might need some help a findin' 'em, but I reckon the army's got records," Will spoke confidently.

"Good, Presley. Make that your first order of business. We have a telegraph machine here in this office. You can contact the War Department today and request the information you need."

Speaking to the soldier operating the telegraph, Will said, " I need contact information on these fellers right here. Will you send a telegram to the Department of War and find them for me?"

"Yes, Sir Mr. Presley, right away, Sir." He then typed these names: Norville Hill, Tony Stansberry, David Stansberry, Darrell Hensley, and Clyde Coker. "Are these friends of yours, Sir?" he asked.

"Yep. All a these boys 'er from East Tennessee 'n' wuz in my outfit with General Howard. Figgered they might wanna help fix thangs here in ther' state," Will explained.

TWO HOURS LATER

Mr. Presley, the War Department, has just returned the information you requested.

You must know somebody up there," he was impressed.

"Well, my fiancé and her cousin both work there. Guess they got it speeded up," Will grinned. "Send this message to every one of these men." I have a new position in Memphis. I'm working for the Freedman's Bureau. We can help fix what's been broke. Are you interested in helping?

"Please send tha message to these boys on tha list. I 'preciate it."

Joe Caldwell entered the telegraph room and spoke to Will, "Got ye all set up to stay in the City Hotel until Saturday mornin', Sir. Oh, I'm sorry. I meant to say Will," he apologized. "It's a nice place on the Public Square downtown. It's got a great view of the Cumberland River on the back side. There's good food in the restaurant, and your favorite cold beverage in the bar, if you're so inclined," he grinned.

"Thank ye, thank ye very, very much, Joe." Will curled his lip as he smiled. "I'm gonna go on down ther' and git checked in. I'm kinda tarred from all this travelin'."

When he arrived at the City Hotel, Will was dazzled by its size and splendor. A large brick building adorned with massive columns on the facade, greeted guests.

The first floor was filled by a public dining room 30 feet x 70 feet, appointed with nineteen tables and Windsor chairs. Chandeliers glistened, flooding the room with light. An adjacent barroom offered a variety of beverages for weary travelers.

The guest rooms featured feather mattresses and pillows. An outside door opened onto a covered veranda overlooking the Cumberland River. Will thought to himself: *Man, this is much better than the Palmer House back home in Graham. Ain't never stayed in such a fancy place. I like it.*

The next morning at 8:00, Will returned to the office.

"General Fisk wants to talk to you just as soon as you come in this mornin'. We usually get here at 7:00. Thought I'd warn you," Caldwell said.

"Thanks, Joe. I 'preciate it," Will was grateful.

Knocking on Fisk's door, he removed his hat and waited to be invited into the room.

"Sorry I'm late, General. Wuddn't shore what time y'all started in tha mornin', 'n' I was real tarred from all 'at travelin'," he apologized.

"We believe in bein' on time 'round here, Presley, but we'll excuse your tardiness this first time. I suggest you have a strict time to start and stop work when you arrive in Memphis. It's just good military discipline," Fisk opined.

"Yes, Sir, General. I shore will," he agreed.

"Now sit down here, and let's talk about what we want to accomplish in Memphis. The freed-slave population is denser there than any other place in Tennessee. Your job will be tough, but you're a man who has been innovative and resourceful as a soldier. You've done the best you could with what you had. I feel terrific about having you on board down there.

"Our first-priority must be to educate these folks. Plantation owners never saw a need to teach them anything, except to work 'til they dropped. Do you have any interest in doing this task?"

"Yes, Sir, I do. My Maw taught all nine of us kids ta read an' rite. Then she started a school for all the kids in our little town down in North Carolina.

"Lenora, my fiancé, graduated from High School in Washington, D.C., 'n' has been workin' at the War Department. When we get married next month, she wants ta come here an' work for Reconstruction. I thank she would be excited ta help me git things goin'," Will was exuberant.

"I'll telegraph Colonel Benjamin P. Runkle at Fort Pickering. He heads up the Freedman's Bureau in Memphis. His office is at the Fort. Ben's a good man, fought with Grant along the Mississippi River, and at Shiloh and Vicksburg."

"General Howard has good friends in the American Missionary Association who are eager to teach these young black children. I think the first school should be at the Fort. We have a large group of black soldiers there. Then, we can build other schools out closer to where the families live. The black population in Memphis is over 16,000 and a lot of those are children."

Fisk was passionate. "I hope to start a college here in Nashville to train some black teachers, too. I want to build schools in Chattanooga and

Knoxville someday."

"Sir, ye shore got big plans. It's my understandin' tha Bureau's only supposed ta last one year. Do ye thank they'll keep it goin' long enuff ta git alla that done?" Will wondered.

Fisk answered thoughtfully, "General Howard's optimistic that Congress will extend and vote some funding for it. Right now, we're taking War Department funds, but we can't keep doing that. We need money to provide food and housing and jobs for these former slaves. Many of them don't know how to do anything but pick cotton. We'll try to rebuild the cotton business and get some of these folks jobs as free-market laborers on plantations, train a few of them in trades and crafts, turn pieces of the unclaimed land into small farms, and set up a court system for them.

"Tennessee state laws prevent blacks from suing or even appearing in court rooms. As you said, it's a big job, but we gotta try to get it done. President Lincoln envisioned it this way."

"I shore like the plans y'all have made. Maybe me 'n' Lenora can help ye make it happen," Will smiled wryly.

"We have some on-base housing available where temporary people can stay, and I'll arrange with Colonel Runkle for you and your bride to live there for a while. When we get an extension of the program and some more funding, you can look for more suitable housing. When is the wedding?" Fisk wondered.

"Sometime around the first of August, Sir. I'll need to take a few days off and go back to Falls Church for that. Will that be alrite?"

"Yes, I'll arrange for that with Runkle. In the meantime, familiarize yourself with things around here, and we'll get you to Memphis on Saturday."

Caldwell spoke to Will just before noon. "We have responses from your contacts, Sir. Norville Hill is interested in moving to Memphis, but the other four want to stay on their farms back home."

"OK, Caldwell. I don't blame 'em boys fer wantin' to stay home. Wish I could go home myself," Will sighed. "Guess ther's plenty of folks in Memphis needin' a job. Some of 'em freed slaves 'd be good workers if ye treat 'em rite."

Before he left the office on Friday, Caldwell handed him a train ticket to Memphis, and a letter of introduction to Colonel Runkle from General Fisk.

The next phase of his life was about to begin.

Chapter Five

MEMPHIS, TENNESSEE

The 5:00 A.M. departure of the train bound for Memphis found Will still a little bit sleepy. Although he was not yet fully awake, the steam engine sounds and the whistle as they pulled away from the station quickly awakened him.

Leaving the outskirts of Nashville behind, the rolling landscape of the Middle Tennessee countryside rushed past. It would take twelve hours for the two-hundred-mile ride to Memphis. A forty-five-minute layover in Jackson for fuel and passenger turnover gave Will time to stretch and grab a quick snack in the dining car.

As the train pulled away from the station in Jackson, Will laid his head back to take a nap. It would take four more hours to finish his ride into Memphis; so he would catch up on his sleep.

He was happy when the sound of the train whistle abruptly aroused him from his fitful attempt at sleep. His unspoken burden seemed determined to haunt his dreams.

Peering out the window, he could see the station in Memphis. From the station, he glimpsed the Mississippi River, and was surprised at how wide and broad it was. At the port of Memphis, he could see riverboats docked, and bales of cotton being unloaded. It was an impressive sight. He made himself a mental note to explore the river dock when the opportunity arrived.

Finding a carriage driver who would take him to Fort Pickering, he made the short ride, and breathed a sigh of relief. His long journey from Washington D. C. to Memphis was over. Fetching his bag, he paid the driver and thanked him. Sally Presley had raised her children to be polite

Fort Pickering

Fort Pickering was an impressive site for Will. Built along the south bluffs overlooking the Mississippi River, it was initially constructed during the Revolutionary War and was named for the Secretary of War, Timothy Pickering. Its strategic location made it a valuable site.

Taken over from the Confederates (who refurbished it for use during the Civil War) by the Union Army after the capture of Memphis in 1862, it was expanded to nearly two miles long. Reaching all the way to Beale Street, it became the central supply depot for the Union troops on the Western Front.

With the end of the war, many of the barracks were left empty, but a full contingent of troops was necessary to continue the entire operation of the Fort. The Freedman's Bureau had located in the Fort and provided accommodations for all personnel assigned there.

Will pulled out the letter from General Fisk and presented it to the guards at the gate. "Yes Sir, Mr. Presley, we had orders to expect you today. Colonel Runkle will see you on Monday. In the meantime, I'll show you to your quarters," a young PFC informed him. "Follow me, Sir."

Concealing his surprise, Will was escorted to officer's quarters, a small four-plex apartment building. Settling in, he could see that this would be suitable for Lenora when she arrived. There was a living area, a bedroom, and a small kitchen area. A bright fire was already burning in the fireplace. *"Yep, this'll do real good."* Will thought. *"Cain't hardly wait ta git Lenora down here."*

MONDAY MORNING

Colonel Benjamin P. Runkle was appointed as Superintendent of the Memphis Freedmen's Bureau. Like Howard and Fisk, he was a man of strong faith. He was tall, slim build, and had brilliant blue eyes, his most striking feature. A full, dark beard adorned his face. With an air of sophistication, he was an imposing figure.

Precisely at 7:00 A.M., Will arrived at Runkle's office to present himself. (He did not dare be a minute late.)

Extending his hand as he rose, Runkle smiled and said. "Happy to have you with us, Presley. I've heard about your accomplishments."

"Happy ta be here, Sir. I wanna try ta improve things down here."

"Are your accommodations satisfactory?" Runkle inquired.

"Oh yes, Sir, the place is especially nice. I know Lenora will be happy to see it."

"Lenora?"

"Yes, Sir, she's my bride-to-be," Will smiled. "She works for the Department of War's office in D.C. but wants ta come here and work in Reconstruction. Her Daddy 'n' Mama run a farm near Falls Church, Virginia, 'n' supply meat and vegetables to the War Department."

"Hey, it will be helpful to have someone who's experienced from the War Department. Her contacts there can be helpful, too. When's the wedding?"

"If it's alright with you, Sir, we're a plannin' it 'bout August 1. I'll need a few days off ta go back fer tha weddin'."

Answering, Runkle replied, "Fisk told me you are interested in schooling these black children. Tell me about that."

"Yes, Sir, my Maw learnt all us kids ta read an' rite, then started a school fer tha kids in our little town. I know she'd be proud knowin' I wuz doin' sump'in like that."

"Do you know any Union soldiers who'd like to help us? We have a building here at the Fort to start our school, but we'll hafta build some schools for children outside the Fort."

"Yes, Sir, a Sargent named Norville Hill wuz with me at Gettysburg. He lives in Knoxville 'n' wants ta help."

"OK, you get started on furnishing our school here at the Fort. We can buy surplus desks and books from the local schools here in Memphis. After your wedding, we'll see about bringing in your friend from Knoxville."

"Sounds good ta me, Sir, I'll get rite on it."

JULY 30, 1865

With great anticipation, Will boarded the train for the three-day ride back to D.C. he would arrive on Wednesday at 6:00 P.M. The telegraph operator at Pickering had sent a message to Lenora at her War Department office. She would meet him at the train depot, and they would go directly to her parent's home near Falls Church.

The wedding would take place on Friday, August 4, 1865, at 2:00

P.M.. It seemed like a tight schedule, but Lenora assured him they could make it happen.

Three days seemed like an eternity, as Will expected seeing his bride. It had been almost a month since he had last seen her. Finally, when the train pulled into the station in D.C., his heart skipped a beat. "Was that Lenora standing there waiting for him?" While the train was stopping, he passed her and waved jubilantly.

Before it had completely stopped, he jumped off and ran into her arms. "Will, I've missed you so much," she was sobbing.

"Me too," was all he could say. Tears were rolling down his cheeks. She kissed him passionately, and as he responded, she pulled back.

"What will people think of us," she blushed.

Noticing a man and woman peering at them, Will said, "We're a getting' married Friday. Ain't seen my Sweet Lady in a month."

The couple smiled and nodded approvingly.

"Come on Will, let's go. If we go now, we'll be in at Mama and Daddy's before dark," Lenora directed.

"OK, darlin', I'll tell ye all about Memphis while we're a ridin'."

Parker Home

The ten-mile ride to the Parker farm took just over an hour in the Parker's carriage. Lenora described the wedding details that she and her mother had planned during his absence. They had arranged for someone from the Virginia Theological Seminary to perform the ceremony and publish the required pre-marital Bans.

Her cousin, Judy Parker, would be Lenora's Maid-of-Honor, and Carl Fain, Will's assistant at Fort Whipple, would stand as his Best Man. (Fain and Will had a rocky start when they first met, but became good friends as time passed.)

The ceremony would be conducted using the standard rite from the Episcopal Book of Common Prayer. Will had been raised in a Methodist-Episcopal congregation, so he assumed it would not differ from his home church.

Reverend John Wesley Henderson was his Pastor at Roaring Fork Methodist, a small country church in Graham, N.C. He had attended the old Falls Church with Lenora and her parents while they lived at Surratt House in D.C. At the time, the church was being used partially as a hospital for Union Soldiers, bringing back unpleasant memories for Will.

Arriving at the home of Lenora's parents, they were greeted by Alice and Harry Parker. "Welcome home Will, we've missed you around here," Alice Parker hugged him.

The Parker House was a clapboard construction built with a wraparound porch with white railings. A white picket fence surrounded the lawn, and roses decorated the front of the house. Will loved this place.

"Yes, we sure have, boy," Harry echoed Alice. "Things have been busy here. It's a big job marrying this girl off. Course, she's the only one we've got, so I didn't know what to expect."

"I shore 'preciate what y'all done fer us. I wudda helped if I'd a been here," Will assured them.

"Well, come in the house and rest up some from your trip," Alice welcomed him. "Tell us all about Memphis, and what you've been doing down there."

"Thank ye, Miss Alice. It shore is good to be back here again," Will smiled. "They've got big plans for the Freedman's Bureau, schools, job trainin', housin', land grants, court systems, even a black college ta educate teachers. It's gonna be great, 'n' I'm proud ta be a part of it. Me 'n' Lenora has a chance ta really help this country back to normal."

"Where will you live in Memphis," Harry Parker wondered.

Hesitantly, Will answered, "For right now we have officer's quarters at the Fort. Ther's a livin' room, a kitchen, and a bedroom. Three other apartments 'er next to us. We got close neighbors, and we'll be safe inside the Fort. Lenora will work with me to start a school inside the Fort for the children of the black soldiers stationed there. Then, later, we'll build some more schools for black children who don't live inside. Those will be built out in the section where they live."

Hearing this news for the first time, Lenora got excited. "I hadn't thought about schools, but I think it's wonderful to have that kind of opportunity. I'll be proud to help you, Will."

"My friend from Knoxville, Norville Hill, wants ta come down 'n' help us, too."

"Whadda ya gonna do if they don't extend it," Harry Parker worried.

Lenora joined the conversation, "General Howard said they'd find us a job somewhere in the government."

"And if they don't, we'll come back here 'n' help you 'n' Miss Alice," Will was grinning.

"Colonel Runkle said he'd see 'bout gittin' Norville a job with us. We'll git married on Friday; spend Saturday with our friends here; go to church on Sunday; then head out on Monday for Memphis."

"Don't you get any time for a honeymoon?" Alice scowled.

"Just the weekend, Miss Alice, but we'll have three days on tha train a holding hands 'n' pitchin' woo," Will smiled and winked at Lenora.

"Come on, Will, I've arranged for you to stay at the Fairfax Inn until Monday morning," Harry directed.

As he delivered Will to the Inn, Harry said, "I'll pick you up in the morning for breakfast. Alice and Lenora want to walk us through the ceremony, so we know what to do."

"Yep, ain't never been in a weddin' a'fore. I wuz worryin' 'bout gittin' it rite," Will confessed.

Chapter Six

THE WEDDING

Harry Parker asked one of his long-time employees to fabricate simple wooden benches for seating, set up on the church lawn in two sections with a middle aisle. A small rustic altar and arch were positioned at the front of the benches. He also hired a family of local musicians to play their collection of stringed instruments before and during the ceremony.

FALLS CHURCH EPISCOPAL

Several church members volunteered to bring flowers from their gardens. One lady created a lovely vase for the altar and a matching bouquet for the bride. The weather cooperated, and the freshly cut lawn made a soft carpet.

Will and Carl Fain walked to the right side of the altar and stood with great anticipation.

Alice Parker beamed as she was escorted to her reserved seat on the left front bench.

Carrying a wooden cross festooned with cut flowers, a young first-year Seminary student entered, followed closely by the officiating Seminarian.

The small group of family and invited guests watched as Judy Parker entered from behind the church building and marched down the aisle. Then, as the quiet music morphed into a march, Harry Parker, with Lenora on his arm and a tear in his eye, escorted his lovely daughter down the aisle.

Taking a deep breath, all that Will could muster was a whispered, "Wow." As Lenora, with a glowing smile, came closer, he couldn't believe his good fortune to have captured the heart of such a beautiful woman.

Alice had cleverly refashioned her own wedding dress, preserved for almost twenty-five years, into a more casual style appropriate for the pastoral event. As she helped her daughter secure the ivory lace bodice and fasten the matching headpiece, she held back tears of joy mixed with sorrow at the impending separation from her only child.

When Harry and Lenora reached the altar, the Officiant spoke. "Who gives this woman in marriage?"

Harry very quietly replied, "Her Mother and I do."

"Dearly beloved, we are gathered together here in the sight of God and in the face of this company," the Officiant began, "to join this Man and Woman in holy Matrimony; which is commended of Saint Paul to be honorable among all men and therefore is not by any to be entered unadvisedly or lightly, but reverently, discreetly, advisedly, soberly, and in the fear of God to witness and bless the joining of this man and this woman in Holy Matrimony."

Will was smiling from ear to ear as Lenora glanced at him lovingly. His mind wandered as he glanced once again at Lenora and fantasized of delights yet to come, and she smiled knowingly.

"Into this holy estate these two persons, George Wilhelm Presley and Lenora Mae Parker, come now to be joined. , . . ," Will's mind hurried back to the words as he heard his name mentioned.

Lenora slightly chuckled under her breath as she had never known Will's name was George until the Bans were published.

"Wilt thou love her, comfort her, honor and keep her, in sickness and in health, forsaking all others, keep thee only unto her as long as ye both shall live?"

Will nodded, then smiled as he looked straight into Lenora's eyes and intoned, "I will."

Lenora repeated the vows the Rector recited to her, including, ".... will thou obey him and serve him, love, honor, and keep him, in sickness and in health..." Will made a mental note to remind her of this vow whenever the occasion arose.

When the ceremony was completed, all the attendees returned to Harry and Alice's house for a country feast. The wedding guests enjoyed a sumptuous meal of fresh meat, savory garden vegetables, and a selection of sweets, including an unique wedding cake.

After a relaxed visit, everyone extended their well-wishes to the newlyweds and bade them God's speed as they went home.

The happy couple relived their special day with the parents for a respectable amount of time, then hurried to the Fairfax Inn to consummate their marriage.

The manager of the Inn had left flowers and a basket of fruit in the bridal suite. He smiled at Lenora and winked at Will as they ascended the stairs.

On Sunday morning, they returned to the Parker's home for breakfast, an extended visit, and dinner. Will filled them in on all the details of the train ride back to Memphis. Promising to stay in touch by letters and an occasional telegraph to Judy Parker at the War Department.

When Monday morning dawned, they boarded for the three-day train ride to Memphis.

Chapter Seven

MEMPHIS SCHOOL

A s they waited to board the train, Will tried to prepare Lenora for a less-than-glamorous ride to Memphis. "It takes three days ta git ther, and it'll 'wear ye out," he warned. " I cain't afford no sleeper car, so we'll jist hafta nap a-sittin' up.

"You kin sleep on my shoulder, then I'll sleep on yer's," he apologized. "Ther' is a dinin' car, so we kin eat, but we hafta go ta the necessary-room when they make a stop fer fuel or a big station."

"Oh, it's gonna be fun," she smiled. "Being Mrs. Presley is gonna be great. We'll be workin' together, and I really believe, we're good together, Mr. Presley."

Will liked her attitude.

He placed her in the window seat for her first-ever train ride and pointed to landmarks along the countryside. Lenora enjoyed it for a while, but soon, everything began to look the same.

As they crossed over into West Virginia, Will was remembering his trip to Harper's Ferry. Just after a significant battle at Chancellorsville, his unit stopped there to re-supply with ammo and weapons.

He asked his Captain to allow him to carry a pistol. This was an unusual request for an enlisted man, but the commanding officer complied with his desire, and he was given a side-arm besides his rifle.

When the pivotal engagement occurred at Gettysburg, this acquisition proved to be an essential addition but a double-edged sword for Will.

"If I'd neva asked fer tha pistol, I most likely bin dead rite ther on tha hill," Will thought as he remembered running out of ammunition.

"On tha otha hand, it wouldn't bin me tha killed Johnny. We'd prob'ly all three bin dead. Somehow, I'm not believin' Maw woulda been any sadder either way. Jist anotha rich man's war'n many a us poor boys wuz lost

in tha fight."

For now, he would keep his secret about the pistol.

Will recalled the beauty of the small valley where Harper's Ferry was nestled, and began to describe it to Lenora.

"It's a small town surrounded on three sides by mount'uns. President George Washington picked the place in 1794 'cause it wuz real purty, and the mount'uns made it easy ta pertect it. He built tha armory and arsenal of tha United States here. The meetin' of the Shenandoah and Potomac rivers give a real good way ta transport materials inta and outta tha area.

"John Brown raided tha town in 1859, and he wuz tha one who fired the first shots in tha 'war over slavery'. It didn't last very long 'n' didn't git much dun ta stop slav'ry, but it got more people tryin' to, 'n' talkin' 'bout it."

Lenora looked at him and smiled. "Thank you Will. I remember my Daddy and Mama talking about John Brown and worryin' about war. I'm sure glad it's over and we can help with Reconstruction."

"Well, why didn't ye tell me ye knew all about Harper's Ferry? Ye'd a saved me a lotta trouble."

"You described it very well, Will. Thank you for sharing with me," she smiled sweetly. "I wanted to hear about your experience there, not to mention I love to hear your voice."

"I'm really not trying to impress ye with how much I know. I jist didn't know if ye had heard 'bout it," Will was apologetic. "Guess we gotta lotta learnin' ta do about each other."

He placed his arm around her shoulder and hugged her close. "It's a long ride to Charleston, West Virginia, so you may as well lay your head on my shoulder 'n' rest a while. I'll wake you when we get there."

***

The two-hour layover in Charleston gave the couple a chance to take a necessary break and eat. Soon, after continuing the second day of their journey, Will saw the sun rising and decided to take a nap himself.

The trip was much more pleasant with a companion. As the train slowed, the whistle blew, and the brakes hissed. Will was awakened.

He smiled, kissed his pretty wife, and said, "Good mornin' Darlin'. Guess we made it to Louisville."

"Yes, I heard the conductor say Louisville. Can we get off here and stretch a little bit?" she asked.

"Yep, we hafta git off here and change trains. It's a different' one to Nashville and Memphis. We'll have time ta eat sum'thin, and find er other train," he advised her.

***

Lenora was amazed at the changing landscape as she had gazed out the window. West Virginia and Eastern Kentucky were all mountainous terrain.

As they neared Cincinnati, then Lexington and Louisville, the land became rolling hills of horse farms. From Nashville to Memphis, it would flatten out into cotton plantations. The diversity was noticeable to a first-time visitor.

"Where are you going to find teachers for these black children in Memphis?" Lenora inquired.

"General Howard has some friends in the American Missionary Association," he answered.

"I've never heard of them. Who are they? Are they qualified to teach children?"

"These Association people have been active since 1840, building schools for black children in the north.

"According to Colonel Runkle, they are mainly women, white and black, who are Congregationalists and Abolitionists. Colonel Runkle, General Fisk, and General Howard are all ardently religious men. They want these children to have a Christian education.

"I reckon that even the Christians don't want black children going to school with white children. We'll just hafta git them educated anyhow," he responded.

"We'll work with these teachers; do our best ta git 'em what they need, then hope fer tha best," he continued. "Our first school will be at tha Fort for the children of tha so'jers. Then we'll go out inta tha neighborhoods 'n' build schools.

"It ain't gonna be easy, my Sweetheart. Ther's still a lotta bad blood 'tween the southern whites and blacks. Ther' a blamin' tha blacks fer tha war. Claimin' they tha reason white boys turned agin' ther brothas.

"But that ain't true. I fought fer the Union, 'n' I didn't thank nobody otta be slaves to sum rich white men. We wuddn't much more than slaves our ownselves ta tha man who owned 'er farm. He let us make a livin' off it, but he got haffa what we made fer ever."

"Yes, it's really hard to get ahead if you don't own some land," she replied. "Maybe someday we'll own land close to my family farm," Lenora was wistful.

"Yep, but first we gotta git thangs straightened out down here. We got a lotta work ta do, my Darlin'."

***

Settling into their apartment at the fort, Lenora was pleasantly surprised. "Well, it's small, but nicely furnished. This is better than I expected."

"Yeah, officers' quarters are finer than enlisted men. I've lived in both. I like the officers' much better."

When they entered the office of Colonel Runkle the next morning, Will introduced Lenora.

"We are happy to have you with us Mrs. Presley," Runkle smiled.

As she smiled and extended her hand, she thought, *"Mrs. Presley has a nice sound to it."*

"Why, thank you Colonel, I'm happy to be here. Will and I have looked forward to this day for a long time. We want to help in the recovery of our country from the great tragedy of this war."

Runkle looked at Will and said, "OK Presley, let's get on with it. Central Supply has the desks and other equipment we bought from the Memphis school system. Two rooms have been readied for you. Four teachers will be here next week to begin classes."

When they found Central Supply, they discovered the school desks, chalkboards, and teacher's desks acquired from the Memphis Schools. It was apparent from signs of use and abuse that the equipment had seen better days.

"I suppose we'll have to make do with these," Lenora complained. "All our finances are coming out of the War Department's funds. Congress still hasn't appropriated any money for the Freedman's Bureau."

"Yeah, I've heerd talk 'round 'er that President Johnson ain't too keen on spendin' a lotta money on these blacks. Shore hope Congress'll extend Reconstruction and give us some money ta operate on."

"Guess we'll just have to see what happens," Lenora mused.

***

With some help from two soldiers working in the supply room, they moved everything to the designated classrooms.

She continued, "Let's turn these desks toward the wall on this end. We'll put the teacher's desk up here with the chalkboard behind her.

"Then we'll turn the other desks toward *that* wall, dividing the two classes with their backs to each other. Maybe they won't be distracted as much that way."

There was a distinct separation when they placed three worktables between the two sets of students' desks. Satisfied with this arrangement, they moved to the other room and set it up identically.

"Let's go git Colonel Runkle and show him what we've done," Will suggested. "I'll go to his office ta see if he's available."

Runkle nodded his approval as he surveyed the classrooms. He remarked, "Teachers will be here on Monday, August 15, and we'll start classes on Monday, September 5. That'll give them three weeks to prepare, and us some time to round up students.

On the opening day of school, fifty-four pupils arrived for classes, and the first school in Memphis for black children was off and running.

Chapter Eight

FORTY ACRES AND A MULE

"Good job on that first school, Presley. You and Lenora worked well together and got it done. Now we have to find jobs for the freed slaves," Runkle announced.

"Whatta ya got in mind Colonel?" Will asked.

"Well, we got a lotta freed slaves with no jobs and no livelihood for their families. There's much abandoned land lying vacant because plantation owners can't farm it without slaves."

Runkle continued, "These black families could build small farms and raise enough livestock and vegetables to provide for their families. Fisk calls it Forty Acres and a Mule. In addition, there's a shortage of human resources here in Memphis because of so many being killed in the war. Workers are needed down at the river docks to unload what little cotton still comes in, and workers in the warehouses where they sell it."

"Where are these freed people gonna live, Colonel?" Lenora inquired.

"For those who have jobs, there's rental housing available, but many of these families are headed by single mothers. We will need to build some housing for them," Runkle explained.

"Don't you have a friend from Knoxville who wants to help us, Presley?" the Colonel asked.

"Yes, Sir. Name's Norville Hill. Me 'n' him was in tha same outfit in tha war. He'd be some good help fer us," Will answered.

"They're gonna open a Freedman's Bureau in Knoxville, but if he wants to come here, we can use him. We got a big job to do here," Runkle said.

"Colonel, do you think we can git any of 'er people's jobs with tha city gub'ment here in Memphis?" Will asked.

"Maybe, but I don't wanna push that too much. We got a lotta Irish immigrants here who want those jobs. Don't wanna start no trouble," Runkle rubbed his chin.

"I'd like to get started settin' some people up on farms. Lincoln thought it was important for freedmen to own land and have the means to support themselves. General Sherman has already started it in South Carolina. Think you could handle some of that Presley?" the Colonel asked.

"Yes, Sir. My Paw come ta 'merica as a 'dentured servant, an' worked several years' ta pay fer 'er land," Will reported.

"Good, then you understand what we have in mind with the *forty acres and a mule* program. Hundreds of acres of land are just lying dormant. We wanna put them to good use, Presley."

"When do we start, Sir?" Lenora joined the conversation.

Runkle replied, "There are two lists in the main office here - one for people who have applied for land, and one for tracts of land. It'll be your job to match them and make assignments. Central Supply can get them what they'll need to get started."

He continued, "Lenora, you can make the initial contacts, then Will can show them their land. That should be a rewarding job for both of you. We need to get it done as soon as possible. There are rumors that President Johnson is restoring land rights to some of the more-wealthy owners.

President Andrew Johnson

Will asked, "Why would he do that?"

"Its pure speculation, but Representative Thaddeus Stevens has been working with us. He says since Johnson is a Southerner, he sides with them. Many of them are begging him to give back their land."

Continuing, Runkle said, "Stevens wants to stop it, and when Congress re-convenes in December, he will try to do that. Until then, we want to get as many as possible settled on this unclaimed land. That was Lincoln's plan, but Johnson thinks differently."

"Yes Sir, Colonel, we'll git rite on it," Will replied. "Headin' fer tha main office now. Come on, Lenora, let's git ta work."

***

Speaking to the Sargent staffing the front desk, Will spoke. "Hello, Sargent, Will Presley 'n' this is my wife, Lenora. We're a workin' fer Colonel Runkle in the Freedman's Bureau."

"Yeah, I heard about you, Presley. Did ya get the school all set up yet?"

"Shore did, Sargent. Now Runkle wants us ta git sum a these folks started on a farm. Do ye have tha lists a 'em people?"

"I sure do, Presley. I'll get it from the file. Here's the list of people, and this one is the list of divided properties. They've all been approved."

"OK, thank ye Sargent. Let's go Lenora."

***

Smiling, Lenora spoke, "Well, that was easy enough. Seems that somebody has been busy."

"Now comes the hard part fer us. We gotta git 'em settled on tha land with a place fer 'em ta live. Ther'aint no houses on 'at land."

"Who's gonna build those cabins?" Lenora was puzzled.

"Norville will be here next week. I'll line up tha first five men. They can all work on tha house with Norville showin' 'em how. Then, they'll build another 'un, then another 'un.

"When we got five cabins, I'll pick five more men, and do tha same thang with them."

"Oh Will, you are so smart," Lenora gushed.

Will grinned, "Yep, I ain't as dumb as I look."

Chapter Nine

FIVE SETTLERS

W ill, here's the note I'm sending to the prospective settlers," Lenora spoke. "Tell me what you think of it."

You have been chosen to receive forty acres and a mule to homestead. We will build five cabins for five such places. You will be required to help in the construction of all five.
If this is acceptable, please give your consent to this messenger, and report to the Fort on Monday morning at 8:00 A.M.|
Thank you,
Lenora Presley Freedman's Bureau

"Yes, 'at sounds great, Len. I'm a thankin' ye'll hafta tell tha messenger ta read it ta 'em. 'Spect these Freedmen cain't read much," Will said.

"OK, I'll go ask the Sargent to find some messengers to deliver this to the first five," she smiled. "Sam Jennings, Otis Wilson, Luther Kaine, Malcolm Nance, and Roscoe Gaye," she read.

"Sounds good ta me. Let's do it," Will was eager. "These folks need fer sum'thin good ta happen fer 'em."

"When will Norville be here, Will?" Lenora asked.

"Supposed ta be on tha train this Sat'adee. At's whut Colonel Runkle tol' me," he answered. "We'll hafta help 'im git settled in, I reckon."

***

Standing on the station's platform, Will watched the passenger train from Nashville pull in at precisely 2:27 P.M. *"Now I know what they mean by railroad time. They don't miss it by much at all,"* he thought.

As passengers exited the cars, a tall, slender, clean-shaven young man with dark hair and eyes *stood out* in the crowd. Will recognized Norville and waved to him. His old friend, who was not much on smiling or talking, returned his wave and walked toward him.

"I wuz a wonderin' how I wuz gonna git ta tha fort. It's good ta see ye again' ol' buddy," he grinned.

Will grinned and shook his hand. "Shore am glad ye decided ta come down here 'n' help us. Thought ye might wanna stay in Knoxville."

"Well, I wanted ta start here wit' ye 'n' yer' bride. Maybe I'll transfer ta Knoxville when they git open up ther'."

"Let's git ta tha fort. You've been assigned a bachelor room in tha Officer's quarters. I know yer wore out from tha ride a commin' here, so tanite an' ta'morra, ye can rest.

"We'll git up early Monday mornin' 'n' load the wagons. Tha boys'll be in here 'bout 8:00, so if we loadin' 'bout 6:00 we otta be ready fer 'em."

As they rode to the fort, the two old friends reminisced about their days together in the army.

Both men served with General Meade at Gettysburg. Later, after the Gettysburg Cemetery was dedicated, Will requested his discharge from the army. Now they were reunited in a new cause - the reconstruction of this ravaged region.

***

Monday morning arrived, and at 5:00 A.M., the bugle's sound roused the residents of the fort from sleep. After breakfast and a quick trip to the stables for wagons, the lumber and tools were loaded from the supply yard.

Malcolm Nance and Luther Kaine were the first of the new landowners to arrive. Both men were recently discharged soldiers who suggested they carry rifles with them to the construction site.

Will quickly accepted the suggestion and accompanied Norville, Nance, and Kaine to the arsenal. Seven lever-action, breech-loading rifles with ammunition were issued to the cadre of settlers. Now, they were ready to venture to the first home site.

The eighteen-mile trip to the Callahan Plantation's abandoned land took almost two hours because the wagons were so heavily loaded.

Will spoke to the group," It won't take so long going back tanite, 'cause 'em wagons'll be unloaded. Let's git 'er dun, men."

First, the crew of men unloaded the wagon filled with stones for the foundation, then the lumber for the floor.

As the unloading was almost finished, two men on horseback rode up to the wagon. "What tha hell do ye people thank yer doin' here?" a bearded man with a large protruding stomach demanded

"Yer truspassin' on my land."

"Not truspassin' a'tall, mister. This here's land owned by the United States Gub'ment. Hit's abandoned land 'n' hit's been gave ta the Freedman'a Bureau. These five men here 'er gonna work it and own it."

"Like Hell thur gonna work it 'n' own it," Callahan yelled. I'm a gonna see tha judge 'n' git a court order ta git ye scalawags off my land."

When the conversation got heated and loud, Norville picked up a rifle and stood beside Will. Kaine, Jennings and Nance picked up guns too, and stood ready to fight.

As Callahan and his accomplice, Shawn Hammond, turned to leave, Hammond yelled, "Ye two white scalawags 'n' them five black asses had better look out. We'll be back fer ye."

Roscoe Gaye spoke up. "I'sa knowed ther'd be a fight. What we gonna do Mista Will?"

"We gonna do what we come here ta do, Roscoe—build a house fer Jennings. Now let's get ta work. Norville will hold his rifle and be ready fer anything that might happen."

At 6:00 P.M., Will spoke to the group. "OK men, we got tha foundation set and the floor trusses placed. We'll come back tomorrow 'n' work some more."

***

Driving back to the fort, Norville spoke to Will. "Do ye thank we'd better report ta Colonel Runkle what happened taday?"

"Yeah, I reckon so. We might need a squad of soldiers to stand guard while we work."

"I shore would feel a lot better if we had some military guards. I thought this fightin' 'n' feudin' wuz over 'n' dun with when Lee surrendered," Norville said.

"I reckon not," Will replied. "These Rebs down here in Mississippi 'n' Alabama ain't give up yit. They might not never give it up."

When they arrived back at the fort, Will and Norville reported to Headquarters. Colonel Runkle, returning from the Officer's Mess, spoke.

"How'd it go today, men?"

Smiling wryly, Will answered, "Hadda little problem ta report, Colonel. A feller named Callahan claimed we wuz truspassin' on his land. Feller with him named Hammond claimed they'd be back, and we'd be sorry."

Runkle said, "I suspected Callahan might show up down there. That abandoned land belonged to his family, but it now belongs to the United States of America.

"I was hoping he'd fold, but I guess that's a no-go."

"Me 'n' Norville thanks we're gonna need some soldiers to guard us as we work. Can that be arranged?" Will asked.

"I can make that happen, Presley. I'll have a squad here in the morning."

"Thank you, sir," Will replied. "I shore 'preciate it."

As they walked back to their barracks, Norville spoke, "Them Rebs ain't a-gonna give up too easy, Presley. What'll these Freedmen do when the soldiers leave?"

"My Paw used ta say 'Cross 'at bridge when ye come ta it'. I reckon they'll hafta deal with it as best they can when they git there."

Chapter Ten

A CONFRONTATION

On Tuesday morning, with the wagons loaded, and the Freedmen ready to go, Sargent Eddie Murphy rode up with his cavalry squad of African Descent soldiers to escort the builders to the site selected for the first house.

Acknowledging them with a salute, Will and Norville started to move out. Six soldiers hurried to the front of the wagons, and the other six followed at the rear.

"Norville spoke to Will, "I feel good about having 'ese troopers with us now, but I still worry about tha fam'lies of 'ese farmers when ther' pertection leaves."

"Yeah, me too," he answered softly. "But I ain't got no answer fer 'at rite now. We'll jist hafta see what happens.

***

As the group neared the homesite, a large contingent of men on horseback rode in from the other direction. Led by a thick-waisted man wearing a tin star on his chest, they stopped about ten yards from the homesite.

Their leader spoke quickly and loudly.

"I'm Sheriff Joe Ashe of Marshall County, 'n' ye boys 'er truspassin' on Callahan's property here. Now ye'd best jist turn around and head back ta tha fort in Memphis. Ye ain't got no bizness here."

Will looked him straight in the eye and replied, "This here's abandoned land, and hit's now owned by tha United States of America.

"Hit's being deeded to 'ese farmers here, and they aim ta work it and own it. Now if y'all will jist git outta 'er way, we got work ta do."

"Maybe ye didn't hear me, boy. I'm tha high sheriff here, and I said yer truspassing. If ye don't leave, I'll place ye all under arrest."

Sargent Murphy rode up beside Will with his rifle cradled in his arms. Firmly, he spoke to the sheriff,

"I got orders from Colonel Runkle at the fort. He tol' me 'n' my men ta pertect 'ese folks by any means necessary. My men's got repeater rifles 'n 'they'll use 'em if they hafta."

Will spoke, "We don't want no trouble sheriff, but somebody's gonna git hurt if y'all don't leave us alone."

"We'll be back with orders from tha judge in Holly Springs. Ye scalawags ain't a takin' my land," Callahan vowed.

Turning to leave, Hammond yelled to Will and Norville, "Ye Nigger-Lovin' white boys'll regret tha day ye started takin' up for 'ese black boys. Write this down sum'wher's."

***

"Do ye thank we orta report this ta tha Colonel when we git back, Presley?" Norville asked.

"Yeah, I do. He needs ta know what's goin' on."

Back at the fort, they entered the administration building and encountered the Colonel returning from the mess hall.

"Evenin' Colonel, got a minute? Will spoke.

"Sure, Presley. You and Hill come on into my office.

"Be seated, men, and tell what's on your mind."

Will replied, "We hadda lil' trouble agin' taday with Callahan. He brung tha sheriff with 'im and threatened ta arrest ever' one of us.

"We stood 'er groun' 'n' didn't let 'em skeer us nun, but they said they'd git a court order from a judge in Holly Springs."

Slowly and softly, Runkle replied, "I've heard rumors that President Johnson is quietly returning land to plantation owners. Some of them are giving money to his campaign fund. Thaddeus Stevens, from Pennsylvania, is trying to stop it, but Congress won't be back in session until December. It doesn't look promising for Lincoln's plan.

"Besides, *black codes* make it even more challenging to do our job. Wanting to ensure the availability of cheap labor on the plantations, local laws force freedmen to sign annual contracts of indenture if they don't have jobs. Many are charged with vagrancy and sentenced to be indentured servants.

"We'll get these first five houses built, then see what happens in D.C."

"If we had four more crews a men, we cud git 'ese houses built a lot quicker. Kin ye spare us 'bout twenty more men?" Norville asked. "We'll need sum guards fer 'em, too."

"I'll check with the Sargent of the African Descent company. If they have Freedmen soldiers guarding them, they'll feel safer."

"Norville is worried 'bout what'll happen when we leave 'em."

"Yes, that's gonna be a problem, but we'll handle it when we have to."

"But that ain't what Lincoln had in mind, is it?" Will was disappointed.

"No, but Lincoln's gone and Johnson's in charge now. We'll do what must be done to handle it now.

"We still have to build more schools for these black children. The teachers say they need their own schools separate from the white children."

"Do 'ese white young'uns thank ther' too good to go to school with black un's?" Will wondered.

"Not at all, Presley. These educators are concerned that little black children will be intimidated by the white ones. If they have their own buildings, they'll be more comfortable."

"OK, but let's git these houses built first. Can we expect some extra workers in tha mornin?"

"Yes, Presley. Be in here at 6:00 am. I'll have them waiting for you," Runkle answered.

As they left the office and walked back to their living quarters, Will spoke to Norville. "Whad'da ya thank 'bout all tha' stuff tha Colonel tol' us?"

"Well, I don't like it much, do ye?"

"Naw, but Paw used ta say, do tha best ya can wit what ya got," Will answered philosophically.

"Yeah, I like that. Believe I'd a liked yer Paw."

"He didn't have much education except what Maw give 'im, but he wuz a purty smart ol' buzzard."

"Did yer Paw die young?" Norville wondered.

"Yeah, hadda accident whilst we wuz loggin'," Will choked up.

"Did ya see it happen?"

"Yeah, guess ya could say I'se partly responsible."

"Sorry ta hear that, Presley." Norville dropped his head.

"I'll tell ya the whole story some time, my friend. Good nite. See ya in tha mornin'."

Will remained silent during the rest of the walk home, but his mind was anything but quiet.

He remembered the details of that horrible day at the logging site in Roaring Fork. He could see his father's lifeless body lying under the fallen tree.

He could see himself helping to carry J.W. Presley into the home he had built for his family with his own hands.

He could hear his sister, Maggie, sobbing as she prepared to carry the news to their Mother at the school.

Worst of all, he could see their Mother sitting silently by her husband's coffin for days unable to speak or move.

"I'll always feel tha I coulda helped ta prevent Paw's dyin'," Will thought, trying to hold back the tears.

"Why didn't I run 'n' push Paw outta the way 'fore it wuz too late?"

"Why wuzn't we payin' more attention ta where Paw was 'fore lettin' tha tree fall? We knew he wuz a drankin' more'n a bit a his corn liquor tha day.

"I gotta stop this now," he told himself, wiping his eyes with his sleeve.

"Cain't let Lenora see me cryin' like a baby. Gotta act like a man fer her sake."

He entered the living quarters shared with his wife, and Lenora met him at the door. "I was worried about you, Will. You're late. Did you have trouble again today?"

"Shore did. Callahan showed up agin' wit his gang a men 'n' the high sheriff a Holly Springs. Feller named Ashe. Said they's gonna git a court order 'n' make us leave."

"Isn't that property abandoned land?" Lenora questioned.

"Yep, but Runkle says Johnson wants ta give it all back ta them former plantation operators. He's a Southerner, and sides with them."

"But that isn't what Lincoln had planned for Reconstruction. His plan was forty acres and a mule for these Freedmen. I heard him talking about it with Secretary Stanton while I was still working at the War Department."

"That's rite honey, but Johnson's in charge now, Lincoln's gone."

"Isn't there anything we can do? I didn't come down here to watch Lincoln's plan be reversed." she lamented.

"Colonel Runkle sez we gonna git 'ese houses built, then go back ta buildin' schools here in Memphis outside tha fort.

"He's gonna give us sum extra men ta help us finish 'ese five houses, then we'll move on ta tha schools."

"I brought you some food from the mess hall. Sit down here and eat a bite before bedtime," Lenora patted his shoulder.

Chapter Eleven

TROUBLE RETURNS

With the help of the men's extra crews, all five houses were finished in the next four weeks. Sam Jennings and his wife, Mandy, and their four children, were the first ones to move into their new house.

Will and Norville found some surplus furniture in the storage room of the supply depot. Arriving early at the house, they started to unload the wagon.

Coming out of the house after carrying a table and six chairs inside, they heard a loud scream of joy. Mandy and Sam had just arrived with their children and saw the furniture.

"Praise the Lawd," she yelled. "I's a won'drun' what we gonna do fer furnishin'."

Sam Jumped down from the wagon, grinned and said, "Thank ye, Mista Will, 'n' Mista Norville. We shore 'preciate what ye dun fer us."

"Let me git 'ese here boys ta helpin' us unload tha stuff. Abe, ye 'n' Ike git 'em bed rails an' headboard inta tha house. Jake 'n' Joe can carry 'em bed sheets 'n blankets."

"Lawd bless you, Mista Will," Mandy exclaimed. "Ye dun got us a stove 'n' ever' thang else we gonna need ta live here. We shore 'er obliged ta ya."

"Glad we could help ye Miss Mandy," Will nodded as Norville smiled proudly.

"Guess me 'n' Norville better mosey on down ta Luther Kaine's place 'n' see what more needs ta be dun ther'. Ye folks kin git settled in today, maybe."

"I shore hate ta leave 'em people without pertection out here. Callahan ain't give up yet," Norville said.

"Well, I give Sam a repeater rifle 'n' sum ammo, but I hope he won't hafta use it," Will said.

"Hope yer rite, Presley, but I got a bad feelin' 'bout 'ese folks."

"Come on, let's go on down to Kaine's place. Then we'll try ta check on tha other three this aftanoon."

***

When they arrived at Luther Kaine's property, Cicely, Kaine's wife, greeted them. "Good mawin' Mista Will 'n' Mista Norville. What brings ye men out this way?"

"Just checkin' in Miss Cicely." Will was polite.

"They's puttin' tha roof on now. Should be finished by tomorrow or tha next day. That's what Luther's a sayin'," she informed them.

"OK, we'll see if we can find some furnishin's fer ye at the fort. We found a few thangs fer Sam and Mandy."

"Has ever'thang been purty quiet 'round here, Miss Cicely?" Norville asked.

"Yas Sir, so far. Er ye 'spectin' anythang?" she asked with a worried look.

"I'll get a rifle for Luther when I get some furnishin's too," Will told her. "Just to be safe."

"We're goin' on down ta Otis an' Lucy Wilson's house. We'll see ya tomorrow, Miss Cicely."

***

Driving the wagon east from the Kaine house, they could see the Wilson house in the distance. Some white men on horseback were gesturing wildly and yelling.

As they got closer to the house, they could see the Freedmen's squad of soldiers with rifles ready to oppose the intruders.

"What's a goin' on here, Sargent?" Will asked.

The young white man spoke first, "These here niggers is truspassin' on my daddy's land. They gonna hafta leave now."

"Who are ye, 'n' who's yer daddy?" Will asked.

"My name is William Callahan, Jr., and William Callahan, Sr.'s my Paw."

"I've explained ta yer Paw afore that this here's abandoned land is owned by the United States of America, Mr. Callahan."

"My Paw 'n Sheriff Ashe is gone ta Washington D.C. rite now to talk to President Johnson. He's a gonna give 'er property back to us. Sheriff said he would."

"Well, rite now it belongs ta Otis 'n Miss Lucy, so yer tha one a truspassin'. Now Sargent Jordan 'n' his men is got repeater rifles 'n' know how to use 'em. Ye best jist be movin' along."

"We've got sum surprises fer ye scalawags 'n 'ese niggras. Ye best be watchin' out fer us. We'll be back soon."

"Whatta we gonna do, Mista Will?" Otis asked and rubbed his head.

"For rite now we gonna finish 'is here roof on yer house. We'll leave a rifle with ye. Since ye served in tha Union army, I guess ye know how ta use it, don'tcha?" Will reassured him.

"Yas Suh, Mista Will, but I don' wanna be killin' nobody lessen I hafta ta pertect my fam'ly."

"I know whatcha mean Otis, but sometimes ya gotta do it."

"We're headin' back ta tha fort. Try to see ya agin' tomorrow.

"I'm a huntin' fer sum house furnishin's fer Miss Lucy. We gonna talk ta Colonel Runkle 'bout how ta handle 'ese bad boys comin' 'round 'n botherin' ye."

"Keep yer kids in tha house 'n' yer eyes 'n ears open," Norville said.

While they rode back to the fort, Will was musing. "Hope we can figger out a way ta keep 'ese folk in their homes, but I ain't a bettin' no money on it."

"We might hafta give up on this project 'n retreat. We done that in tha army several times." Norville said.

"I heerd Gen'ral Meade say, better ta live 'n fight another day."

Chapter Twelve

A NEW STRATEGY

H eading immediately to the Colonel's office upon arriving back at the fort, Will knocked on the door.

"Come in, Presley and Hill. What can I do for you, gentlemen?" Runkle asked.

"Colonel, we need ta tell 'ese folks what's a gonna happen ta 'em. They wanna git on with ther' lives, 'n' not hafta worry 'bout 'ese landowners all tha time," Norville spoke first.

"Tell me what happened today," Runkle sighed.

After a quick recount of the day's events, Will continued, "We're 'bout finished with this first group of settlers. I thank we orta hold off on buildin' any more houses," he reasoned.

"Agreed, Presley. I have written a letter to General Fisk in Nashville requesting permission to build some schools in the African areas here in South Memphis.

"We have the school here in the fort, but none out where the civilians live.

"Most of the Freedmen families live here in close-proximity to Fort Pickering. These children need to attend school close to home," Runkle continued.

"General Fisk has also given me the authority to negotiate with Callahan and Hammond for a share-cropper deal for our Freedman families."

"I ain't so shore 'ese settlers is gonna like it, if they ain't working ther' own place," Norville was skeptical.

The Colonel spoke emphatically, "They will just have to adjust to whatever deal we can get for them; otherwise, they can just leave and find other means to make a living.

"President Johnson has decided to re-establish the plantations with the pre-war owners."

"He's completely changing the whole outcome of the war, ain't he, Colonel?" Will was incredulous.

"Yes, he is, but as President of the United States, he is Commander-in-Chief of the Army. My only choice is to obey his orders."

"It don't rightly seem fair ta me," Will replied. "But it ain't my decision to make."

"Do ya thank we can gather up some surplus furniture outta the storeroom fer tha rest 'ese folks in tha settlements?" Norville inquired. "We promised we'd git 'em sum stuff, 'n' they gonna need it regardless of whither they stay 'er not."

"Yes, of course. That needs to be done this week. It's the 28th of August now, and we need to build schools next week.

"Presley, if we can find some space down around Beale Street, we can rent it. The more area we don't have to build from scratch, the cheaper it will be.

"We think we'll need eight schools for all the youngsters in South Memphis. Some teachers think some adults will want to learnt o read and write, too.

"We're still operating on the War Department budget. Congress hasn't appropriated funds for the Bureau yet. General Howard is hoping to get Congress to give us some money next year."

"Do you really think Johnson's gonna give money to the Freedman's Bureau, Colonel?" Norville was angry.

"Well, if Congress approves it, he'll have to veto it. Word is that there's already talk of impeaching him. Thaddeus Stevens, a congressional representative from Pennsylvania, is irate at Johnson for what he's doing for the Rebels.

"Presley, your lovely wife could be extremely helpful in finding locations for schools. Renting or building, they should be accessible to the homes where these children live."

"Yes Sir, Colonel, I shore will talk ta Lenora 'bout helpin' ta find space for schools. She's real eager to help all she can."

Turning to his friend, Will said, "OK, Norville, I'll see you in tha mornin'. We'll load out some stuff fer the settlers 'n' try ta git them took keer of this week.

"I'll meet ya at Central Supply at 7:00 in tha nornin'. We'll get two wagons 'n fill 'em up. I thank we kin git enough stuff for Luther 'n Cicely and Otis 'n Lucy."

THE NEXT MORNING

"Alright Norville, looks like that's all tha wagons'll hold. Let's git 'ese unloaded, then tomorrow, we'll git Malcolm Nance 'n Roscoe Gaye sum stuff."

Arriving at the Kaine home, they were met by Luther and Cicely and their five children. "Good Mawnin', Mista Will 'n' Mista Norville. I's a hopin' y'all would be he'ah early," Luther greeted them.

"Yep, knew ye folks wuz wantin' ta git moved in 'is place," Will replied.

Cicely spoke to her children, "Aw rite ye young'uns git to moving this stuff inta tha house. 'Ese men ain't got all day ta wait on you'ns."

As Norville directed the children in the unloading, Will spoke softly to Luther. "Looks like Johnson's gonna give this here land back to tha plantation owners. Runkle, thanks ther ain't much we kin do 'bout it. Only choices I'm a seein' is start another fight; bow our heads 'n' take it; or figger out 'nother way round it," Will surmised.

"Well, what's tha use in doin' all this work on this place, Mista Will? Don't make no sense to me."

"Ther's a possibility we kin work out sum'thin with Callahan fer y'all ta work this place as share-croppers and keep half of what ye earn.

"He'd get tha other half, but ye'd have yer own place ta live 'n' raise sum hogs 'n a garden ta feed yer fam'ly. Callahan wuddn't own ye, 'n' ye cud leave any tine ye wanted to."

Will continued, "This here furniture belongs ta you 'n Cicely, too."

"Wher'd we go to if we don't like it?" Luther was puzzled.

"Well, ya cud move ta Memphis 'n' find a job, iffen ya don't wanna raise cotton. Ye 'n Cicely kin make up yer own mind 'bout what to do. Leastwise ye ain't slaves no more. I'm awful sorry, but that's 'bout all we kin do rite now."

"OK, Mista Will. We do 'preciate what ye dun fer us." Luther dropped his head.

"Let's go Norville , we gotta git on down ta see Otis 'n Lucy."

As the wagons pulled onto the Wilson's property, the children ran out to greet them. Three stair-step sized boys aged ten, eight, and seven were eager to see what was on the wagons. When the cart stopped, Norville jumped down and started the unloading process.

Eagerly, the boys began to work as Norville directed them.

Coming outside to greet them, Otis smiled, "Good afta'noon, Mista Will. Lucy fixed us sum lunch 'n' brung it with us, but yer welcome to share it wit' us."

"We'll pass on lunch, but 'preciate tha offa. I need ta talk ta ye 'n Miss Lucy, though."

As Lucy joined the group, Will took off his hat and smiled at her.

She did not overlook the show of respect-a gesture that was rare for black women.

"Shore "preciate ye a bringin' us all this nice furnishin's, Mista Will," she smiled.

"We found these surplus household items in Central Supply. The army replaces tha officer's furniture every five years, and this was just sittin' ther collecting dust."

"We ain't neva had nuthin' of 'er own afore, Mista Will, so it's looks good ta us," Otis grinned.

Will nodded, then dropped his head as he began to explain the situation to them. As he finished, he looked at Lucy, whose face was contorted in anger.

"Ye mean ta tell me we ain't gonna be able ta stay here? That ain't rite," Lucy was sobbing.

"Miss Lucy, I know it ain't rite, but ther ain't nuthin' much I kin do 'bout it," Will shook his head.

"Y'all kin, maybe stay here, if ye share-crop with Callahan. The Colonel ain't got it all worked out yit, but he's thankin' it kin be dun." He smiled and nodded.

"If ye ain't happy with tha deal, ye kin move back inta town 'n' find a job. Ye kin take all this stuff with ye when ye move. It's yours."

"But Mista Will, we don't know how ta do no jobs in town. We's ah'ways jist been fah'mers," Otis dropped his head.

"Well, ye 'n' Lucy, decide what ye wanna do, then let us know. We'll help ye whatever. We gotta git back ta tha fort 'n find sum stuff fer Malcolm 'n Roscoe. I'll try ta stop in a'gin tomorrow after our delivery to tha other folks."

As they started back to the fort, Norville was pensive. "I shore hope 'ese folks don't get hurt out here. Ese Mississippi Rebs 'er still fightin' tha war. I've heerd sum people call it a *Lost Cause*."

"Yep, I heerd that too. Guess we jist hafta pray a lot fer 'ese Freedmen, I reckon," he nodded.

Hurrying back to Fort Pickering, they arrived in time to load the next day's delivery.

At 7:00 the next morning, they pulled out to make their last furniture run and explain their options to the Nances and the Gayes. Neither family was happy, but they were well accustomed to resigning themselves to the reality of the current situation.

Chapter Thirteen

SOUTH MEMPHIS SCHOOLS

O n Monday morning, September 26, 1865, Will and Lenora made an excursion down to Beale Street in South Memphis.

They were searching for an empty building to locate a school. The couple walked about five blocks east of Front Street.

Located on a corner lot, they found a building in need of repair, but well within walking distance of several homes occupied by black families with children. Inquiring at an office building across the street, they secured the name of the owner.

The pair continued to walk through the area, and found another empty facility about five blocks north on Third Street.

"Alright, Lenora, let's go back ta tha fort 'n' talk ta Colonel Runkle. Two places ta start with is enough. We'll let tha Colonel negotiate tha rental contract wit tha owners. I do thank we got sum good spots fer schools."

As they walked back to their living quarters, Will said to Lenora, "Let's stop in at Norville's room 'n' tell him what we found taday."

"OK, but we can't stay long. They'll be serving dinner in the Mess Hall soon, and I want to freshen up a bit before we go," she reminded him.

"Aw sweet lady, ye'll be tha purtiest gal in tha place anyway," Will gushed.

"Oh Will, how you do go on," she smiled while brushing her hair back with her hand.

***

Norville very quickly opened his door as Will knocked. "Hello Presley 'n' Missus Presley. Come on in 'n' set a spell. Did y'all have a good 'un taday?"

Lenora said, "Yes we did, and please call me Lenora.

"Missus Presley sounds so formal."

"Yeah, Hill," Will replied. "Found a couple a good spots fer schools over in South Memphis. One of 'em's gonna take some serious work ta git it ready fer a school building, t'other 'un needs sum paint 'n' a li'l cleanin' up."

"Alright, sounds good ta me. When do we start?" Hill was eager to go to work.

Lenora replied, "The Colonel will have to approve it before we can proceed. We'll report to him and ask him to contact the owners of the buildings."

"'Matta a fact, I'm headin' ta his office rite now," Presley responded.

"If he's OK with it, I'll ask fer sum help ta fix up tha first 'un 'n' ta clean 'n' paint t'other 'un. 'At's where ye come in, Norville. 'Er ye OK on it?"

"Count me in. Fixin's a lot easier than building from tha ground up."

"Let's go talk ta the Colonel, Lenora," Will was eager to get started.

***

Will knocked on the Colonel's office door, and barely constrained himself, waiting for Runkle to invite him in.

"Good afternoon Presley and the Missus. Come in. Do you have some news for me?"

"Shore do Colonel. Found a couple a places that'd make good schoolhouses. Both of 'em close to where families live there in South Memphis."

Lenora asked. "How many schools are you looking to open, Colonel?"

"We need to open several, probably eight or nine, to get all these black children off the streets. Memphis police officers are arresting many of them and charging them with being vagrants. I heard a report the other day that some teenaged boys walking home from school here at the fort carrying spelling books were arrested.

"When they go to court, the judges are requiring them to sign contracts of indenture. These children are then sent to plantations to work the cotton crops. They're doing the same thing to adult blacks too. It's slavery all over again."

"Why 'er they a bein' allowed ta do that ta 'ese folks?

Tha war's over 'n' we're a tryin' ta make things right 'n' ther jist keepin' it a goin'," Will exclaimed.

"Yes Presley, but many of these policemen and judges are Irish. They resent the fact that the freed blacks are taking many of the jobs they consider being theirs.

"Then, too, the plantation owners are putting pressure on their Congressmen and even President Johnson. The cotton business is struggling without slaves to provide labor."

"Well, this is just a sneaky way to get around what the war was fought over," Lenora replied. "It just seems so unfair to me."

"Alright Colonel, we'll jist wait 'til ye find out sum'thin' on tha buildin's."

"In the meantime, you could be scouting for locations to *build* schools. We won't be able to find enough vacant sites," Runkle said.

"OK, Colonel. Me 'n' Lenora'll be on the lookout fer sum land ta build on. In the meantime, kin ye give us sum construction help from here at tha fort? Norville kin oversee them on the first 'un, and me and Lenora kin git tha paintin' and cleanin' dun' on t'other 'un.

Chapter Fourteen

THE IRISH SQUAD

Standing on the corner of Third Avenue and Beale Street, Patrick O'Brien enjoyed the beautiful early fall day in Memphis. At 8:00 A.M., the sun shone its brilliant rays of light from the east side of the Mississippi River. A gentle, southerly breeze caressed the back of his head and lifted his spirits.

As he twirled his hickory-wood nightstick with the leather strap around his wrist, he whistled a tune his father sang to him. Before his father had gone on to his heavenly reward, Pattie (as Pop called him) and his Dad were almost inseparable.

Robert O'Brien had served in the U.S. Army during the Mexican War. After his left leg was amputated just above his knee, he was discharged and returned to Memphis.

Sargent Patrick O'Brien, a ten-year veteran of the Memphis Police Department, was a tall, heavy-set man. His size and exaggerated gruff demeanor intimidated many people who met him for the first time.

Will and Lenora walked out the south gate of Fort Pickering and crossed Front Street to Beale. Walking east toward Third, they could see the Sargent standing on the corner.

As they approached, Patrick spoke, "Top a tha Mahnin' ta ye. What's a couple o' nice white folks like ye doin' down 'ere in Shanty town? It might be dangerous in dese pahts fah ya."

Lenora replied, "We're here looking for some vacant property to build some schoolhouses. Maybe you can help us, since you're so familiar with the area."

"I didn't know de Memphis school system was goin' to build mahre schools in dis black district." he looked puzzled.

"Oh, it's not the Memphis system that's going to build them. It's the Freedmen's Bureau. Will and I are working for them out of Fort

Pickering."

Will winced as Lenora rattled on about their plans. He quickly took her hand and said, "Excuse us Sargent, but me 'n' Lenora's got work to do. Thank ye, Sir."

As they walked on toward Jefferson Avenue, Will spoke. "We don't wanna be tellin' too much 'bout what we're aimin' 'ta do. If word gits out it's tha gub'ment wantin' property, tha price'll go up. A lotta 'ese people prob'ly don't want schools fer blacks ta be built anyhow."

"Oh, my goodness, I didn't think of that. I suppose these southerners aren't keen to be helping freedmen's children."

"Ye kin bet yer bottom dolla' on 'at, Sweet Lady. So many blacks moved in 'ere after tha Union Army took over Fort Pickering. Colonel Runkle said ther' wuz 16,000 er more what come here," Will informed her.

Musingly, Lenora replied, " A lot of these southerners are still fighting the war. I heard somebody in D.C. talking about the Lost Cause."

"Yep, they cain't tolerate tha thought a losin' tha war, but ther gonna hafta, I reckon."

As the Presleys walked away, O'Brien watched and slowly began to seethe. His face turned red, and he tapped the nightstick on his left palm.

Thinking out loud, he whispered, *"By Gahd dese carpetbaggers are thinkin' they can just take over ahur town 'ere. I guess de Irish squad needs to know 'bout dis.*

"When I take me lunch break, I'm goin' to tell all the bahys what dese carpetbaggers is up to."

Sitting at a long table at the back of the dining area, four Irish cops were sipping beer and waiting for the others to arrive. Every day at 11:30 A.M., the Irish officers of the Memphis Police Department gathered at Gus's Irish Pub for lunch. With the one exception of Spencer, they all walked a beat in South Memphis, which was almost totally populated by black freedmen and their families.

Mostly, they knew the residents in their district, and were contemptuous of them, resenting that freed slaves were becoming the majority inhabitants. The Irish populace opposed them at every turn. O'Brien was eager to make his pals aware of the Bureau's plan to build schoolhouses in South Memphis.

Before he sat down at the table, Patrick began to speak. "We gaht trouble brewin' in de destrect bahys."

Raising his eyebrows as he looked up, Lieutenant Tim Spencer inquired, "What's goin' ahn, Pattie?"

All eyes turned to O'Brien. "The United States Army is buildin' schoolhouses in South Memphis. At least dey are 'untin' vacant prahperty to build dem ahn."

Patrolman Mike O'Malley asked, "'ow do you know dat Patrick?"

"Spoke to a female carpetbagger and a scalawag from the fahrt dis mahrnin'. Dey told me what they wuz doin' walkin' in me destrect that wuz full 'o blacks.

"I told dem it wuz dangerous fahr dem to be walkin' here, but the country white folks didn't seem nervous."

Lieutenant Spencer exclaimed, "Looks like we ahr goin' to 'ave to crack down on dese neggers and show dem who's boss 'round 'ere, bahys."

Speaking up, officer Johnny Murphy interjected, "Me block 'o blacks already knows who's boss. that 'ick'ry stick across an ahrm or a shin keeps dem in line."

Richie Flynn inquired, "When is dis all supposed to stahrt?"

"Well, I reckahn very soon. Dey ahr lookin' fahr land, but dey won't be able to buy any from Irish ahwners."

Officer Larry O'Donnell spoke, "My uncle Jack rents three 'ouses to blacks down dere. They might try to rent land."

"De federal government won't rent no land. If dey want it, dey'll get it one way or de ahther." the Lieutenant informed them.

He continued, "Best thing we can do is try to 'vince dese blacks to go back to de plantations. Dey might want to leave if some bad egg cops use Deir sticks on 'em."

"'Ey Lieutenant, what's goin' to 'appen to an ahfficer who breaks a freedman's ahrm or leg?" Arnold Ryan asked.

"Ye might get a prahmahtion," he chuckled. "Chief Garrett and Mayahr Park would be 'appy to get rid o' some o' dese neggers."

Spencer continued. "If ye see one o' dem standin' 'round on a street cahrner or lahterin' at a cotton ware ahuse door, put dem in jail fahr vagrancy. A little 'arassment won't 'urt de cause."

As they finished lunch, paid their bill, and started out the door, O'Brien spoke, "Let's go kick some black arse, bahys."

Will and Lenora, after locating vacant properties on Jefferson Avenue, Peabody Avenue, Central Avenue, Madison Avenue, Second Street, and Front Street, started back to the fort. Approaching Beale and Third Avenue's corner, they noticed Sargent O'Brien standing over two black men lying on the sidewalk.

Sargent O'Brien spoke as they drew nearer, "Be real careful ma'am, dese low lifes ahr goin' to jail."

Shocked, Lenora gasped, "What did they do?"

"'Hangin' ahut on the cahrner ma'am, prahbably plannin' some mischief instead o' wahrkin'. De law calls it vagrancy."

Incredulous, Lenora raised her voice. "Do you mean they are going to jail for doing nothing?"

He replied, "I don't make de laws ma'am, I just enfahrce 'em," slightly raising his voice. "Now move along 'ere an' don't be a 'inderin' law enfahrcement."

"Come on, Lenora, We gotta git back ta tha fort. We'll go talk ta Colonel Runkle 'n tell 'im what we found."

Chapter Fifteen

OPPOSITION

"Evenin', Colonel," Will spoke as they entered the office building.

"Can we talk with ye fer just a minute?"

"Certainly, Presley. You and the Missus have a seat. Did you find anything that might work for a schoolhouse location?"

"Shore did. Found six spots right in tha middle of where a lotta freedmen-families live. Most of 'em er close ta churches, too. I'm a thankin' sum a 'em preachers'll wanna help in tha schools since tha teachers 'er a workin' fer churches."

"Yes, that's good thinking, Presley. Give me the addresses and I'll see what we can do with the owners."

Lenora joined the conversation, "Colonel Runkle, I'm afraid some of the folks here in Memphis are not happy about schoolhouses going into these neighborhoods. We met a police officer who wanted to know why we were walking down Beale Street. I answered him honestly, and he gave me a puzzled look.

"When we started back to the fort, that same policeman had two freedmen lying on the sidewalk with handcuffs on them. He said he arrested them for doing nothing."

"Yep, said it wuz vagrancy or sum'thun like 'at," Will added.

Answering slowly, the Colonel replied, "Yes, that has been a problem for quite a while here in Memphis. The Irish population, not just the police, are resentful of the freedmen's rapid growth here.

"The black population swelled right after Memphis was occupied by the Union army in '62. Freed slaves left the plantations in Mississippi and Alabama and Tennessee to move here.

"Some of them were hired by cotton warehouses as laborers and paid lower wages than the Irish people were paid. Also, the

City Government hired some as garbage collectors and street sweepers. Irishmen thought these jobs should be theirs because they were here first."

Lenora furrowed her brow as she spoke. "We seem to know what the problem is, but what can we do about it?" she asked.

"After talking with many business owners who employ freedmen, I am told that the Irish want to drive the former slaves back to the plantations. Cotton growers want them back, too. It's challenging to grow cotton without a lot of labor.

"Consequently, police are encouraged to harass these people, and force them back to picking cotton."

"It was my understanding that our goal in the Freedmen's Bureau is to educate black people and help them be qualified to perform other jobs besides picking cotton," Lenora added.

"Well stated, Mrs. Presley," Runkle replied. "We have some folks in Congress who are working to that end. It is our responsibility here to do whatever is necessary to accomplish this goal."

"So, in the meantime we got to get some schools opened 'n' start educatin' 'ese young'uns I reckon," Will responded.

"I've got an idea," Lenora volunteered.

"Yes, go ahead, Mrs. Presley. What's on your mind?"

"I'm sorry Will, I just had this thought as we walked back from our excursion today. Colonel, if we could hire some freedmen to work preparing the buildings and constructing the new ones, vagrancy is not a problem.

"Somebody has to do the work. Why not freedmen?"

"That's an excellent idea ma'am. We really can't spare soldiers from the fort to do construction work. We'll have to hire workers," he replied.

"Me 'n' Norville can oversee the work 'n' show 'em what ta do. I thank it's a *great* idea. If 'ese men work on construction, it'll be more important to 'em ta send ther' kids ta school," Will noted.

"I'll have to get permission from General Fisk to take that step, but I believe he'll be receptive to it. I'll send him a telegram in the morning. As soon as I get approval, I'll inform you to proceed. Check in with me about noon tomorrow."

***

Will knocked on the office door and spoke, "Are you busy Colonel?"

"No, come on in Presley. I told the General I wanted to hire some freedmen to get the buildings ready for our students to occupy. He thought it was a *great* idea, and I told him you and Mrs. Presley agree with the idea."

"OK, but actually Lenora is the one who had tha idea in tha first place, Colonel," Will protested.

"I am well aware of that, but I believed that the General would be more receptive to it, if it came from me."

"Yeah, I guess yer' rite. I'm shore Lenora will understand," he shrugged.

"Well, we both know where it came from, but it might be best if we don't tell her. Take it from an old married man."

He then added, "As a Christian, I do believe that men should take the lead, and women should follow them. The Apostle Paul taught us that."

"Alright, that's settled, I'll tell Norville, 'n' me and him kin git started tamorrow. We'll go to Central Supply Depot 'n' git what we need to fix tha first building. It needs a lotta work."

"Yes, that building was a *grand house* several years ago. General Grant used it as his office when he was first assigned to Memphis. It was called the Hunt-Phelan House. That's a perfect spot for a school.

Hunt-Phelan House

"The Hunt-Phelan House was built between 1828 - 1832 and owned by William Richard Hunt when the war started. A Federal-Style architecture building, it features brick construction with symmetrical windows. The two-story structure's portico is adorned with Ionic columns.

"A grand house indeed, it hosted the likes of Andrew Jackson, then Jefferson Davis, and Nathan Bedford Forrest during the Civil War. Sadly, the beautiful abode was severely damaged in 1862, when the Union army captured the city of Memphis."

Runkle continued, "Go on down there this afternoon and tell them what you need. Take Norville with you. The two of you can load the wagon, then you'll be ready in the morning." he directed.

"I'm gonna take Lenora too. She kin hire us some freedmen to work. At first, just hire a few, then add some as we go along. The second building will only need some paint and a good cleaning. I'll work a couple of days with Norville, then move on to tha other one."

***

Will knocked loudly on his friend's door and spoke, "Hey Norville, er ye in ther?"

Just as he spoke, Norville walked up behind him. "No, I'm rite here, Presley. What's a goin' on?"

"Goin' ta supply depot ta git what we gonna need ta fix that old buildin'. Don't' look like nothin's been fixed on it since 'er army took over here in '62. Floors got holes in it and tha roof's a leakin'. Colonel says we kin hire sum locals ta help us work. Gonna git Lenora ta help with that. We kin load out tanight and start work first thang in tha mornin'."

"Alright, I'm ready. Let's go."

***

"Hello, Sargent Walters. Colonel Runkle sent us down here to git lumber and materials ta fix up a place on Beale Street for a schoolhouse for freedmen's children. Here's a list of what me and Norville thank we gonna need."

Walters, a short, stocky, balding man from Ohio, answered, "Yes Sir, Presley. I'll get a couple of my men to get it together for you." When do you need it?"

"We wuz hopin' ta load it this eve'nin' so we can leave first thang in tha mornin'. Is 'at possible?"

"Yeah, I got two men just real eager to work. Hey Smitty and Flatt, need you men to get some material together for the Freedmen's Bureau. They need it loaded now. Come on, let's get it done."

Norville winked at Will and said softly, "I ain't shore 'em two wuz as eager ta work as the Sargent let on."

Chapter Sixteen

CONSTRUCTION

Lenora climbed into the wagon with Will and Norville as they prepared to leave the Supply Depot. Holding the hand-lettered sign that read "Now Hiring Laborers - Freedmen Preferred."

Norville wryly observed, "Ye might hear sum complainin' 'bout preferrin' Freedmen, Miss Lenora. 'Ese Irish boys ain't a gonna like that much."

"They prob'bly don't wanna see no schools fer black young'uns, anyhow," Will answered.

Lenora then spoke, "Colonel Runkle liked my idea of using freedmen to build these schools. I think we need to make it clear that they are preferred. Many of them wouldn't even try to get these jobs if we didn't."

"Yeah, we kin deal with it if we hafta. Otherwise, jist fergit it," Will observed.

As the wagon turned onto Beale Street, six young black men noticed the hauler loaded with building material. Curious, they followed behind to the location. When they stopped, one of them asked, "What y'all fixin' ta do, Missy?"

"We're going to open a school for the children of former slaves, and we need some help to get it done. Do you want a job?"

"Yas ma'am, I shore do. You gonna pay us."

"Of course, we'll pay you. You will get the regular pay that all laborers are paid here in Memphis."

"Hey Missy, I wan' me a job, too."

"Yeah, me too ma'am," the other four chimed in.

Smiling, she retorted, "I think we can use all of you. Start unloading the wagon."

Norville whispered, "Don't thank ye'll need tha sign, Miss Lenora.

Jist lay it down in under tha seat. No sense in causin' a ruckus 'round here."

Will then took charge. "Stack all that stuff inside the buildin'. Try ta put it all over agin' that far wall out of tha way. Don't wanna hafta move it three 'er four times."

As the men finished unloading, Lenora said, "Come over here and give me your names. I need to make a list for Colonel Runkle, so we can pay you."

"Willie Johnson, ma'am," the tall, wiry man who appeared to be the leader of the group volunteered.

"Joseph Robinson, ma'am," a short, thick-waisted man with a heavy mustache added.

"George Johnson, ma'am," the smallest and youngest man in the group answered.

"Thomas Preston, ma'am," as he dropped his head in respect for the white lady.

"Charles Jackson, ma'am," a heavily muscled man with large rough hands replied.

"Robert Pierce, ma'am," he smiled with his white teeth flashing through the full beard on his face.

Noville joined the group and said, "OK men, I'm Norville Hill from Knoxville, Tennessee, 'n' I fought in tha Union army. I been on your side for a long time. We gonna build at least eight schools fer black young'uns, so you kin have a job fer a long time if ya want it."

Willie asked, "Where ya gonna build all a 'ese schools, Mista Norville?"

"Right here in South Memphis, close ta where y'all live."

"Ain't none a us got any kids big enuff ta go ta school. Won't help us none," he replied.

Joining the conversation, Will asked, "Have ye got bruthers 'n' sistas big enuff, 'er other fam'ly members?"

"There are plans to have some classes for adults too," Lenora added. "Reading and writing and counting are skills that will help you find a job besides just labor. Can you read and write, Willie?"

"No, ma'am," he dropped his head. "Nobody on tha plantation never learnt us ta read 'er 'rite."

"We didn't have ta read ta pick cotton, Missy," Robert said.

Joseph chimed in, "I don' wanna go ta no school wit a bunch a young'uns."

Presley offered, "This here building's got lots a rooms. They kin have a room jist fer grown folks."

"Also, it's possible they will have night classes for adults who have jobs," Lenora added.

"This here is shore, a fine house fer a school. It do need sum fixin', but it'll be nice fer black chil'lun," Thomas spoke.

"Alright, let's git ta workin' men. The Colonel's gonna wanna know how much we got dun taday," Norville ordered.

Speaking to Norville as the day wore on, Will said, "Can we wrap thangs up a little bit early? Lenora needs to git this here information about 'er workin' men to the Colonel's office. Tell 'em we'll pay fer a full day's wages."

"Alright men, let's call it a day. Y'all will git a full day's pay. Be here at 7:00 in tha mornin' with yer workin' britches on. We finished tha floors in two rooms taday, and I wanna git tha rest a tha downstairs rooms finished this week," Norville said.

"OK, boss man. We be here tomorrow bright 'n' early." Willie spoke as the other men nodded in assent.

When they arrived back at the Fort, Will and Lenora went straight to Runkle's office.

"Come in Presley and the Missus. Did you have a good day?"

"I would say it went purty good, Sir. Didn't have no trouble 'n' Lenora hired us six good men ta work. You kin tell 'ese boys been on a plantation, 'cause they worked hard 'n' steady, 'n' followed orders real good. They'd a been good soldiers."

"We gotta do the rest a tha downstairs floors, then move upstairs. We need ta fix a leakin' roof and paint everything. Prob'bly take 'bout four 'er five weeks on this 'un.

"Me 'n' Lenora's gonna work ther tomorrow, then go ta t'other place 'n' start on it. We'll take two a Norville's man's wit us 'n' try ta hire two more."

Lenora said, "Here is the list of men we hired. Told them they'll get regular laborers' wages here in Memphis. I wasn't certain what the prevailing wage is, so I wasn't specific."

"Sounds to me as if you have made a good start, folks. I am happy to have you two here with me to tackle this big project.

"As soon as we get these first two schoolhouses ready, we'll find some desks, chalkboards, and other furnishings, and start classes. When we get the others built, they can be started as ready."

As they walked back to their living quarters, Lenora smiled and said, "I feel real good about what we're doing here, Will. Thank you for convincing me to attempt this huge undertaking. It's rewarding to make a difference in the lives of these people."

***

At precisely 7:00 A.M., Will, Lenora, and Norville pulled up in front of the Hunt-Phelan House to resume work. Six men were sitting on the front porch, awaiting their arrival.

Norville ordered, "OK men let's go to work. Y'all know what we wanna git dun taday. Let's git on it."

"Mista Norville, if we split up 'n' two men work in each room, we kin git dun quicker," Willie suggested.

"Yeah good idee, Willie," Hill replied. "That way we kin work on three rooms at a time."

"Little Georgie, ye kin work wit me. Joey 'n' Tom kin help each other, 'n' Charles 'n' Robert tagetha. That makes good teams, Mista Hill. I worked with 'ese boys a pickin' cotton 'n' knows 'em purty good." Willie took charge.

"At's fine by me," Hill nodded his assent, "Let's git ta work."

As they watched from a distance, Lenora whispered to Will, "We got ourselves a good team."

"Yep, yer a good picker, Sweet Lady."

"I picked you, didn't I."

Will said to Norville, "Check your materials this afta'noon before you leave. If ye need more, make a list 'n' we'll git it outta tha Supply Depot in tha mornin'. Me 'n Lenora's goin' over ta tha other building 'n' see what we gonna need there.

"I'm gonna need two a yer men ta help us tomorrow. Charles 'n' Robert kin work wit us. Ye kin keep Willie 'n' tha other three here with you."

"We'll see you back at the fort after dinner tonight," Lenora smiled as they left the building."

***

Recounting all that had happened in a short period, Lenora and Will felt a shared sense of accomplishment. At the end of each busy day, they spent a few quiet hours alone in their quarters at the Fort. On this evening, they were sharing their thoughts.

"It has been a tiring but rewarding experience for us, Will. I am so glad to have been by your side," Lenora said softly as she reached for her husband's hand.

"Even though much of Lincoln's plan has been stalled by politics and local resentment, I believe we are on the right side of history. It's most likely going to take a long time for our country to get where it needs to be, but I am proud that you and I are playing a small part in that journey."

"Lenora, ye 'ave a way of sayin' what I'm a thankin' much betta than I eva could. Ye're the best thang eva happen to me."

"Hold on, Will, I have something to tell you that may be even better," she said with a wink and a smile.

"What could tha be, my Darlin'?"

"Well, I'm pretty certain that sometime next spring, our family is going to expand."

Will looked puzzled for a few moments, but when he realized what she was saying, he let out a loud yell and grabbed her in his arms.

"I'm goin' be a Paw! Ye've made me happier than I already was, Lenora. I love ye so much, my Sweet Lady." Will swung Lenora around in a circle, shouting for joy.

"Now calm down, Mr. Presley, there's still a lot of work to do before the blessed event. This needs to be our secret for a few months. I don't want anyone to think I am not able to continue in my job."

"It's gonna be purty hard fer me not ta tell everybody, but I'll try to do what yer askin' of me. Guess I'd betta be startin' ta act like a real fam'ly man, plannin' fer the future 'n' evathang."

"I have no doubts that you will do everything necessary to make our future secure and that you will be a wonderful father, Will. To be on the safe side, I'm planning on visiting Doc Harrison at the Fort in a few days to confirm my suspicions. I'll ask him to keep our secret for a while and to advise me on how long I should keep doing our regular activities."

"Yer such a smart lady, Lenora. Ye think of evathang," Will smiled at his wife and thought again how fortunate he was to have found her and convinced her to build a life with him.

"Yer gonna be the best Maw in the world, next to my own, of course," he said with a wink.

"Someday I want to meet your mother, the famous Sally Presley," Lenora responded with a slight air of jealousy. "Just remember, I ain't your Mama."

***

Doc Harrison examined Sally, agreeing with her diagnosis, and promising to hold her confidence until she wished to share it with those in charge. "I don't see any reason for you not to continue with your work until late February or early March unless complications arise, Lenora. Please be sure to eat well, get plenty of rest, and come see me again if anything unusual happens or you have questions."

"Thank you, Doctor. I feel safe knowing that you are so close," Lenora smiled as she left his office to meet up with Will.

Freedmen's School

By this time, the first Freedman's School located inside the Fort was up and running. Children from military families were the first to be enrolled. Several volunteer teachers divided the thirty into three smaller groups and organized a beginning curriculum. Although all three groups had a similar starting point, the teachers felt divisions by age would create a better learning environment. The younger children would not be intimidated by the older ones, and the older ones would not be embarrassed by comparing their success with younger brothers and sisters.

Lenora enjoyed getting to know the volunteer teachers, most of whom were sponsored by the American Missionary Association. She admired those who traveled from as far away as Pennsylvania and Ohio to be part of this worthy experiment. Because of a reduction in troops based at Fort Pickering, barrack space was available to house all the teaching staff, and they were eligible to take their meals in the Mess Hall.

***

At breakfast one morning, Lenora struck up a conversation with Charlotte Peterson, a recruit from Pennsylvania. "Why did you decide to move so far from home to take on this challenge?"

"Most likely, for the same reason, you and your husband left home and signed on to help people you had never met," Charlotte answered. "If you believe it is your responsibility to follow the Great Commission to carry the Good News to all the world, you can't be too particular about what part of the world needs you.

"These children were born in a time and place where they have little to no opportunity to fulfill their God-given destiny. The odds are all against them, but as I see it, we can at least arm them with the tools of basic literacy. They will always have to fight for a place in the world, but we can't send them into battle unarmed."

"Oh Charlotte, I am so proud to know you and proud that Will and I are helping in some small way to right the wrongs done to them,"

Lenora said with a tear in her eye. "I guess we are all Missionaries in our separate ways."

Chapter Seventeen

MORE SCHOOLS

W hen Norville, driving the wagon, arrived at the worksite on Beale
Street the next morning, he quickly alit and spoke. "Charles 'n
Robert, you two go with Presley 'n' the Missus over ta Third Street. Willie,
Li'l Georgie, Joey 'n Tom kin stay here wit me."

"How many schools y'all gonna build, Mista Will?" Willie asked.

"So fer we got locations fer eight, but we might need nine. We
already got one school inside the fort for soldier's young'uns, it'll jist
depend on how many students we git 'n' how many teachers. We'll have
enough ta han'le 'er students. You kin bet on that."

"Whatta we gonna do at the other place Mista Will?" Tom asked.

"Yeah, I wondered.'bout that too," Charles added.

"We got ta do a lotta cleanin' 'n' paintin', men," Presley answered.

"Well, I didn't see no lumber 'ner nothin'. Didn't thank we could
do no buildin'."

As the wagon turned onto Third Street, Officer Harvey Kelly
looked and saw a white man, a white woman, and two young black
men. Quickly following them down the street, he approached when they
stopped.

"Top 'o tha mahrnin' ta ye folks. What's a goin' on taday here on
me street?" Kelly prided himself in knowing everything happening on his
beat.

Lenora, stepping down from the wagon, spoke, "We are going to
open some schools here in South Memphis for freedmen's children. They
need to learn to read and write."

"Where I come from tha wahmen ain't in charge, Mista," Kelly was
sarcastic.

Irritated, Will fired back at him. "Officer, this here's my wife 'n'
we're partners in this here project. She kin speak good as I kin. Now what's

yer problem?"

"I 'eerd ye scalawags 'n' 'carpetbaggers wuz gonna try 'n educate dese ig'nernt neggers, but it won't take. "Dese people cain't take no book lahrnin'.""

"The United States Army is a gonna do it, 'n' me 'n' Lenora is aiming ta help 'em. Now if ye don't mind we got work ta do."

"Does Mayahr Park 'er Chief Garrett know what ye people is up to?" Kelly sneered.

"Don't rightly know 'bout that, but if he's got a problem, tell 'im ta take it up with tha Freedman's Bureau at tha fort.

"Come on, Tom 'n' Charles, let's git this stuff unloaded. We got work ta do," Will ordered.

Kelly stood outside the door and watched them work until lunchtime. He was eager to get to the Irish pub and inform his fellow officers of this morning's development.

***

Kelly opened the conversation and announced, "De damn Freedmen's Bureau's buildin' one a dem black schools on me beat. I talked to a scalawag 'n' a wahman. Dey 'ad two neggers wharkin' fahr dem. Looks to me like dey could o' 'ired white men to do de wahrk. "Dem neggers cain't do nothin' bot pick cotton. Dey thank dey kin lahrn dem to read 'n' write. Dat dohn't make no sense to me."

"Aye, I seen dem too. Der over on Beale Street fixin' up de Hunt-Phelan place fahr a school. Dat's a mighty fine buildin' to turn over to a bunch a blacks," Pattie O'Brien joined in.

"I asked dem if de Mayahr knows what dey wuz op to, bot I dedn't get a straight answer," Kelly added.

Lieutenant Spencer volunteered, "I don't think Chief Garrett knows 'bout it. I'm goin' to skedaddle on over to de office afta' lunch 'n' tell 'im. He'll prahb'bly want to talk to de Mayahr. All o' de Big Bugs at City Hall needs to know 'bout it."

"Dese neggers ahr goin' to take over dis town if we dahn't do sahmethin'," Mike O'Malley offered his opinion.

"Aye, ye got dat right, O'Malley. I 'eerd de Chief 'n' tha Mayahr talkin' de ahther day. Damn Republicans in Washington is wantin' to give dem full citizenship rights. Fourteenth Amendment dey's' callin' it," Spencer replied. "Dey'll be gettin' highfalutin'."

"White people ahr naht goin' to go fahr it ahr dey?" Richie Flynn inquired.

"I 'ope not, bot dat Stevens guy from Pennsylvania's pushin' it," Spencer answered.

"Well Lieutenant, what ahr we goin' to do 'bout it?" O'Malley repeated his question.

"Looks ta me like we hafta make dese neggers so meserable 'n' skeered dey'll want to go back to de plantations, 'n' quit dis foolishness," Spencer scowled. "If ye ketch one just standin' 'round on a street cahrner, put 'is arse in jail. Don't take no sass ner backtalk neither. Use 'at 'ick'ry stick."

"If de Fourteenth Amendment passes, dese neggers'll be wantin to vahte." O'Brien observed. "Mayahr Park'll 'ave a conniption fit."

"Aye, and de Chief 'll be fet to be tied, too." O'Malley added.

"Hey, Pattie, 'ow many o' dese schools are dey a goin ahpen?" Ryan asked.

"Don't rightly know, but dese two dey ahr workin' on is two too many, if ye ask me," he frowned.

"Alright men, don't allow 'ese neggers to get too uppity. Show dem who's bahss. 'At's de only way ye kin deal with dem," the Lieutenant said.

When he returned to the Third Street project, O'Malley walked in the door. Speaking to Will, he asked, " 'Ow many 'o dese schools ahr ye fixin' ta ahpen, Boss Man?"

"Depends on how many students we sign up. Could be jist two, but might be more." He was evasive.

"Der's fahr sure goin' be a lotta yellin', screamin' dahrkies runnin' up 'n' down dese sidewalks 'ere. Me job's goin' ta be a lot 'arder. When's it set ta ahpen?" O'Malley complained.

"Well, we ain't got too much ta do here, jist cleanin' 'n' paintin'. Time we git desks 'n' chalkboards set up, it'll be 'bout two weeks, I reckon."

"I 'eerd ye wuz ahpenin' one in de Hunt-Phelan House on Beale. Is it goin' ahpen in two weeks too?" the inquisitive cop persisted.

"No, it'll take a little longer. Needs sum repair work on it."

"We hope to have both schools open before Christmas," Lenora added.

"I 'ope ye folks know whart yer doin'. I ain't fahr certain dese darkies kin even laharn ta read 'n' write," O'Malley smiled contemptuously.

"We have well-qualified teachers, who are good at what they do. The freedmen and their children are ready and willing to learn. We'll teach them," Lenora assured him.

"Dem young'uns better behave. Memphis police don't tolerate rahwdyness ner vagrants," he warned.

***

As they rode back to the fort, Lenora asked Will, "Do you think we can get Third Street open by November 1st? Can the Colonel get us desks and chalkboards?"

"I thank he kin. Fort Pickering has been tha main supply depot fer the Union army in the South ever since we took it over in '62."

The couple met Runkle as he entered the Mess Hall. Will spoke, "Hey Colonel, wait up a bit. We need to talk ta ya fer jist a minute."

"Good evening, Presley and the Missus. What can I do for you?"

Lenora spoke first. "We will need desks, chalkboards, chalk, and slates by next week. Are they available that quickly?"

"But of course, Mrs. Presley. We have been gathering school furnishings since the time of your arrival in Memphis. Many school systems from the surrounding areas have a surplus, and with older equipment they replaced.

"Then, too, we got some from abandoned lands on plantations. Some owners had private schools for their children."

"That sounds great, Sir. We gonna need enough fer four rooms at Third Street," Will was excited.

"Norville thanks it'll be three or four more weeks on Beale Street. There's six rooms on that place - four downstairs 'n' two upstairs, plus storage space."

"We can handle all of that," Runkle assured them.

"This weekend you and the Missus need to visit our forty-acre homeowners, I got a notice from General Fisk that Johnson has restored the abandoned land back to the original owners. It will be necessary to inform our settlers."

"Oh, Colonel, these people will be devastated. For the first time in their lives, they've had something to call their own. Now, we're going to make them give it back," Lenora lamented.

"I am totally sympathetic with what you are saying, Mrs. Presley, but it's out of my hands. There's nothing I can do.

"Callahan and Hammond will be here in my office on Monday at 10:00 A.M. Jennings, Kaine, Wilson, Nance, and Gaye will all need to be present.

"I've been instructed to negotiate a sharecropper's agreement with all parties concerned. It's the best I can offer."

"Well, we kinda prepared 'em fer this here a while back of this,

Colonel." Presley reported.

"I guess we kin ride out ther' Sat'dee mornin', Sweet Lady," he sighed with resignation. "You jist do what hasta be done I reckon."

"Alright, Colonel, we'll be the bearers of the bad news." Lenora shook her head.

Chapter Eighteen

BUILDING MORE

"That was one of the most difficult things I've ever done in my whole life, Will," Lenora said as they drove back to the fort.

"Yep, I know what ye mean, Sweet Lady. I almost cried myself," he answered. "We'll go to Runkle's office and stand with 'em on Monday mornin' when Callahan 'n' Hammond show up. I shore do hate it fer 'em good people."

"I guess the only thing we can do now is finish these other schools we have planned," she reflected.

"Yeah, I been a thankin' 'bout that, 'n' if we put tagether three crews a men we kin build 'em in a couple a months.

"I kin take Tom 'n' Charles, then hire two 'er three more. Norville kin take Joey 'n' Bobby 'n' add some more. Willie kin head up a crew with Little Georgie 'n' some more.

"I thank we kin build a four-room schoolhouse in 'bout a month. Buildin' three at a time, we kin have six a them open 'round first of February."

"That sounds like a wonderful idea, my Darling. If the Colonel will approve the funds to hire some more men, it'll create some jobs and these freedmen can learn new skills for later."

"Yep, I'm a thankin' a whole lotta new houses 'er gonna be needed in Memphis when word gets out ther's schools fer ther' young'uns. Freedmen 'er gonna wanna move here fer that," Will said.

"Uh huh, I think you're right, Mr. Presley," Lenora smiled. "We already have over 20,000 freedmen living in Memphis now. It's going to grow faster when the schools are open."

"I'll tell Norville to keep Tom 'n' Charles with him on Monday mornin'. Since we're goin' ta stand with tha settlers when they sign tha papers ta work fer tha plantation owners, we'll be late fer tha Third Street buildin' work. Don't want Officer Kelly ta put 'em in jail fer doin' nuthin'."

"OK, we can swing by the Beale Street location and pick them up when we finish with Callahan and Hammond," she replied.

"I wanna talk ta Runkle 'bout gittin' sum more help to start tha new buildin'. Hope he'll let us do that." Will was pensive.

When Monday morning arrived, Lenora was fidgety and nervous. Fearing that the settlers would be dis-served by the plantation lords, she spoke to Will. "If Callahan or Hammond get too arrogant or disrespectful to our friends, I will speak out and tell them just what I think. I won't stand silently by and let them be mistreated."

"I'm proud a ye, Mrs. Presley. I won't neither." he assured her.

Encountering the settler families outside Colonel Runkle's office, the Presleys greeted them warmly. "Welcome to Fort Pickering folks. I'm thrilled to see you this morning." Lenora smiled.

Will shook hands all around with the men, then spoke, "This ain't what we hoped would happen, but I reckon it's tha best we kin do under tha circumstances. The Colonel will git y'all a good deal with 'ese owners. I feel real good 'bout that."

"Oh, I wanted to tell all of you about the schools we are about to open here in Memphis for your children. It's solely for freedmen's children.

"We have some wonderful teachers. They will teach reading, writing, arithmetic, and religion. It's a great opportunity for them," Lenora was enthusiastic.

Luther Kaine spoke first, "We 'preciate it, Miss Lenora, but we gonna need tha chil'lun to work in tha cotton fields 'n' to help raise tha garden, so we kin eat."

Cicely then sadly nodded her head and said, " I do want my babies ta learn 'n' git ed'cated, but it don't seem poss'ble now, Missy. Maybe a li'l later on."

Sam Jennings dropped his head and said, "Got to have 'em pickin' cotton fer rite now, I su'pose. Maybe sum day we all kin learn to read 'n' rite, Miss Lenora. I shore hope so."

Mandy nodded in agreement with Sam. Each of the others nodded their assent.

Will then spoke, "OK let's go on in tha office 'n' git this biz'nus over with. Looks like Callahan 'n' Hammond's already in there."

The plantation lords both refused to rise when the entourage entered the office, but Runkle stood to greet his guests. Lenora then introduced the settlers to the Colonel.

"Come in, folks, and have a seat. Presley, you and Mrs. Presley sit over here beside my desk.

"Now I know we all are aware of our business today, so let's get right to it. I have prepared contracts for all parties to sign. If any of you freedmen can't write your name, just place your X on the line and I'll witness it with my signature."

As Runkle spoke, Callahan and Hammond sat smirking and casting condescending glances at the former slaves.

When the Colonel finished, Callahan loudly proclaimed, "I told ye people dat I would 'ave me land back and me black labor. I told all ye slaves and yahr scalawag benefactor, Presley, too."

"Now that's enough, William," Runkle cautioned him. "You will have contractual relationships with Kaine, Jennings, and Wilson. Hammond's are with Nance and Gaye. They are not your slaves, they are contractors. If you attempt to treat them as slaves, you will violate your contract, and will make it void."

"The land will then revert to the ownership of these families. The same goes for you, too, Hammond. The United States Army can, again, declare your land contraband.

"We will protect the rights of these settlers as long as necessary. There is a movement already underway for a Constitutional Amendment to give freedmen full citizenship in the United States of America."

Smirking as he approached the desk to sign the contract, Hammond said, "I've 'eerd enough. Let's get this ahver with so dese neggers can get to wahrk raisin' cotton fahr us."

Standing outside the office with the freedmen after the signing, Will and Lenora wished them well and bade them goodbye.

Chapter Nineteen

NINE SCHOOLS

"Let's git on down ta Beale Street and pick up Charles 'n' Tom," Will said as he smiled at Lenora.

"I'd like to stay at the Fort and talk to some teachers. We'll need four of them at Third Street in two more weeks. You can go on to Beale Street, then to Third when you pick up the men," she suggested.

"Alright, Sweet Lady, I'll see you when I git home tonight."

By the time Will arrived at the Beale Street site, it was almost noon. A pleasant surprise greeted him.

"Hey Norville, yer men has got a lot done taday. At this rate, ye won't be too fur behind Third Street fer Openin' Day."

"Yep, I hope ta start on tha roof this afta'noon afore quittin' time. Havin' all six of 'ese men makes a diff'rence."

In an aside to Will, he said, "'Ese boys know how ta work. I reckon workin' all 'em years fer a slave driver learnt 'em how ta git things dun. Havin' 'ese extra two men's helped too."

"Why don't I jist stay 'ere with ye taday, then we'll fer shore git started on tha roof. Finish tha roof this week, and paint next week. We kin open soon as we set up desks 'n' blackboards.

"I figger three more weeks here, 'n' two more weeks over on Third Street."

***

Back at the Fort, Lenora talked with the lead teacher from the American Missionary Association, Miss Charlotte Peterson. "We're going to need four teachers at Third Street and six more for Beale Street. We should be ready for teachers by the first part of November.

"Plans have been made to construct seven more buildings. Those will be four-room schools. Twenty-eight or thirty teachers need to be prepared to start by February 1st."

***

When they finished for the day, Norville dismissed his men, then turned to Will. "We dun real good taday, Presley. Got a good start on tha roof, should be ready ta paint next week. After paint dries, we'll set the desks."

"OK, I'll make sure Runkle has 'em fer us. Me 'n' my boys'll finish up this week with paintin' 'n' set desks next week. I'm a gonna need four more men. You'll need four more. Willie 'n' l'il Georgie'll need four more. Reckon we kin find twelve freedmen who wanna work?"

"Yep, Willie knows a lotta 'em huntin' jobs. Seems he's got several half-brothers. His Mama's husband'd git sold off 'n' they'd bring her another 'un. He's got cousins too, who lived on his plantation. L'il Georgie's his brother."

***

On Friday, November 17, Presley and Hill reported to Colonel Runkle's office. Will spoke, "We have tha first two schools ready for classes. Teachers kin show up Monday 'n let tha folks in tha vicinity know they're open. We got enuff men ta start buidin'on Monday. That's tha 20th, I thank."

Runkle looked at his calendar, then replied, "Yes, that's right Presley. If everything goes well, you can be ready to open at least six by February 4th."

"If we need another school, we kin git it ready in three more weeks, 'bout tha 25th, tha Good Lord willin' 'n' nuthin' don't happen." Norville counted on his fingers.

"What we're a plannin' is four-room schools. Make 'em forty-foot wide by sixty-foot long. Leave a four-foot hallway down tha middle with a door in tha front 'n one in tha back. Outhouse out back," Will suggested.

"Yes, that sounds about right, Presley. Each room will be about eighteen feet by thirty feet. That will be a good-sized classroom," Runkle agreed. "I'll make certain we have furnishing for that many schools, and that they are here when we need them."

"We have ordered material fer buildin' three schools at a time. We got three crews ta work. Kin we pick this stuff up Monday mornin'?" Norville asked.

"Yes, I'll get the order to the Supply Sargent, and have three wagons loaded by 7:00 A,M.," the Colonel promised.

Will, arriving at 6:55 A.M., found Norville and Willie awaiting him. "Looks like you two are full of *vim and vigor* this mornin'," he smiled a greeting.

"Yas Suh, Mista Will," Willie smiled back. "We gots ta git 'ese schools open fer the young'uns. They need ta learn ta read 'n' rite so theys don't have ta pick no cotton. That there's hard work."

"Yep, me too, Presley. I went 'n' fit a war, so's 'ese people wuz'nt forced ta pick cotton fer 'em rich folks. It ain't right." Norville set his jaw.

"OK men, let's roll. Willie, you pick up your crew at Beale Street, then go on over ta Central. Norville, you git your team, then head ta Jefferson. I'll take mine and go ta Madison.

"Let's all see if we kin git the foundations set taday."

"At quittin' time, head back ta tha Supply Depot 'n' park yer wagon. They'll load out tha floorin' we gonna need tomorrow," Will instructed.

*** *

When he arrived the next morning at 6:45, he found Norville and Willie had once again preceded him. "Dang, how early does a feller hafta git up ta beat ye boys?"

"I'se used ta startin' work at 5:30, Mista Will," Willie grinned.

"Ye know I've always been an early riser, Presley," Norville added with a bit of a taunt. "When I wake up, I gotta git up. Cain't lay in no bed awake."

Will made himself a mental note to arrive at 6:30 the next morning. It had become a game of motivation. By making the work a competition, it was much more fun.

By the end of the first week, all three crews had the floors installed and the sidewalls standing. When they met at the Supply Depot on Friday afternoon after work, they were tired.

Will spoke first, "I hate ta admit it, but I'm plumb tuckered out. Git plenty a rest this weekend boys. We gonna knock this out in no time."

"Yep, I'm tarred too, but I wanna git this job done," Norville smiled wearily.

Willie just grinned.

'Kin, we git tha roofs on next week, men?" Will was pushing. "That'll git us in ta tha first part of December. "I'd like ta finish 'ese three afore Christmas."

"Yas Suh, Mista Will, we be finished by Christmas."

"We'll be done 'er bust a gut a tryin'," Norville volunteered.

***

On the morning of December 22, 1865, Colonel Runkle and Lenora accompanied the three leaders to inspect their completed school buildings.

"I am thrilled," Lenora gushed, "We will get these children well versed in the four R's.

Will looked puzzled. "Four R's? I thought it was three Rs."

"Reading, Riting, 'Rithmetic, *and* Religion. Remember all of our teachers are missionaries from their churches."

"Oh yeah, I forgot that," Will blushed.

As Runkle, Will, Lenora, and Norville made their way back to the Fort, the Colonel decided to offer a special invitation.

"Monday will be Christmas Day and Mrs. Runkle always makes enough food for an army, so how about the three of you joining us for dinner? We can celebrate the results of your hard work and toast to the new year."

"That's so kind of ye, Sir. We don't want to create more work for Mrs. Runkle, but we would be happy to join ye." Will responded for the group.

"The more the merrier, Venetia loves having a crowd to swoon over her cooking. Mrs. Presley, do you want to invite anyone?"

"If it's not an imposition, I would like to ask Charlotte Peterson. She was our first teacher at the Fort and has helped all the others get started," Lenora replied. "May we bring anything?"

"No, just bring your smiling faces and a bit of Christmas cheer. We'll have us a party, for sure." Runkle laughed.

***

On Christmas afternoon, Will, Lenora, Charlotte, and Norville walked together to the home quarters of Colonel and Venetia Runkle. Lenora had baked a Christmas fruit loaf, and Charlotte had made a lovely arrangement of evergreens and berries. The men just brought themselves and a great hunger for a good meal.

Venetia welcomed the foursome with a warm smile. "Merry Christmas. Ben and I are so happy to have you join us today. Thank you for the lovely gifts. Please make yourself at home."

The men congregated in the living area, where they were offered a cup of holiday cheer. Lenora and Charlotte followed Venetia to the kitchen and began to pitch in with the final preparations.

Runkle questioned Will and Norville about their experiences over the past few months. He was curious to know how they felt about his prospects for continuing this experiment. "What do you hear from the locals, boys?"

"First, Sir they don't like us none," Norville quickly responded. "They feel like we's a takin' away what rightly belongs ta them."

"Don't they understand tha they lost the war, and it is a new day?" Runkle asked.

"They mite know it, but that's a long way from understandin' 'n' 'cceptin' it, Sir," Will spoke out without thinking.

"Lenora and I are worried the black families who signed those contracts are not gonna 'ave anything close ta what wuz promised," Will added remorsefully.

"Well, at least they are not owned by anyone anymore. They have a little protection from the government, and it looks like there's more coming soon," Runkle proposed.

"You should feel mighty good about the part you have played in changing their lives and the lives of their children. The grown folks have a bit more control over what they do, and the younger ones are having time to learn enough to find jobs away from the land."

"Somehow, I get the feelin' this war ain't neva gonna be over," Will sighed.

"Come on boys, It's Christmas. Let's celebrate by stuffing ourselves at Venetia's table," Runkle invited them to the dining area.

The ladies laid out the feast of roasted foul with stuffing and gravy, potatoes, both white and red, fruit compotes, and warm fresh-baked breads.

Runkle offered grace, and with much anticipation, the group began to fill their stomachs.

"What were you ladies discussing in the kitchen?" the Colonel inquired.

Lenora spoke first. "We were telling Mrs. Runkle about the

schools, the teachers, the children, and the progress we have made in a short time."

As Charlotte began to fill in the details, Norville found himself staring at her. Although he had seen her around the Fort, he did not notice her shiny blond hair and her beautiful smile. His palms became damp, and he could feel a blush on his cheek.

Lenora decided this happy occasion was the perfect time to share the good news. Smiling at Will and touching his hand, she announced, "Will and I will have a blessed event in the spring of the new year."

Ben, Venetia, Charlotte, and Norville raised their glasses and mugs to congratulate their friends. "That's wonderful news," the Colonel said. "Does that mean you will not be working alongside Will anymore?"

"Oh no, Doc Harrison has assured me I can continue my duties until March if there are no complications. I want to be part of getting the rest of the schools up and running," Lenora responded.

The conversation returned to work yet to be accomplished and hopes for a successful 1866.

After dinner, everyone thanked the Colonel and Mrs. Runkle for the lovely afternoon and the delicious meal. As they left the Runkle home, Norville got the courage to say, "Miss Charlotte, may I walk you to your barracks?"

"That would be very nice of you, Norville," she replied with a smile on both her lips and eyes.

As Charlotte and Norville veered off the trail to her barracks, Will winked at Lenora. "I believe my ol' pal has been *smitten.*"

Chapter Twenty

COMPLETING THE PROJECT

January 1866 began the push to finish building the schools in preparation for classes in early February. Will and Norville had established an efficient method. Each school had the same dimensions, used the same materials, and went up in the same order.

The three teams of six men each could work on three houses at a time and join forces for the ninth and final one later in February.

The winter weather was mild, but cold enough to require the team to build fires in metal containers at each building site. The workers took turns, warming their hands and returned quickly to relieve another man.

"Dang, Norville, we're gittin purty good at this buildin' stuff," Will exclaimed with pride as the two pals stood back to admire their work.

Lenora, with Charlotte's assistance, had standardized the instructional process at the fort. They would replicate the orientation process with each new school.

As each new teacher was recruited and arrived in Memphis, Lenora welcomed her, gave her a tour of the fort, including the mess hall, the infirmary, and central supplies. She then helped her settle into the assigned barracks.

As the group of teachers grew, assigning more than one teacher to each available space became necessary. Fortunately, the young women did not seem to mind having a roommate.

Charlotte would bring the new recruits up to date on what had already been accomplished. She explained how the student age groups were divided. She let them sit in on classes at the fort to understand the level at which a teacher would begin with each group of students.

"Lenora, I think you and I should take these new ladies out to visit the other schools that are ready. They need to understand that the ones in town will not be precisely the same as in the fort," Charlotte suggested.

"That's a great idea, Charlotte," Lenora agreed. "We should also prepare them for the fact that the students will not be at the same level as the children of our soldiers. And they may run into some folks in town who are not happy about the new schools."

"We don't want to scare them off before they even start," Charlotte said with a bit of worry.

"No, but we want to be truthful with them. They need to be told what they may be dealing with when they actually start teaching."

Volunteer Teachers

***

By mid-January, twenty-five volunteer teachers were living at Fort Pickering. "Since the sun is shining today, let's take a field trip," Lenora suggested to Charlotte.

"I will tell the teachers to dismiss classes after lunch time and I'll roundup the other twenty-one. We will look like a parade marching down to Beale Street," Charlotte chuckled.

"Ladies, I hope you are wearing your walking shoes, because we are about to put some dirt under our feet. You are going to get a first-hand look at what may become your second homes. Let's meet next to the big gate at 1:00. Don't be late," Lenora advised them.

It was most likely an unusual sight to see a procession of twenty-six young white women walking in unison toward the mostly black section of downtown Memphis.

Reaching Beale Street, the group was stopped by a large uniformed man. "'Old yahr horses, ladies," Sargent O'Brien shouted, holding both hands out with palms facing the crowd. "Wahr would ye be goin in such a hurry?"

Lenora spoke up, "Sargent, we have met before and you know

that we are opening more schools in this area. These are some of our new teachers and we are on our way to examine the facilities."

"And whar would yahr men folks be? Do dey know yahr aught 'ere with no protection?"

"Why would we need protection when we are peacefully walking together to look at schools?" Lenora responded.

"Dahn't ye know des a lot of Neggers down 'ere and ahther low lifes?"

"Sargent, we have work to do, so kindly let us get on with it. Come on Ladies, we are wasting time." Lenora said indignantly.

***

The first stop was the Hunt-Phelan House on Beale Street. Lenora explained, "This historic home was used for several purposes during the war and suffered much damage. The Freedman's Bureau was fortunate to rent this space. There are six classrooms, including two that are used for night school."

"Night school?" Emma Baker, one of the newest recruits, asked. "Why are we having school at night?"

Charlotte answered, "Some of our students are grown people who work during the day and have never had a chance to learn basic literacy. They want a better life for themselves as well as their children and we want to help that happen."

"I feel so stupid because I didn't even think of that," Emma said. She lowered her head.

"Don't be reluctant to ask questions. Most of you have grown up in different environments. You have not seen first hand the results of treating people like property for hundreds of years," Charlotte added.

***

The next stop was the Third Street school, another rental refurbished by Will's team and contained four separate classrooms. "All the other schools will also have four classrooms, as you will see," Lenora informed the group.

"I like the idea that there will be at least four of us in each school," a young brunette from Ohio said. We can walk together to and from school each day for safety."

"Now don't let that Sargent frighten you," Lenora quickly advised.

"We are legally here to do a job, and we're not going to let a few blowhards prevent us from fulfilling our mission. Just keep walking with your heads up and don't stand for anyone trying to intimidate you."

Charlotte added, "That is the same attitude we want our students to develop. We want them to have confidence that they can learn, they can become independent, that they are as good as anyone else. We want them to believe that their lives matter."

"It will take patience to help them learn these things," Lenora sighed. "When you and your family have been treated like property instead of people for generations, it doesn't always come naturally to hold your head up and march forward."

"Ladies, that is your mission," Charlotte proudly proclaimed. "You will be teaching more than the Four R's here. You will also be teaching Respect. They need to learn to respect themselves and to expect respect in return, despite constant evidence to the contrary."

After visiting each of the completed schools, where the teachers could get a better idea of what their classrooms would resemble, they stopped by the ongoing construction sites.

***

Norville's crew was working at one of the sites as he saw the ladies approach. He removed his cap, brushed off his hands, and walked out to greet the group, which was led by Charlotte.

"Aftanoon, ladies," he smiled and bowed his head respectfully. "Whatta ye thank of our schools?"

"We think you have done a wonderful job," Charlotte replied, locking eyes with Norville. "We are all eager for the first day of school and we appreciate how hard you all have worked to make this happen."

Norville felt the same rush of heat in his cheeks he had felt at Christmas dinner with the Runkles. In his eyes, Charlotte looked more beautiful each time they met.

He was thinking, "*She's such a smart lady with a good education. She knows how ta get things dun 'n' she could prob'ly 'ave 'er pick of any man she fancied. I'm not 'n tha same class as 'er but, by Gawd, I'm goin' ta try it.*"

"Miss Charlotte, ifen ye'd like ta stay behind fer more inspectin', I'll walk ye home safe."

"Don't mind if I do, Norville. Lenora, you go with the group; I'll be back in a little while."

To interrupt the giggling, Lenore heard behind her as they walked toward the fort, she decided to change the conversation.

"We will make sure that as each school opens, the teachers will be escorted for the first few days," Lenora promised. "By that time, the local folks should have adjusted to seeing black children coming and going during school hours."

***

The next morning in the Mess Hall, Charlotte saw several teachers looking at her as if they knew a secret. She decided to get them talking about their jobs and their fears rather than about her.

"Those of you who have not yet been assigned a classroom will go with Lenora and me to recruit students from the community," Charlotte explained. "Sometimes we have to convince the families that it will be alright and that it is perfectly legal to get an education."

While the remaining school buildings were being completed, Charlotte helped the new recruits become comfortable with the standard curriculum and expect the various obstacles they might encounter.

During this period, Lenora began to feel her baby move. She was excited but also aware that life would be permanently changed in a few months.

Doc Harrison told Lenora that she seemed to progress normally. He talked with her about what to expect in the remaining months of the pregnancy. He introduced her to his wife, Martha, who was an experienced midwife. "Martha will be right by your side when the time comes. She will treat you like her own daughter."

She realized she had not told her Mother and Father they would soon become grandparents. In fact, she had only written to them twice since arriving in Memphis.

January 21, 1866
Dear Mama and Daddy,
Forgive me for being so slow in writing to you. I do miss you and think about you every day.
Will and I have been extremely busy getting the schools started. There were many more details involved We found two vacant buildings that could be cleaned up and repaired. Then we had to find land and hire workers to build six more schools. Will has overseen all the construction projects.

It became my responsibility to coordinate the recruitment of teachers and students. I have had to adjust to some things I had never seen before. It hurts my heart when I meet these former slaves and hear how simple their dreams are. They only want a chance to have a safe home for their children and an opportunity to work for a better life. Unfortunately, many of the white folks here do not want that to happen. They resent us for trying to create opportunities. They have not accepted the fact that the war was lost and that the country will remain united. When we get the chance to come home for a visit, we will share the whole story. I'm not sure how soon that can happen since we are obligated to completing this project in Memphis before making a change.

I do have some exciting news for you. Sometime in May, you are going to become grandparents. Now don't get worried. I am fine. There is an infirmary at the fort, and I have been given permission by Doc Harrison to continue my work for another month or so. I hope this letter finds you both well and that you are happy for us.
Will and I send our love,
Lenora

Chapter Twenty-One

LOVING TO LEARN

Opening day for the six newly built schools was hectic, but energizing and rewarding. Will and Norville were proud as they made the tour of their handiwork. "We's dun a good thang, Norville," Will smiled.

"What am I 'posed ta do now?" Norville asked. "Do I jist go back ta Knoxville 'n' try ta find sum work?"

"Not so fast, Pal," Will said with a surprised tone. He had not thought about what would happen when the work was completed. "I'm a bettin' thar's plenty otha work needed here, 'specially wit sum one like you. Let's talk with the Colonel at the fort. I got me sum ideas."

Will met with Colonel Runkle that afternoon.

"Sir, I don't mean ta be too pushy, but I'm thankin' thars a need fer a lotta livin' spaces down here in South Memphis with so many more black folks movin' in. I thank I've seen sum vacant lots 'n' unused farm-land close nuff fer workers ta walk ta ther jobs." Will was talking more than either the Colonel or Norville had ever seen him speak at one sitting.

"Alright, Presley, slow down before you give yourself the vapors," Runkle said, chuckling. "I believe I follow your train of thought, but let's try to keep that train on the rail long enough to make some deals.

"It is always a good strategy when trying to cut a deal to understand how the other person will benefit. Lead with 'what's in it for them' before talking about the need you are trying to fill."

"Oh Colonel, yer so smart. I knew yer tha one we needed ta work out a plan," Will replied after catching his breath.

"Course, I have my own reasons fer wantin' ta keep Norville here and keep his crews a workin'. They all have skills tha kin be helpful in most any project 'n' they's got a good relationship agoin'."

Norville had been quietly listening and trying to picture in his mind what Will was suggesting. "I'd be happy ta stay in Memphis a while longa 'n' work wit my Pal. Ifen we could build sum homes whar these freedmen could live, work, and send thar chil'ren ta school, it mite seem like something' good come outta tha damn war afta all," he said with a sigh.

"You boys relax a bit," Runkle said as if giving an order. "Let me pull together information on landownership and start to make some contacts. I'll call you back when we are ready to move forward."

As Will and Norville left Runkle's office, Norville had a funny smile on his lips. "What's ye thankin' 'bout, Norville?"

"Jist happy tha I don't hafta say goodbye ta Miss Charlotte so soon."

"Oh, I can see ye got it real bad, my ol' pal," Will chuckled.

***

Over the next few weeks, Colonel Runkle cut deals with several landowners to front the rental housing cost on their property. He painted a picture of how these units would create an ongoing source of income for the owners.

Will and Norville accompanied Runkle when the contracts were signed to assure the owners that they would oversee all the workers.

"They's gonna be no loafin' 'round wit our crews. We work hard 'n' fast. We clean up behind our ownselves. You jist wait and see what we can do," Norville said proudly. "Ye won't hafta worry 'bout gettin' yer rent neither."

Will added. "Tha folks rentin' from ye will be good people with jobs. They's jist tryin' ta be good citizens a Memphis."

***

Back at Fort Pickering, Lenora and Charlotte were getting daily feedback from the teachers about how classes were going. In a group meeting held in the Mess Hall, Lenora asked, "How is it going so far?"

Ida Williams, one of the Hunt-Phelan teachers, spoke first. "The children are mostly sweet, but quite timid about speaking up in class. We spend a lot of time encouraging them and reminding them they are capable of learning anything.

"Our biggest problem is outside the school-house. There is always some angry white man hanging around the door to harass the children and us when we leave for the day. They laugh at the children and say things like,

,"You dumb Niggers ain't gonna learn to read. You're only good enough to pick cotton."

Ida's co-worker, Minnie Smith, added with more than a little fury, "Then they turn on us."

"What do they say to you?" Lenora asked.

"Things like, 'Only ugly women would be wasting their time trying to teach darkies. You might as well try to teach a pole cat to paint a picture. You should be looking for husbands fore you get too old."

Charlotte stepped in to calm the discussion. "We knew we would meet opposition when we signed on for this project. There will always be people who are afraid of progress and will try to stop it if they can. If the law is not on their side, they will try to frighten the change makers."

"Well, they are doing a good job of that," Emma Baker said. "Our classes in the new buildings had barely begun when we had white boys throwing trash at us through the windows."

"Try to keep your eyes on the prize," Lenora said. "You are not just volunteers; you are pioneers leading the way to a better future. I am proud of each one of you and grateful for the chance to have been part of this project."

"That sounds like a going away speech," Ida looked puzzled." Are you leaving us?"

"No, I am not leaving, but as you may have noticed, I've got a *bun in the oven* as some people say. I will be here at least until August but will be restricted to work inside the fort. If I can be of help to anyone, please call on me."

April 1866 brought many happy moments as the teachers watched their students open up and actually begin to read. The younger children were obviously proud of themselves, and their parents were overjoyed with their progress.

The night classes at the Hunt-Phelan House had attracted a good number of working adults. Among them were Bertha Lewis and Anna Lou Miller. Bertha was the Mother of Willie and Lil George Johnson. They both had day jobs as maids at the most elegant hotel in Memphis, the Gayoso.

Bertha told Ida Williams, "I ain't gonna pass up a chance at learnin' ta be a proper schooled lady 'n' my lil girl ain't neether. We does a good job at cleanin' up afta white folks, but I kin see more is poss'ble now tha I'm a readin'."

Mostly, the teachers had learned to ignore the daily taunts, but they were careful to always walk together.

***

After class on April 6th, Ida and Minnie were comparing notes on some of their success stories. The students at Hunt-Phelan had been in school at least a month longer than most others, and some of the older ones were reading reasonably well.

The teachers, who were also missionaries, always used both the Bible and the United States Declaration of Independence as texts.

"I think it would be a wonderful idea to have a special program for the parents this month," Ida suggested. "We could have it here at Hunt-Phelan and invite the students and their parents from all the Freedman's schools.

"We could have a group of younger children read Bible verses. Then all the children could sing several hymns," Minnie offered. "At the end, I would like to have my student, David Brown, read the Declaration of Independence. He is only twelve years old, but he has learned really quickly, and he has a wonderful voice."

"It could be just what we need to inspire all the younger students and to encourage their parents to keep the children in school," Ida thought aloud.

"The only thing that worries me is what kind of trouble the locals might drum up when they see several hundred black folks walking together down Beale Street. I'm sure Sargent O'Brien is not going to be happy," Minnie was tense.

"We might have to ask for some protection from the fort. Four or five men in uniform outside the school might be enough to discourage trouble-makers," Ida said.

"We'll talk with Charlotte about our idea. She knows Colonel Runkle and he could probably arrange it."

***

The next day, Ida and Minnie shared their idea with Charlotte, who was excited about the plan. Charlotte immediately brought Lenora and Will into the loop.

Before they knew what happened, Ida and Minnie were sitting in front of Colonel Runkle, supported by Lenora, Will, and Charlotte.

"This must be something big to have an entire contingent seek my attention," Runkle said. "What's going on?"

After listening to the proposal, Runkle had only one question, "When is this celebration scheduled?

"Yes, we can provide guards to prevent any disturbance during the program. I think this is a great idea. It will be proof that all our efforts are paying off. Although you didn't say it, I assume I am invited." Everyone laughed.

"Sir, we were planning to have the program after classes on Friday, April 27th if we got approval from you, and of course you are invited," Ida said respectfully.

Lenora helped prepare posters, programs, and invitations for the *Loving to Learn* program, as Ida and Minnie called it. The other teachers pitched in to help by ensuring that all parents received a letter of invitation, and in any way they could, but mostly by drumming up excitement among the students.

***

The next two weeks were filled with practice sessions. Two girls and one boy were selected to read from the Bible. All the children in the Hunt-Phelan House practiced singing the hymns. David received private tutoring to prepare him for his starring role.

Excitement was in the air on Friday, April 27. For some reason, all the students had shown up in clean clothes and freshly groomed hair.

Not much additional teaching happened at the Hunt-Phelan House that day, but there was a lot of Bible reading and singing. Sargent O'Brien heard the restrains of 'Onward Christian Soldiers' as he walked his beat on Beale Street. "Damn Neggers, des naht good for much, but dey shahre can warble nice."

The children were dismissed at 3:00 and expected to return to the Hunt-Phelan House by 6:00 with their parents. The teachers told them not to be afraid because there would be soldiers from the fort on guard before and after the program.

Around 5:30 P.M., groups of black adults holding hands with their children began to walk down Beale Street toward the school from both directions.

O'Brien started to approach one group with his hickory stick in his hand when Will and Norville touched him on the shoulder. "Jist want ye ta know yer invited to watch tha program ifen ye want ta," Will said, handing the Sargent a printed program.

"I'm naht goin to let a bunch a neggers take ahver me street dis eve'nin, no matter whart deys up to," O'Brien shouted. "I'll be puttin' an end to dis."

When five mounted soldiers from the fort ambled quietly toward the school, O'Brien backed off. Other Irish men were gathering to see what was taking place.

O'Brien showed them the program. "Des neggers and der negger-loving scalawags frahm the Naraht, is getting' too big for der britches. Der just shahin' ahff ahver der."

Inside the school, the teachers had arranged a makeshift stage in the central hall. It would be crowded, but they were hopeful that everyone could see and hear.

Colonel Runkle was asked to introduce the program. He rose to welcome all the families. "I want to thank all of you for supporting our new Freedman's Schools in Memphis.

"I want to thank Will and Lenora Presley for leading this project. I want to thank all the workers who have restored this fine home and who built the others. I especially want to thank all the teachers who left their homes in other states to come here and start this program."

Ida stood and escorted three children to the stage. "Let us begin by listening to our children read from the Holy Bible."

Sarah, age 9, read, "Jesus said, suffer little children, and forbid them not, to come unto me, for such is the kingdom of heaven." Matthew 19:14

Nellie, age 10, read, "For God so loved the world, that he gave his only begotten Son, that whosoever believeth on him should not perish, but have eternal life." John 3:16

Fred, age 11, had to be pushed to come forward. After a long silence, he read, "Children, obey your parents in all things, for this is well-pleasing in the Lord." Colossians 3:20

That was met with tremendous applause from the crowd. Fred's Father shouted out, "Don't ya be forgittin' tha one, boy."

Next, the multi-class choir bounded onto the stage and began singing.

The first selection was "Jesus Loves Me."

Next came, "Zaccheus."

They ended with "Onward Christian Soldiers" complete with marching down the aisle.

By this time, the crowd was clapping and singing along.

"Our final presentation will be a reading of the Declaration of Independence by David Brown," Minnie announced as she proudly escorted her student toward the front of the stage.

David took a moment to compose himself, and with his mellow baritone voice began:

"When in the course of human events, it becomes necessary for one People to dissolve the Political Bands . . . .

When he got to the part, "We hold these truths to be self-evident, that all Men are created equal, " sobs were heard.

". . . that they are endowed by their Creator with certain unalienable Rights, that among these are Life, Liberty, and the Pursuit of Happiness."

When David finished, the room was silent for several moments. Then, as if rehearsed, the crowd shouted, *"Amen."*

The crowd left the school with smiles on their faces. Many took the time to thank the teachers. When they reached the street, they saw that the guards were still waiting for them. For this, they were thankful.

As the five guards rode behind each group toward their homes, they could hear quiet conversation. They could sense the pride of these families having witnessed something they never thought they would see. They saw their children being transformed into fully equal human beings.

O'Brien was watching all of this with his teeth gritted and his fists clenched. He turned to his Irish pals and said, "Dawn't be thinkin' dis is de end. Dey gaht away with it tahnite, but dey wahnt 'ave dem sahld'ers with dem fah eva."

Chapter Twenty-Two

MEMPHIS MASSACRE

Tuesday morning, May 1st, dawned with a beautiful sunrise over the east end of South Memphis. The Third Heavy Artillery (African Descent) had completed their tour of duty on Monday, April 30th, and were preparing to muster out.

Three Sargents, Eddie Jones, Frank Smith, and James Pippen were chatting. "We gonna cel'brate gittin' out a da ahmy in da mawnin' men?' Smith smiled.

"Ye got dat rite, man. I got me a bottl' a red-eye, n I ain't sharin' it wit no'body. It's all mine," Jones grinned. "I'se heavy-on-da-hip afta I got ma payday. Pocket full a greenbacks, otta git me a girl ta pahty wit me."

"If yer huntun'a girl, ya betta go easy on dat red-eye. Ya don' wanna git wall papered. Might slow ya down wit yer girl," Smith cautioned.

"Ain't nuthiin' gunna slow me down, man. I been thankin' 'bout dis fer a lawng time," he bragged.

Laughing out loud, Pippen said, "I'sa gunna git me a big mug a John Barleycorn wit a big head a foam on top. I'sa jist gunna sip on it all day. Git loose, not plastered."

The Captain of their unit heard the conversation and walked over to join them. "Be keer'ful, men. Dat big po'lice Sargent down ther on Beale Street's a bad egg. Likes ta swang dat hick'ry stick he carries. Dat baby'll put sum hurt on ya."

"Dat po'lice ain't gon' hurt me. I got me a pig sticker in ma pocket. I'sa put sum hurt on him," Jones bragged. "I ain't takin' no trash from no I'rish cop."

"Just stay outta trub'le, men. We all goin' home in de mawnin'," the Captain assured them.

As they walked out the gate of Fort Pickering, several small groups of men from their outfit joined them. Soon Beale Street was filled with soldiers.

The large crowd of black men quickly attracted the attention of local citizens. Celebratory shouts and loud laughter from blacks were not the ordinary behavior expected of them.

Sargent Pattie O'Brien heard the commotion and looked to see what was happening. Sensing his need for help, he spotted a young boy and gave him a message. "Go ta de station 'n' tell dem I need 'elp dahwn 'ere. Dere's a big bunch o' neggers in de street makin' trouble."

Running in the door at the station, the boy blurted, "Sargent O'Brien needs 'elp on Beale Street. A big gang o neggers ahr tryin' ta kill 'im."

"Alright men, everybahdy 'ere go dahwn ta Beale Street 'n' he'p O'Brien with a big gang o' neggers. Dey tryin ta kill 'im."

When the reinforcements arrived, O'Brien approached Eddie Jones and said, "'Ey negger, you can't carry dat bahttle ooeht in de street. Give me dat."

"No Suh, Mista Po'lice. Dis 'ere's ma red eye. I paid fer it 'n' I'sa gunna drank it by myself."

Hearing that, O'Brien raised his stick and struck Jones across his left arm, causing him to drop the bottle and yelp in pain.

Without thinking, Jones pulled out his large knife and slashed the Sargent on the hand holding the stick, severing two fingers. At the sight of blood, the group of police officers attacked the crowd of soldiers in the street.

Unarmed and defenseless, the nearly discharged army men raised their arms to fend off the blows. General George Stoneman, the local Commander, sent out orders for his men to return to the fort.

When they turned to obey their Commander, shots rang out from the Memphis police. Five soldiers, shot in the back, fell dead in the street.

Jones, Smith, and Pippen were placed under arrest. Charged with assault with a deadly weapon, Jones faced a felony charge. The other two soldiers were charged with disorderly conduct and resisting arrest.

White bystanders who witnessed the altercation were outraged at the army. Many of them were former Confederate soldiers and resented the presence of Union troops in Memphis. One man shouted, "These niggers cain't be allowed ta git by with this. We gotta show 'em who's boss in these parts."

Mike O'Malley, who was sent in to replace O'Brien, joined in the conversation. "If we dawnt nip dis in de bud, ahr tahwn ain't gonna be wahrth livin' in," he said louder than was necessary.

As the crowd of mostly Irish men grew on Beale Street, tempers raged. Shouts were heard from both older men and young boys.

" Negger's gaht to be kept in line."

"Nahtin' but trahble since de damn Yankees came to tahwn."

"De darkies cain't leern nahtin' but wahrkin' with der hands."

"It was bad enahgh seein' neggas dressed up in unifahrms but then dey attach ahr awn, Sargent O'Brien, like de savages dey ritely is."

"Whart shahld we be doin 'bout it, Mike?"

O'Malley responded with a sly grin, "It's naht for me to be a tellin' ye what to do. Use yer imagination, bahys. Just dahwnt be doin anythin' ye'll be a regrettin', at least naht awn me beat."

Several men moved down the corner, so O'Malley could not be accused of hearing their plans. Their anger became elevated as they talked about grievances old and new.

The desire for revenge shared within this group was spawned by multiple factors. Losing the war, the occupation by Union troops including black soldiers, the growth of the Freedman population in Memphis, the building of schools for black children, the hiring of black people at lower wages, and the increasing demands for equal treatment for those people these men considered inferior, all stoked the flames of their resentment.

Joining the expanding group on the corner were Andrew Kelly, Samuel O'Brien, and Martin O'Malley, all brothers of Memphis police officers.

Andrew spoke up, "Listen, men. Dis standin' awn de carhner ain't getting' us nahwhere. We need a plan of action."

"We're listnin', gah awn," an older Irishman said.

"De ahnly thing that'll wahrk with dese darkies is to put de fear o de Lahrd in dem. Dey ahr gettin' der heads filled up with nahnsense 'bout bein' equal to us. Dey startin' to dream 'baht readin' 'n ritin', 'baht takin' mahre o' ahr jahbs, 'baht livin' whare we live, 'baht bein citizens, 'baht votin'. Next thing ye knahw, dey be dreamn' 'baht 'aving our fine I'rish lassies in der beds."

The crowd was cheering and waving their arms at this point as Andrew continued laying out his plan.

"Let's us divide into three grahps. Samuel, you and Martin each take some men. I'll take the rest. We each need to get sahm of ye pals to jahn us. Bring yer yahng lads, too."

"Den what?" someone yelled from the crowd.

"Den, we're gahn to make it clear to dese neggas waht der place is. Dey'll get a taste o waht der future's gahn to be if dey dahwnt get back in line.

Martin was getting excited and added, "It's easy to scare dese darkies. Dey soop'astishus anyway.'

Andrew continued, "When ye get at least twenty in yer group, start shahin up at the places dey wahrk. Meet afahre dey can get hahme. Tell dem dey best naht be sendin' der chil'ren to de yankee schools nah mahre."

Samuel, as Pattie's brother, thought he should contribute to the plan. "Tell yer yahng lads to go to each o de schools 'n put a scare awn de black kids. If dey spot a nice lahkin' girl, dey mite find a way to make 'er wahnt to think twice 'afahre cahmin' back." The men all laughed.

Within two hours, mobs of wrathful white men could be seen waiting by employee exit doors for black men to emerge. Other gangs stationed themselves close enough to each school to await class dismissal.

The Irish police officers clearly saw the angry men marching in a coordinated pattern toward their targets. They could hear the shouts. They had to be aware that something terrible was going to happen; yet they seemed oblivious to any dangers of civil unrest. They walked their beats, swinging their hickory sticks as if nothing unusual was underfoot.

Black workers at a cotton warehouse were met by angry shouts, followed by the throwing of rocks. "Negga, go home! Negga don't come back!"

When they tried to avoid confrontation, they were pushed and shoved. When they tried to defend themselves, they were forced to the ground. Some were stomped, some were beaten and cut, some were bound with ropes and dragged away.

As classes were dismissed for the day, children also encountered groups of fuming white boys and young men. "Better not see ye, here again, neggas.

" Schoolin' is too good for the likes of ye."

"Ye darkies need to get back to wahrkin' de cotton, like Gahd intended."

The teachers, hearing the commotion, tried to disperse the gangs with little success. They told the students to hurry home and to stay together. "Don't respond to the taunts," the pupils were told.

The young men were not deterred. In fact, they became more incensed by having been scolded by Yankee women. Although they held back for a few minutes, they soon followed the students on their homeward march, shouting epithets and threats.

Three of the older boys decided to take advantage of the situation when they spotted a pretty thirteen-year- old-girl walking at the back of the pack. One grabbed her and pulled her into a space between two houses, while the other two stood guard.

"Ye sure are a pretty thing for a negga. Must 'ave a white Daddy sahmewhere. We gonna have a bit o' fun today."

"Please don't hurt me. I aint dun nutin' to ya," she cried out.

Throwing her on the ground, he pulled up her skirt and began to do what she feared, while his pals watched and laughed.

"She's puttin' up a good fite, ain't she? A lively one."

"Me tahrn next. I like me a good tussle. Don't wahnt 'em to just lay dahr."

As the traumatized girl tried to pull herself together, she heard the boys talking.

"Now that we gaht us sum, what's next?"

"I'm thinking we mite set a little farce in dat school house to keep dem black tahes warm if dey be darhin' to cahme back. I 'ave some sticks, some rags, and coal ahl behind 'at buildin'."

"It's ahnly rite 'at we shahld warm up des negga buildins. Don't want dem to get cold and turn blue o nahthin'," another boy said as he roared at his joke.

While the youth continued their reign of terror, the older men intensified their confrontations with the black workers. What started with the throwing of fists and stones escalated into armed conflict.

Crowds can quickly spiral into mobs if the fuel of fury is not doused by the cooling liquid of leadership. In Memphis on May 1, 1866, there was none to be found.

The police looked the other way. The Mayor was missing in action. General Stoneman, who had the authority to stop the carnage, appeared to be tone deaf.

An observant bystander would have witnessed the completely unfiltered venting of rage. Men who normally might have behaved in at least a somewhat civilized manner, became crazed fanatics, acting out revenge for their imagined insults and injuries.

The mobs were indiscriminate in their attacks. Any black person who dared show his or her face on the streets was fair game in the minds of these men.

One older black man who made the mistake of coming out of his house on Beale Street because he heard all the noise, was hit over the head with a club and left bleeding out in the dirt.

A younger black male was bold enough to ask a white man, "What's goin' on?"

"I'll shah ye what's goin' on, negga! We ain't takin' nah mahr. We 'ad enough of ye darkies actin' like yer same as us, takin' ahr jobs, poppin' oout mahre pickaninnies ever' day, and spectin' us to mahve ahver to let ye wahrk by us on ahr ahn street." With that rant, he slit the young man's throat.

Strutting and shouting down Beale, another parade of agitated white men were searching for their next targets. Two black women returning from their jobs as laundry maids were talking and were not fully aware of the uprising on the street.

As their paths crossed with the mob, they were accosted with slurs and threats. "Whare dah ye thank yer goin'?"

"I'm bettin' ye got no wahrkin' men at hahm ahr ye woodn't be carryin' dem bags a rags."

"Maybe ye need us fine white men to shah ye whart ye be missin'," one bearded Irishman laughed.

Four of the group eagerly jumped toward the women. Two men grabbed one, and two of them grabbed the other as they attempted to run away. Screaming for help, the women were dragged off the street behind a grove of trees where they were brutally beaten and repeatedly raped.

As the women lay bleeding and sobbing, they heard their attackers laughing. "Dey be lookin' fahr mahre o' dat, I'm thinkin'. Dis will be a spay'shul day fahr dem to remember."

Other packs of overstimulated rioters concentrated on setting fires in the new schoolhouses. The more damage and violence the horde was victorious in perpetrating, the more reckless they became. They felt empowered to do whatever they wished because so far, no one had tried to stop them.

Colonel Runkle had been successful in selling the concept of building rental housing to several landowners with whom he had negotiated contracts. Will and Norville were returning to the fort after inspecting several sites when they heard the shouts coming from the Beale Street area.

The first person they met was stopped to inquire about the unrest. They saw several black men lying in the street, either injured or dying. Soon, they learned that fires had been set at some schools.

The two split up to cover more territory and checked on each of their schools. Their first concern was to ensure that all the students and teachers had safely escaped.

They searched for signs of fire and found two, one at the school on Madison and one on Main. Being less than successful in snuffing out the flames and finding no official help in town, they raced to Fort Pickering to report the damages to Colonel Runkle.

With the support of General Stoneman, Runkle sent a small contingency of men back to town with Will and Norville to minimize the damage to the schools. They carried written orders to present to both the Police and Fire Departments requiring their help.

SCENES IN MEMPHIS, TENNESSEE, DURING THE RIOT—BURNING A FREEDMEN'S SCHOOL-HOUSE.
[SKETCHED BY A. R. W.]

www.alamy.com - BTKH0S

Burning Freedmen's School House

The city officials did not interfere with efforts to quiet the mobs. However, they offered little support.

While the newly freed black population could not, mostly, afford any protection other than knives, the white civilians showed up with clubs, rifles, shotguns, and handguns. This was not exactly a level fighting ground.

Consequently, by the end of the day, twenty black male civilians had been murdered, three black females had been raped, and fires were still smoldering.

Chapter Twenty-Three

WEDNESDAY, MAY 2ND

One thousand three hundred and fifty men from the Third Heavy Artillery lined up in a single file. Assembled on the Drill Field at Fort Pickering, they would receive discharge papers and a train ticket to Nashville.

Waiting in line, Henry Jacobs, Johnny Campbell, and Jackson Claiborne discussed the events of the preceding day. "'Em cops dun shot 'n'kilt five a 'er men, yes'tidee. ***Shot 'em in da back. Shot 'em in da back,***" Henry was outraged.

"Yas Suh, dey sho' did. Shot 'em in da back. Em dirty, rotten muggins cain't get by wit 'at kinda con'duct. 'Ese cops 'er still fightin' da wahr," Jackson waved his finger.

"Man, dey fer sho' still fightin' da wahr. We's got's ta fight back. I got me a *Arkansas Tooth Pick*. Tuck it offen a dead so'jer. 'At big blade'll put sum hurt on da damn' killa cops," Johnny bragged.

"Uh huh, as fur back as we is in dis line, 'er train won' leave he'ah 'til one o'clock. We gon' have sum time ta take keer a biz'ness 'fore we go," Henry observed.

"Yas man, I'se gots me one a dem pig stickers like Jones had," Jackson said softly.

"I went 'n' got me a officer's sword outta da Supply De'po'. I thank Walters seed me, but he didn't say nuttin'," Henry nodded his head.

"Uh huh we gon' put sum hurt on dem I'rish boys," he added.

Gayoso Hotel

Adjacent to Fort Pickering on the north end of Front Street, the Gayoso Hotel was located. Built in 1842, it was the most elegant structure in the city of Memphis.

Sitting on the bluffs overlooking the Mississippi River, it was highly visible to river-boat visitors and road travelers. A state-of-the-art building, it boasted its own wine cellar, gasworks, and sewer system.

This luxurious structure had served as the headquarters for General Ulysses S. Grant while he was the Commandant of Fort Pickering from 1862 to 1864.

***

Bertha Lewis had moved to Memphis in '62 shortly after the takeover of the city by Union forces. Liberated from the West Tennessee plantation where she was enslaved, she brought her three remaining children to live a new life in the city.

At sixteen, she bore her first child and named him William. His father had the last name of Johnson, so Willie (as his father called him) was given that last name. Her second child was named George and called Li'l Georgie by his father.

When Johnson was sold, Bertha was given another husband, who gave her three more babies before being sold. With the next two succeeding husbands, she bore five more babies.

Anna Lou, her first daughter, was fathered by a man named Miller, and received his last name. Bertha's remaining seven children had been sold, and she had no knowledge of where they were or their fate in life.

Living in a camp just outside Memphis's city limits for a while, she got a job as a maid at the Gayoso. When Anna Lou turned twelve, she was hired by the hotel. With two small salaries, they could rent a four-room house on Beale Street-just a few blocks from their job. Willie and Li'l Georgie did odd jobs around the cotton warehouses along Front Street.

As Bertha and Anna Lou walked to work on Wednesday morning, they encountered a gang of Irish youth who began to yell and harass them. "Look at de arse ahn de young 'un. I wahnt me sun o' her."

Hearing that remark, the two women were scared. "C'mon Lou

we's got's ta git ta da ho'tel. Run, baby, run."

Arriving at the hotel just about ten yards ahead of the pursuing gang, the doorman opened the front door for them and stared angrily at the youths. "Ye bahys move ahn a'long nahw, ye 'ear me? Git ahn away from 'ere."

***

Mike O'Malley, substituting for the injured O'Brien and Harvey Kelly, who worked the Third Street beat, were standing on the corner where their assigned areas intersected. Expecting further trouble from the soldiers, they had alerted several Irish policemen to stay close. Three bursts on a whistle would signal that they needed help.

Immediately upon seeing the soldiers ambling down the street, O'Malley blew three quick bursts on his whistle. Within seconds, Beale street was filled with policemen. Noticing the sword hanging on Henry's side, Kelly drew his pistol and began to fire.

Henry fell dead in the street with one bullet in his face, two in his chest, and one in his left shoulder.

When the shooting started, Johnny and Jackson simultaneously ran toward O'Malley and Kelly.

With the two large knives, they stabbed both officers several times. Shots rang out again as other officers fired their weapons. When the shooting stopped, two policemen and three soldiers lay dead.

Already, eight soldiers and two Irish officers of the law were murdered. The Civil War continued.

***

Lieutenant Spencer looked at his men and said, "O'Malley went off ahn 'is own hook, and dedn't wait fahr me to give de ahrder. Now 'e's layin' dead. What des dat tell ye bahys? Dahn't ahpen de ball 'til ye gaht ahrders."

Turning to a crowd of several hundred onlookers, he said, "Me and me ahfficers ahr goin' abaht ahr business 'ere. If yah people wahnt to get rid o' dese neggers, now's yahr chance. Yah need to avenge me dead pahlicemen, and get red of darkies at de same time. We ahr goin' tah walk away, bot when we retahrn I 'spect to find sahm dead neggers. That's as clahr as I can mahke it tah yah peeple."

As the officers walked away, a young Irish man yelled, "Ye heerd de

Lieutenant, make dese neggers pay fahr ahr dead men."

Watching from the fringes of the crowd of white people, little more than a dozen blacks stood in silence. "Ese neggers ova here on tha sidewalk needs ta pay fer tha killin' a 'ese po'lice men. Ther ahr kind 'n 'ese blacks ain't."

Facing off against the mob, Ernie Garner, a large black man six feet tall and weighing more than two hundred pounds, raised his fists to fight. When he did, two white civilians charged him.

The first one hit him in the head with a large wooden pick handle. The other man grabbed him from behind with a chokehold around his neck. Wrestling him to the ground, he placed his knee on Garner's neck while the other man held him down.

As Garner lay on the ground, he repeated, "I can't breathe, I can't breathe." In less than ten minutes, this peaceful freedman was dead.

Wandering the streets of South Memphis, the agitated mob looked for black civilians to assuage their anger. "I dink dat negger's de one who leered at me wife 'n' dahter ahn Soondee afta church. Let's lynch de low-life darkie."

"String 'im up," another shouted.

All the rest of the afternoon, mobs beat, robbed, killed, and raped black men, women, and children. Twenty-two blacks were slain, and more than fifty were maimed or severely injured.

***

Approaching darkness, the violence began to abate. Lieutenant Spencer returned to Beale Street with a few of his men. "I dink de neggers gawt de wahrd 'bout dings in Memphis. Dey'll quieten dahwn nahw."

When they ended their shifts at the Gayoso, Bertha and Anna Lou were more than a little nervous about walking out on the street. They had heard the rioting outside all day, and the bell captain had told them of some of the violence.

"Lou, Baby, we ain't got far ta walk but we need ta go as fast as we kin, make no noise, 'n' fade inta tha shadows."

"Mama, I'm too 'fraid o all tha mean white men out thar. Cain't we just stay 'ere tanite?"

"No, Baby, tha ain't 'llowed. Stay close ta me 'n' don't say nuthin' ta nobody."

Mother and daughter had walked three blocks when they heard drunken laughter coming around the corner. "Grab my hand, Lou. We'se gotta be runnin' now," Bertha whispered.

A group of five well-oiled white men spotted the women. "Look whart I've fahnd. Cauple a darkies o de female persuasion."

"De little ahn looks ripe fahr de picken, if yah knahws whart I mean."

Seizing Lou and separating her from her mother, one man sneered, "Nutin'like tastin' de first harvest, men."

Bertha screamed, "Don't hurt my baby. Take me, take me. Let her go home, please, Mista."

Lou blubbered, "Mama, don't leave me. Why does they want ta hurt us? We ain't dun nuthin', but work."

Bertha continued wailing and pleading, "Please have mercy on my little girl. Let her go and take me instead."

They only laughed as they pulled Lou to the side of the street. "We'll be lettin' 'er gaw when we get whart we wahnt o 'er. Then we 'ave a piece o yah fahr dessert."

An hour later, Mother and Daughter lay side by side, weeping. Bertha tried to help Lou sit up and adjust her clothing. "I'm so sorry, Baby. Lord knows, I coulda killed 'em bastards if I had me a knife."

"What am I ta do now, Mama? I'm 'shamed ta look at ma brothas."

"Nuthin' fer ya ta be 'shamed 'bout, Baby. These poor white crackers wants to think they be like the big-time landowners 'n' we ther slaves."

"Mama, I smell sumthin' burnin'," Anna Lou said as they struggled to walk the rest of the way home.

"Yes, Baby. Tha Bell Cap'in tole me theys also been settin' fires at our new schools. They don' won't us ta 'ave anythin'. Theys 'fraid we might get 'head them iffen we get schoolin'."

Before total darkness on May 2nd, much of the south part of Memphis was in flames. Black families were hiding in terror.

Not only schools, but black churches, and some black homes were caught up in the insurrection. The problematic but noble work of the Reconstruction Team appeared to have been erased.

Chapter Twenty-Four

THURSDAY, MAY 3RD

T wo days of violence had rocked the city of Memphis. Will, Lenora, Norville, Ben Runkle, and Charlotte Peterson were in shock.

Meeting in Runkle's office, they discussed the situation in the city. "What 'er we a gonna do now?" Norville was bewildered.

Charlotte added, "With our schoolhouses all but destroyed, I don't think we can continue what we've started. Our teachers are discouraged to the point of giving up. What shall I say to them?"

Ben Runkle rubbed his chin, then spoke, "As you folks know very well, I am a man of faith. I believe we won the war because God was on our side. I am cognizant of the fact that the Rebs think that God was on their side, too, but ours is the cause that is just, and that, ultimately, right does prevail.

We must persist and continue with our fight. Lincoln, General Howard, and General Fisk are, also, men of faith. Our leaders are expecting us to complete this task. Hopefully, we can change the mindset of the Rebels. We must try."

"I certainly hope you're right, Colonel," Lenora added. "I have a baby on the way, and I don't want him or her to come into a world of turmoil and strife."

"I understand what you're saying Mrs. Presley, but, unfortunately, the world has always been full of turmoil and strife going all the way back to Cain and Abel," Runkle reminded her.

"Yes, the Bible is filled with stories of conflict from Genesis to Revelation," Charlotte added.

Don't know much 'bout tha Bible, but I do know we had more'n 'er share a killin' and maimin' people," Norville observed.

Meanwhile, on the streets of Memphis, the riot continued.

***

Agitated by police Chief Garrett and Mayor Park, gangs pillaged and burned churches and homes in the black neighborhoods.

"We gotta do sum'thin', Colonel. We cain't 'llow this ta go on," Will pleaded.

"I'll confer with General Stoneman," Runkle replied as he left his office in a heated state.

General George Stoneman

Colonel Runkle met for about an hour with General Stoneman, reviewing the damage that had taken place over the past two days and predicting what was yet to come.

"General, we are the only ones with the men and resources necessary to stop this disaster. Everything we have accomplished in the last year will be in vain if we do not step in to re-establish order in Memphis," Runkle insisted.

Stoneman was initially reluctant to get more involved but was finally convinced that action was necessary. Before ordering his troops to stand ready, he sent a wire to Edwin M. Stanton, Secretary of War.

Sir,

It is with deep remorse that I find it necessary to send our troops into the south part of Memphis today to halt the current disturbances. The past two days have produced an untenable level of violence, the exact source of which will undoubtedly be the subject of further investigation. We know at this point that throngs of enraged civilians have been raging havoc out on the streets until after dark. There have been severe injuries, deaths, and multiple acts of destruction involving white men and Freedmen. Our new schools have been burned as have many churches, and some homes used by Freedmen. Since the Memphis police do not seem to deal with the rioting, I see no option but to authorize our troops to control the situation. A full report will be forthcoming.

Respectfully,
General George Stoneman.

With that notice being sent, Stoneman gave orders to the Commander of the Cavalry. He made it clear that the mission was to bring an immediate end to the rioting.

He added, "I will expect you to carry out this order with as little additional force being applied as is necessary to accomplish the mission. You should visit the Memphis Chief of Police to inform them of what you intend to do and that you expect their cooperation and assistance. I am approving the use of infantry if needed to maintain order."

Back at the Fort, Lenora was shaking as she spoke privately to Will. "This is not what I bargained for. I knew it would not be easy to get everything done in a short time, but I did not expect this. Memphis is a horrible place. These are horrible people. I cannot have our baby born in this place. I need to go home now." She was sobbing uncontrollably at this point.

Will put his arm around his wife and held her close while the tears lasted. "Lenora, I'm gonna take care a ye. Ye'll be a stayin' inside tha Fort. Ye won't be a walkin' tha streets. Ye'll be protected here by me an' by all tha soldiers."

She wiped her eyes and put her head on his shoulder. "I know you will try to protect me and our baby, but I still think we need to be moving away from Memphis as soon as we can."

Trying not to upset her further, Will said, "Let's git through the next few days afore we make any movin' plans. Tha General 'n' tha Colonel 'er in touch with tha War Department. I'm bettin' they'll have a plan afore long.

"Don't ye thank it'd be best ta stay 'ere least 'til the baby comes? Ya got Doc Harrison an' 'is wife ta look afta ye. Ya got all tha teachas an' yer friend, Charlotte ta keep ya comp'ny."

Lenora was thinking and listening.

"Don't ye thank ye'd like ta stay 'round ta see tha schools built back?"

"You might be right, Will, but I cain't raise my baby in this town," she replied, still shaking a little.

"We don't 'ave ta raise tha baby 'ere. We kin stay til August. Tha'd be what we signed up fer. I kin work with Norville 'n' the crews ta fix up tha schools. Ya kin stay at the Fort wit tha baby 'n' help keep tha teachas 'ere long nuff to start over."

"Alright, Will, you win. My Daddy was right. You should be in politics with the gift of gab that you have."

They embraced and agreed to stay the course, at least for a while.

Memphis Avalanche

Chapter Twenty-Five

MOVING ON

W hen the streets of Memphis were restored to a semblance of order, the task of assessing the damages began. Will and Norville traveled with the troops to inspect each school.

Hunt-Phelan had significant damage, but the bones were still there, as were those of the Third Street School. A few others were repairable, but most had burned to the foundation.

"How long do ye thank it'll take ta fix ever'thang," Will asked Norville.

"We'll have ta git 'pproval from the War Department, I'm jist guessin'. Tha Colonel'll know what ta do and where ta start."

On the way back to Fort Pickering, Will and Norville made mental lists in preparation for a discussion with Runkle.

"Colonel, it's a sad sight down ther," Will started. "Most a our new schools 'ave been destroyed. We kin prob'ly fix up Hunt-Phelan and Third Street, but we'll hafta start over on tha others."

Norville added, "Them hooligans burned all tha black churches 'n' sum of ther' homes, too."

"Them poor Freedmen' er in a terr'ble way down 'ere," Will shook his head. "Sum 'ave lost members a ther' fam'ly. Sum 'ave lost a place ta live. Sum 'ave been hurt so bad, they cain't hold a job."

Runkle listened patiently. He realized how devasted Will and Norville were by what they had seen. "I know you boys are heartsick over what has happened, not only the undoing of your good work, but the pain of the poor folks involved," he replied.

"The problem for us is that our only funding at this point comes out of the budget of the War Department. Congress has not yet approved any funding for the Freedman's Bureau. We will be fortunate just to get the resources to fix and rebuild the damages to the schools."

"It ain't fair," Will almost cried. "It jist ain't right."

Runkle agreed with Will, then added, "The best use of our time is to get our plan worked out for the repair and rebuilding. You and Norville are good at that. Let me do some talking about the other damages."

***

Back in Falls Church, Virginia, Harry Parker got word of the Memphis massacre. He heard a few details when delivering to the War Department, but read more in the *National Republican.*

When he shared the news with his wife, Alice, she fell into a panicked state. "Oh, no, Lenora can't stay there with a baby on the way. She needs to come home now, Harry. We need to send her a wire at the Fort. If she starts now, she can get that long train ride behind her before her confinement."

"Try to be calm, Alice. I'm sure that the military officials at the Fort are in charge and that she is protected. Of course, I would like to have her home as much as you, but that has to be their decision."

Reporting of the three-day riot varied dramatically. Local Memphis papers characterized the riots as Negro instigated but encouraged by Radical extremists. The *Memphis Daily Avalanche* reported that the trouble began with a dispute between two boys (one white and one negro), and that when the police attempted to separate the boys, they were fired on by armed black men, wounding one of them.

The local paper continued to blame Radicals in the weeks that followed. They even tried to insinuate that the *Chicago Tribune* reporting received from a Memphis correspondent contained at least fifty-seven lies.

Lenora could not believe her eyes as she read the local account to Will. "How could they get this *so wrong*," she said, throwing down the paper.

"They jist tryin' ta cover up what really 'appened," Will replied. "It's tha same thang they dun 'bout slave ownin'. They tole stories 'bout how the darkies jist loved livin' on plantations 'n' workin' fer tha white boss man. Claimed all tha trouble was tha makins a tha Damn Yankees."

The Chicago Paper reported a different view of the riots:

Inhumane brutality of the Rebel Mob.

All the Colored Schools, Houses, and Churches burned.

Homes of Blacks Destroyed.

Cold-Blooded Murders.

Women burned Alive.

"It was in every respect, a policeman riot, although it cannot be denied that these ignorant and depraved cutthroats were ably and ,*heroically sus*tained in their work of murder, by the *first families of Memphis.*"

The *Memphis Avalanch*e responded nine days later:
RADICAL VITUPERATION OF MEMPHIS
Wickedly False Representations of the Late Riots.

"Memphis is the victim of the presence of many radical writers, who are filling the Northern papers with maliciously false accounts of the late negro riots."

In a conversation with Charlotte and Colonel Runkle on Monday, May 14, Lenora began talking about what she had read in the *Memphis Avalanch*e.

"The Memphis newspaper should not be allowed to print such terrible lies about what happened," Lenora angrily declared. "It should be against the law."

"Mrs. Presley," Runkle responded, Freedom of the Press is one of our basic rights and protections. In fact, one of our most famous founders, Thomas Jefferson, said, *Our liberty depends on the freedom of the press, and that cannot be limited without being lost.*"

"Of course, that freedom can promote bad ideas and good. It's up to us, the actual observers of a situation, to set the record right."

"That's something I like about you, Mrs. Presley. You always stand up for the truth and what is right."

"Thank you, Colonel, I just try to live my life according to what I learned from my Mama and Daddy and the church we love so much."

"What church is that, Mrs. Presley?"

"Falls Church Episcopal Church, Sir. It's very old. In fact, George Washington worshipped there."

***

Lenora's father, Harry Parker, had sent a wire at the insistence of his wife.

Your Mother and I know about the Memphis situation. We will welcome you home any time you decide to make a move. Stay safely in the Fort. Write back if you can. Love to you and Will.

Lenora hated the fact that her parents were so far away and worried about her. She had not forgotten her request to leave Memphis as soon as possible. She was determined not to let Will forget it, either.

Later in the week, Lenora began to feel something happening to her body. After visiting Doc Harrison, she told Will, "I think our baby is coming soon."

"I'll ask Colonel Runkle, to send afta me if I'm out workin' when tha time comes," Will promised. "I'm so excited 'bout bein' a Pa."

"Charlotte offered to stay with me for the first few days and Doc Harrison's wife is ready to come when I call," Lenora assured him.

***

By mid-morning, Sunday, May 20, the intermittent contractions had begun. On the advice of Doc Harrison, Lenora moved to the Infirmary. She asked Charlotte to give Runkle the news so that Will could be notified.

Mrs. Martha Harrison, a midwife, made Lenora comfortable in a section of the Fort's Infirmary. Her husband, Doc Harrison, examined Lenora and predicted that labor would most likely take all day.

Charlotte agreed to sit with Lenora until Will arrived. Martha came in and out of the Infirmary every half hour to check on the progress. She asked Charlotte to let her know when the contractions got closer together.

Early in the evening, Will arrived and rushed into the Infirmary in a state of excitement. "Where's my wife? How's she doin'? Why's it takin' so long?"

Martha tried to calm Will and prevent him from scaring Lenora. "Doc's going to go with you to the Mess Hall. You should have something to eat and take a few deep breaths. Your wife is fine, but nature takes her own time."

Against his better judgment, Will followed Doc Harrison to the dining hall, where he discovered that he was famished.

"The best thing you can do, Will, is to show up rested and smiling.

A first-time mother doesn't need an anxious father-to-be hanging over her. It's all she can do to follow the instructions. She needn't be worried about you."

***

It was almost midnight when Doc Harrison summoned Will back to the Infirmary. "I think we are getting close. Are you hoping for a son or a daughter?"

"I jist want my sweet Lady ta be alright. She's tha best thang tha eva 'appened ta me. I'll be 'appy wit either. I'm already blessed."

At approximately 1:30 A.M. on May 21, Will heard a small cry from the back of the Infirmary. He moved closer and was told by Doc Harrison, "You have a son, Mr. Presley."

"Kin I see 'im, please?"

"Wait a minute," Martha said, pushing Will back from the bed.

"Is sum'thin' wrong?" he asked with a frightened tone.

"Not wrong, just unexpected," Doc Harrison replied, placing his hand on Will's shoulder. "I was wrong. You don't have a son."

"Ye mean it's a girl?"

"Will, your wife just gave birth to twins. You have *two* sons."

With his jaw dropped, Will stood in silence for a moment, and then let out a shout of joy. "*Two sons, two sons at one time?* Guessin' I'm even betta than I thunk I wuz."

Doc Harrison laughed, "Don't be getting the big head, boy. That little lady in there probably deserves most of the credit."

"Lenora, I love ye so much. We gonna be raisin' two more Presley boys. Kin we name 'em afta my lost brothas, Buck and Johnny?"

"Slow down, Will, give me a chance to get to know these little boys before saddling them with names of people I never had a chance to meet. What were their Christian names, anyway? I am sure it was not just Buck and Johnny."

"The oldest wuz James Buchanan, tha next wuz John Marshal, then there wuz me, George Wilhelm."

Lenora always laughed when she heard Will's full name. "Those are all fine names, but I would like our sons to have their own special names," she said. "I think we can include your brothers' names, but call them by their own special pet name."

That is how the twins became Ronald Buchanan Presley and John Randall Presley, known as Ronnie and Randy.

"Maw'd be so happy ta know tha names of 'er fallen sons are still livin' on in my lil'uns," Will said with a sob as he held Lenora's hand.

Chapter Twenty-Six

JULY, 1866

"Well, Sweet Lady, how did 'er baby boys do taday?" Will inquired as he returned home from work. "Did they wear you out?"

"It is a chore taking care of *two* at the same time. I admired that my mother had raised one, but two is much harder."

"I'm shore 'at's true darlin', but we 'er goin' home next month. The re-buildin' a tha school is comin' right along, 'n' I thank Norville gonna stay here fer a while after we leave. Him 'n' Miss Charlotte's gittin' along real good, if ye know what I mean," he grinned.

"Yes, I believe there's a budding romance between those two."

"Well, I know Norville's a good man, 'n' Miss Charlotte's a smart woman. She's a good Christian woman too."

Smiling wistfully, Lenora said, "My mother will be such a big help to me with these two babies. I'm eager to see my Daddy too."

"You got 'at right. The Memphis schools are in good hands with Colonel Runkle, Charlotte, and Norville. Maybe we kin help git things moving on the Fourteenth Amendment," he added.

"From what I hear around the fort here, it's gonna need a lot of help. Two Northern states have ratified it, but no southern states yet," she said.

"Guess I'd better tell the Colonel we're gonna be leavin' next month. Our year will be up on Friday, August 10," he calculated. "I hope he'll be happy a knowin' we 'er gonna try to work some in D.C."

"We might need to help my folks on the farm some too," she reminded him. "Daddy's not able to do as much as he used to."

"That kinda work's what I was raised a doin'," he nodded. "We mainly raised 'backer 'n' cut timber, but our little vegetable garden, 'n' hogs 'n' chickens kept us fat 'n' sassy," he smiled and winked at her.

"My Paw said he raised nine a us kids, so's he'd have plenty a help on tha farm. Reckon me 'n' 'you's got a lot more ta go," he teased.

"Now, Daddy's got plenty of hired help. We don't have to raise our own. We can hire more if we need to."

***

Walking into Runkle's office the next morning, Will was pleasantly surprised at the news. "Just got a telegram from General Fisk in Nashville. He says the Tennessee Legislature's going to vote on the Fourteenth Amendment on July 18, Presley. If so, we'd be the first Southern state to ratify. Fisk is very hopeful and confident."

` "How many states hafta ratify fer it ta pass, Colonel?"

Right now there are thirty-six states, and three-fourths of them must vote to pass it. Let's see; that would be twenty-seven. Connecticut was the first state to vote for it on June 30. New Hampshire followed them on July 6. If Tennessee votes to accept it on July 18, that'd be three."

"Looks like it's gonna take some doin' ta git it passed. Me 'n' Lenora'd like ta help git that done. Our year with the Freedmen's Bureau is up on August 10, 'n' we 'er goin' back to Falls Church, Virginia. Her parents has a farm ther' 'n' needs 'er help. But being so close to D.C., we thank we kin help with tha Fourteenth 'n' maybe tha Fifteenth."

"I'm sorry to hear that, Presley. You two have done a commendable job with our school program, but I understand family must come first."

"Thank ye, Sir. It's been a pleasure workin' with ye here in Memphis. Norville 'n' Charlotte will finish re-buildin' 'ese schools, 'n' me 'n' Lenora will do all we kin with the feds up ther'," he nodded.

On July 18, 1866, Tennessee ratified the Fourteenth Amendment. The last remaining pre-condition had been met, and thus it re-joined the union on July 24, 1866 - the first Confederate state to do so. Two more years would pass before Arkansas became the second.

It would be 1870 before Texas became the fifteenth and final state to re-join. Lenora's prophecy was correct. It took a lot of work.

***

Will returned home from working on the re-building of the schools with good news. "Hey, Sweet Lady, we got all but one a tha schools opened back up. Norville thinks we kin open tha last 'un before we leave here on August 10. Ain't ye proud of us?"

"Will, you and Norville have done a great job on the schools. I am especially proud of both of you. It's going to be easier to leave here knowing our job is finished.

"But we got some terrible news here at the fort today. There's been another massacre of black people down in New Orleans."

"Oh no, wuz many a them killed?" Will frowned.

"The news we got was that more than fifty blacks were killed and more than a hundred were injured. I don't think there was a lot of property damage, but it's awfully similar to what happened here in Memphis," she answered.

"White policemen and firemen were involved, and most of them were former Confederate soldiers. The blacks were, mostly, former Union soldiers and freed slaves." she said.

"It don't look like ta me that this here war's over yit. People 'er still fightin' it."

***

On Friday, August 3, when he returned home from work, Lenora had a newspaper that Colonel Runkle had received in the mail -the *New Orleans Tribune.* When her husband sat down, she began to read to him.

Street Mob in New Orleans

"On July 30, the Louisiana State Constitutional Convention was re-convened to consider voting rights for free blacks and freedmen slaves. Former Confederate soldiers and their sympathizers opposed this change to their State Constitution, but Negroes and former Union soldiers were adamant that the male suffrage be included.

"A group of civilian-supporters organized a parade with a marching band. Armed opposers confronted the marchers, and shots were fired. The encounter occurred near the Merchant's Institute. Several marchers fled into the building and escaped unharmed.

"Federal troops were called in to quell the riot. At least fifty blacks were killed and more than a hundred were injured. Four whites were killed in the melee. The Convention was dismissed with no action on voting rights," she read.

"We got a lotta stuff ta work on when we git back to Falls Church, the Fourteenth Amendment and maybe the Fifteenth. If the freedmen get voting rights, it's gonna take an amendment jist like it did for freeing tha slaves, I reckon." Will shook his head.

Chapter Twenty-Seven

TRAIN RIDE HOME

O n the morning of August 10, 1866, a flurry of activity kept Will and Lenora busy. Besides double-checking their luggage, including everything needed to care for two babies, not yet three months old, there was a round of goodbyes.

Colonel Runkle dispatched three soldiers to assist them in safely boarding the first train out of Memphis.

Lenora knew the trip would take a minimum of three days and involve several train changes before reaching their final-destination at the depot in Washington, D.C.

Will tried to explain the complications of making connections because some lines destroyed in the war had not yet been restored. Lenora attempted to pay attention but was preoccupied with her two babes in arms. Finally, she said, "Will, it is your job to get us there. I have both my hands full, so I'm counting on you."

***

Settling in on the first leg of their journey, both of them felt excitement and apprehension about the future.

Lenora was looking forward to seeing her mother and father after a year's absence. She was eager to introduce her boys to their grandparents.

As most first-time mothers, she was also uneasy about handling everything that goes with caring for two nursing infants at once, other domestic duties, and helping Will with their shared mission.

Will was excited about becoming involved in the next phase of the Reconstruction efforts, including passing the much-needed legislation. He felt compelled to contribute to something positive.

Remembering how his mountain accent had been held against him when he first traveled north, Will made a promise to himself to unlearn talking like his father, whom he dearly loved and still mourned. "I'll listen to Lenora, her parents, and other people in positions of responsibility. *"A change in my speech might change my future . . . 'n' our future,"* he thought.

Always in the back of his mind, he heard a voice telling him he had a debt coming due. The horrors in which he had participated could never be undone. Although he realized he was a victim of circumstances beyond his control, that knowledge did not absolve him.

The repetitive rhythm of the train wheels on the tracks caused Will to nod in and out of sleep, and in those brief half-sleeps, he would think about the family he left behind.

It had been five years since he left Roaring Fork, leaving his mother, Sally Presley, only a brief note.

Maw,

I can't bring myself to fight, protecting the plantation owners in their fight to keep slaves. Slaves are people just like us. They should not be owned by other people. Preacher Henderson said the United States of America was founded on Freedom. People should be free. I know my brothers think I'm wrong, but I think they are the ones who are wrong. I'm leaving Roaring Fork Farm for now. Don't know where I'm going or what I'm going to do. I love you and all my family. Hope to see you again someday.

Will

He had not attempted to contact her or any of his family during that period. They had no way of knowing if he were even alive. They were unaware of any events in which he had been involved both during and after the war.

The deep regrets he held in his heart had not been revealed even to his wife. He would carry his burden silently for many more years only to be periodically terrorized in nightmares.

Likewise, he had no way of knowing all the changes that had affected his family in his absence.

He did not know that his brothers, Buck, and Johnny, had slipped away from the battlefield in Antietam in September 1862 long enough to assist with the tobacco crop back home in Roaring Fork.

Also, he did not know that his little brother, Matt, and younger sister, Lizzie, had been killed on the street in Graham on April 29, 1865, three days after the official end of the war.

Additionally, he did not know that his grandfather O'Connor had died, nor that his sister, Maggie, had married a young doctor, Doug Mahan, and moved into town.

Finally, he did not know that two Murphy boys were killed at Gettysburg, nor that Andrew Henderson had been crippled.

The scars of war were everywhere in his home community. At a future date, these revelations would only add to his grief.

Sally, the family matriarch, had continued to hold classes for neighborhood children at the Roaring Fork Methodist Church while overseeing activities at the Presley homeplace.

At times, Will would recall his family history as told to him by his parents, probably exaggerating both the good and not so good as storytellers are inclined to do.

The only child of the Graham North Carolina's tailor and seamstress, Sally O'Connor, had always dreamed of becoming a teacher. When she met her future husband, J.W. Presley, he was charming, hard-working, but basically illiterate.

He had emigrated from the old country in search of opportunity and had signed a contract of indenture with an influential landowner in Graham, North Carolina.

During their courtship, teaching her true love to read and write became her initial step toward that dream. The newlyweds started their marriage as indentured workers in a small cabin on land owned by Charles Graham, the town leader.

As Sally and J.W. built a life together, they paid off the original indenture, purchased more land, raised nine children, and constructed a larger home.

Sally honed her teaching skill with her own brood, then added the children of her neighbors. When the family moved into their two-story home, the cabin became the Roaring Fork School.

When their two oldest married and began bearing grandchildren, the cabin was needed for family use.

At the suggestion of Preacher John Wesley Henderson, Sally moved her school to the Roaring Fork Church so that Johnny and Willadeen could have the cabin.

When a tragic logging accident took the life of J.W. Presley, Sally became the spine that held the family upright.

Paralyzed by grief and knowing that life had changed forever, she insisted that the her family would continue the work her husband had begun and that she would continue to teach children.

Sally's strength would continue to be tested as events beyond her control robbed her of four of her nine children. Buck and Johnny were both lost at Gettysburg. Then Matt and Lizzie became civilian casualties as they were killed in the center of town. Will's fate was yet to be confirmed.

In the fall of 1865, Billy Bob, the fourth Presley son, married his brother Johnny's widow, Willadeen.

After the death of his two oldest brothers and the disappearance of the third, he had assumed the role of the senior Presley male and unofficially filled in as father for all the grandchildren. He moved into the cabin with his new wife and her two children.

Martha, Buck's widow, now established herself as the person in charge of the two-story home. Of course, Sally was still officially the matriarch, but was devoting most of her attention to her school at the church. Consequently, Martha could exercise her naturally assertive manner without interference.

Pete, Andy, and Sally were still living with Martha in the big house. Andy, however, was engaged to Grace, Vernon, and Savannah, Willis' younger daughter. Vernon had been J.W. Presley's best friend.

***

"Wake up, sleepy head," Lenora chided Will. "It's your turn to hold these boys. I need to visit the necessary room. What in the world have you been dreaming about while I'm left trying to deal with crying and nursing?"

"I'm sorry, Darlin', I don't know why I am so tired. I was thinking about my maw and wondering how she and the rest of my family are getting along since the end of the war."

Lenora made her way to the back of the car to freshen up and get a bit of exercise. On her return, she was stopped by a middle-aged lady.

"Hello, my name is Mary Agnes Weadon, and I will travel for several days. I noticed that you have two small babies to handle with little assistance. I would be happy to give you a break if you would accept my help."

"How kind of you," Lenora replied with surprise. "Where are you going?"

"I am returning to my headquarters in Washington, D.C. My organization has been active for many years in the Abolitionist Movement and in working for Women's Suffrage."

"That is a coincidence. We are headed to my parent's home outside of Washington in Northern Virginia. You may have heard of Falls Church," Lenora responded.

"My husband and I are returning from our work with the Freedman's Bureau in Memphis where we helped start a system of schools for the newly freed Negro adults and their children. My name is Lenora Presley and I am so pleased to meet you, Miss Weadon."

"Please call me Mary Agnes, and may I call you Lenora?"

"Oh, yes, Mary Agnes. Would you like to move closer to us so that we can talk?"

"That would be lovely. Let me hold one baby to give your arms a rest."

"My husband has them both right now, but I am sure he is eager to be relieved of that duty. Please join us. I want to hear more about your organization," Lenora smiled.

Will was glad to see Lenora walking back to their seats, but was surprised to see her accompanied by a woman he had never met.

"Mary Agnes, this is my husband, Will Presley, holding our sons Ronnie and Randy," Lenora said proudly.

Will attempted to stand to properly greet Lenora's new friend; however, he had both arms full.

"Pleased to meet you, Ma'am," was all he could muster with a smile and a nod of his head.

"Let me take one of those little angels," Mary Agnes offered. There was no objection from Will.

Lenora laughed to see how ready her husband was to hand Ronnie over to a total stranger after less than half an hour of duty. "I'll take Randy," Lenora said..

"Will, Mary Agnes Weedon has been involved with helping people become free for many years. She has worked with abolitionists and suffragettes. In fact, she is headed back to her office in Washington.

"She has offered to help me with the boys on our long trip. It will be wonderful to have two extra hands," Lenora added.

Free to stand up, Will helped the ladies settle in on the opposite side of the aisle. "Let me move some of your hand luggage over by me so you will have more space," Will suggested. "Thank you, thank you very, very, much, Miss Weedon," he smiled with his contagious curled grin.

"Please call me Mary Agnes, and it is my pleasure. It will be good to have other people to talk with on this tiring journey."

He noticed two embroidered symbols on one of Mary Agnes's large straw bags. "Betting there's a story here," he said. "Tell us about the bell and flower, Miss Mary Agnes," Will said.

"The Liberty Bell is a symbol of freedom. It was adopted by the Abolitionist Movement as a reminder of our goal to eradicate slave ownership," she started.

"Ideas set forth during the religious movement known as the Second Great Awakening inspired abolitionists to revolt against slavery. It was a reminder that our Declaration of Independence informs us of a self-evident truth that all men are created equal in the eyes of God."

"That embroidered bell is a beautiful way to remember what is important," Lenora said. "Did you do the needlework?"

"Yes, sometimes in the evenings, I sit in a rocker and do a bit of stitching. It calms me and helps me to forget all the disappointments and work yet to be done."

"What about the flower. What does that stand for?" Will asked.

"That is a sunflower, Will, and it has been used by my sister suffragettes in Kansas to signify how sunlight enlightens the world.

"We hope to make it the official symbol of our movement. Just as sunlight makes plants grow and women make the population grow, so will groups of women organized for universal rights shine the light of truth on our current limitations and demand change. All men and all women should have equal rights under the law."

Will listened intently. This was the first time he had heard a woman profess such strong beliefs about the state of social or political affairs. He had taken it for granted that men, especially men with education or wealth, would be the ones leading the charge for any changes.

"Miss Mary Agnes, I am very taken with the devotion you express," he said. "Preacher Henderson, back home in North Carolina, told us we were all God's children. That's why I disagreed with my brothers and left home instead of joining the Confederate Army and why I can't go home again."

"Never say you can't, Will. That kind of thinking doesn't bring the changes we need. If I thought that way, I would give up and go back home for good. Change comes slowly, but it doesn't come at all unless good people make their voices heard."

Lenora was smiling. "I am so glad we met you, Mary Agnes. You are just what we both needed right now. After all the hatred and destruction, we saw in Memphis, we wondered if things would ever change. Will and I decided to give it another try by coming back to the center of government and play some part in getting the 14th and 15th Amendments passed."

Will asked, "Are there other ladies like you, Mary Agnes?"

She laughed, "Of course there are, Will. There are also some men who share our ideas about equality. There are men and women of good will who have been active in both the anti-slavery and the women's suffrage movements for many years. True equality knows no gender just as true Christian Love knows no boundaries."

The three-way conversation continued across the miles. Lenora and Mary Agnes shared life stories. Will mostly listened and dozed in and out, grateful that Lenora had someone to help her.

Several times over the first two days, Will was awakened from a recurring nightmare. He could see the faces of his brothers, Buck, and

Johnny, lying in the mud at Gettysburg. Buck was looking straight into his eyes as if to say, "How could ye shoot yer own blood?"

Seeing him startled, Lenora asked, "What's wrong, Will? Did you have a bad dream?"

Trying to recover his composure, he offered a different story of remembered guilt. "It's nothing, really. Sometimes, I remember the day my Paw died in a logging accident. I always feel that I should have done more to prevent that." He wondered to himself if he would ever be able to tell anyone about Gettysburg.

Changing the subject, Will asked Mary Agnes to fill them in on what had been happening in Virginia during the last year.

"It is not a pretty story, Will. Just as you witnessed in Memphis, there continues to be strong opposition to allowing free black or newly freedmen to achieve equal treatment and equal opportunity.

"The good news is that some progress has been made. Black Virginians have founded their own churches, reconstituted their families, and started businesses.

"The Freedmen's Bureau helped in this work especially legalizing marriages among former enslaved people. The Bureau was also instrumental in bringing mainly teachers, black and white, to teach school for the freed people of all ages."

"The bad news is that despite Federal occupation, the same people who had run the government of Richmond before and during the war, still run the government.

"The worst news is that you have your work cut out for you if you want to help pass the 14th Amendment."

"Why do you say that, Mary Agnes?" Will was absorbing everything he heard.

"Because the powers that be in Virginia are refusing to do the things asked of them to be readmitted to the Union. They must reject secession, acknowledge the end of slavery, and pledge loyalty to the United States."

"That seems very reasonable," Lenora mused. "What is their objection?"

They don't much like any of it; however, the major barrier is that they must say the Confederacy had been wrong or illegitimate."

Will shook his head, "My Paw used to say, *Ye can lead a horse to water, but ye cain't make him drink.*"

"Exactly," Mary Agnes agreed. "That is why it is an absolute imperative to enact laws that protect the rights of all people. Without the law, people will ignore or deny those rights. Even with the law, people will create ways to keep others in what the privileged think of as *their place.*"

"Guess I'm going to hafta find a way to help get those laws passed," Will said with a new sense of purpose.

"There is no more important mission," Mary Agnes smiled at him.

Chapter Twenty-Eight

PARKER'S FARM

B efore finally arriving at the Washington, D.C. station on the third day of their journey, Lenora exchanged contact information with Mary Agnes. "We must stay in touch," she insisted.

Will thanked Mary Agnes for the help with the babies, and for all the information she had shared. "We feel very blessed to have met you and we wish you the best in your efforts on behalf of women's rights."

"I look forward to hearing from the two of you," Mary Agnes replied. "I am expecting great things from you in the future."

Harry Parker was waiting at the station and greeted them with a broad smile and a waiting carriage. "Alice is so excited to see all of you, she can barely control herself; but she stayed home to prepare a wonderful homecoming meal for you."

Parker's Home

Even though the sun had set, and everyone was tired, the Parkers and Presleys spent hours talking, eating, laughing before calling it a night. Alice could not keep her hands off her two grandsons.

"Oh, Lenora, they are so beautiful. I want to keep holding them, but we all need to get some sleep. Good night, darlings."

***

As Lenora and Will sat down for breakfast, Harry Parker spoke, "Good morning folks, I hope you slept well."

A sleepy-eyed Lenora replied, "As well as expected with two babies in the same room with you. When one falls asleep, the other one wakes up. New mothers don't sleep much."

"Nor new fathers, neither I reckon." Will grinned.

"Alice and I have been talking, and we think you night be more comfortable in your own house. We have plenty of unused land here, and we'd like to give you a plot of ground to build a house of your own."

Grinning, Will said, "I reckon our crying babies are gettin' on your nerves, too."

"Now we're not complaining, but neither of you have had a house of your own; ever. You moved from a boarding house to an army barracks. Not what we had envisioned for our Princess.

"Will has had a lot of experience building structures for schools. It shouldn't be much different for a dwelling house. I have a couple of men who are brothers who work here on our farm. They have built some out-buildings for me.

"Henry and Marvin Rolen are very likable and competent young men who would be a big help to Will on the building." Harry nodded.

"Wow, it seems like you two have really thought about this a lot. It sounds like a wonderful idea to me," Lenora smiled her assent.

"Yes Sir, it will be great having our own place. My maw 'n' paw had two babies when they built their first house." Will added.

Alice carried a bowl of scrambled eggs and a plate of fried pork sausage to the table and sat down. "I heard you talking from the kitchen," she said. "I'm glad you like our idea for your own house, Len and Will. We do want the house close enough to ours so I can help you raise these two."

"I told Lenora we weren't through having babies yet. My maw 'n' paw had nine of us kids. Paw needed help on the farm," he grinned.

"Now Will, I told you we can hire more help on the farm if we need to," Lenora shook her head and smiled.

Alice chimed in, "That's just like a man. You might think differently if you had to bear those babies yourself."

"Just teasing Mrs. Parker. Me and Lenora's got to have a little fun," he said, grinning.

"I suggest we take a walk after breakfast and choose a spot for your house," Harry said. "If we pick a location east of our house with it facing north, the morning sun will awaken you and the evening sun will allow the back of the house to cool down before bedtime. We do need to assure that we don't get too close to the hog pens, though. That aroma gets pretty strong at times."

"I do remember that odor from my childhood, Daddy. It is terrible when the wind comes from a certain direction.," Lenora wrinkled her nose.

"Well, the hog pens and chicken coops are to the south and west from our house, so the east location should be the best spot," Harry reasoned.

"And from there, you can view the cornfields and the other vegetable gardens from the rear of the house, too,' Alice added.

"Mama, can we plant some flowers along the pathway between the houses?" Lenora asked.

"Of course, darling, we'll make this a place of beauty and splendor," Alice smiled and nodded.

Will smiled and said,"Just like my beautiful bride"

"On how you do go on," Lenora blushed.

***

As they walked toward the building plot, Lenora continued, " Will and I are interested in finishing our work for the freedmen. The Fourteenth Amendment has only three states to ratify it so far, Virginia is not one of them, and we promised our colleagues in Memphis that we would do everything we can to help make that happen.

"Daddy, do you know Thaddeus Stevens?" she asked.

"I have never met him, but I do know who he is. He and Senator Sumner are working hard to pass that amendment, and to do something about allowing freedmen and free blacks the right to vote. That might take another amendment," he suggested.

"Yes, we heard about the Fifteenth Amendment too," Will joined the conversation.

"One of our teachers, Charlotte Peterson, is from the same congressional district as Representative Stevens. In fact, they attend the same church. She asked us to contact him and help in every way we can to get those things done."

"I think those are noble aspirations, Will, but Lenora has two young children to raise, and maybe more, if you have your way. Be careful that you don't overload yourselves with ambitions," Alice cautioned.

"We do understand the importance of family, but we believe that we must see the big picture, also, Mama," Lenora asserted.

"We can handle those situations as they arise, Princess," Harry joined in. "Right now, let's just choose a spot for your new house."

He turned to Will and said, "Son, I think you're going to need a parlor, a kitchen, a gathering room, and at least three bedrooms. These two boys'll want their own rooms soon enough. If you have your way, and add children, you can put a second story on the house. Build it so that will be possible in the future."

"That's exactly what my paw did on our farm, Mr Parker. I think that's a good idea."

"Call me Harry, Will. We're family now."

"I certainly will, Harry. It's nice to have family again. I have seen none of mine since the summer of '61 when I left home," he sighed.

"Maybe you can go back some day and show Lenora and the boys where you grew up," Harry suggested.

"I'm not so sure about that. Sir. Most of my family were Rebs. Two of my brothers were Confederate soldiers. And I think the ones who stayed at home were for the Southern side in the war. Just about everybody in town was too," he remembered.

"If they haven't seen you in that many years, they'll be glad to see you again, Take my word for that, Son."

"I do want my maw to meet Lenora, and I want our boys to meet their other grandmother," he replied wistfully. "But for right now, there are plenty of things to get done right here."

Harry smiled, "And the first one is to get this house built. I'll tell Henry and Marvin that they can help you with it. I'm certain they'll be eager to do so. It'll give them a respite from farming for a little while."

Chapter Twenty-Nine

SETTLING IN

"Hey Will, in the morning, I'm making my weekly trip to the War Department. Do you want to accompany me?" Harry asked as they sat down for breakfast. "Henry and Marvin can continue working on the house while we're gone. I'll introduce you around to everyone I know."

"Yes, I certainly would like that, Sir. It is helpful knowing people there. Some of those folks are surely working to pass the Amendments. Lenora knows just about everyone there already." He was pleased to be invited.

"Alice and I were talking about that very thing last night," Harry nodded. "The men will load the wagon tonight, so we can be ready to leave just as soon as we have breakfast. I try to get there by 9:00 A.M."

***

Riding to the War Department warehouse, Will talked to his father-in-law. "Mr. Parker, I mean Harry, I was raised on a farm in North Carolina, and I'm willing to do anything you want me to do here on your farm. I've worked crops and fed hogs and chickens."

"I think it would be good if you work with all the different crews rotating. That way, you can understand all the processes we use and get to know the people involved at the same time.

"One crew works the hogs and chickens, another one works the vegetable gardens, and yet another, works the apple orchard. Someday soon, you will need to assume the responsibility for all of them.

"I know you and my Princess are interested in the political scene here, and I understand the necessity for that too. The contacts you will need can be made right here at the War Department. With your military record, you will be readily accepted here, I believe."

"Yes, General Howard, who heads the Freedmen's Bureau has an office here. He was my commander at Gettysburg and presented me with a medal just after that battle.

"He hired me and Lenora to work for the Freedmen's Bureau, too. I'm certain he's interested in passing the Amendments.

"He has started a school for freed-persons in D.C. and wants to train teachers," Will informed him.

"I've heard a lot about him. He's the one-armed general who they call the *Christian General,*" Harry acknowledged.

"Yeah, lost an arm in '62 in a battle and was awarded the Medal of Honor himself. I was proud to serve under him in the army and in the Freedmen's Bureau."

***

When they arrived at the War Department dock, Harry said to Will, "After we unload and collect for last week's delivery, we'll go in and find my niece, Judy Parker. If we can speak to General Howard, she'll know and arrange for us to see him. She's my brother's daughter.

"Yes Sir, I met Judy once before. She introduced Lenora and me to the General. She, also, kept us informed the night Lincoln was shot."

***

"Good morning, Sargent Moody." Harry spoke to the loading dock worker. "I want you to meet my son-in-law, Will Presley."

"Hello Mr. Presley, I'm Bill Moody. I heard Lenora talk about you while she worked here. You're a war hero, I believe."

Modestly, he dropped his head and replied, "I'm not much of a hero, but they gave me a medal, anyway, I reckon."

"Well, I'm pleased to meet you, and look forward to working with you," Moody smiled.

Entering the building, they walked down a long hall and found the office where Judy Parker worked.

Harry stuck his head in the door and said, "Hi Judy, have you got a minute to chat?"

"Why certainly, Uncle Harry. Come on in. I see you have Mr. Presley with you." Turning to Will, she said, "I thought you and Lenora were in Memphis."

"Yeah, we were for the last year, but we finished our tour and came back here. We're building a house on Parker's Farm. Gonna help there for a while," he informed her.

Harry spoke up. "Will and Lenora want to continue to work for the freedmen and their cause. Can you get him in to see General Howard?"

"Well, I'll check and see what his schedule is this morning. I'm certain the General would be happy to see Will. I'll be right back."

Smiling as she returned from Howard's office, she said, "General Howard is delighted to see you. Follow me, gentlemen."

***

"Come in Presley and Parker. I'm happy to see both of you. What's on your mind?"

"Hello General," Will greeted him. "Lenora and I have moved back to the farm here with Harry and Alice. We have two small boys who needed to see their grandparents.

"Then, too, we want to work with you and the others on the Fourteenth and Fifteenth Amendments. We promised Colonel Runkle we would do that when we got back here."

"Runkle is a good man, and he's doing a great job for us in Memphis.

"We are delighted you want to help with the Amendments. That's a big priority for us at Freedmen's Bureau. Virginia has not ratified the Fourteenth yet. That's one job you and Parker can help us get done," Howard offered.

Harry spoke, "We appreciate your seeing us on short notice, General. We'll move along and allow you to get back to your business at hand.

"I'll speak with our state Assemblyman and offer our services on the legislation upcoming. Alice and I want to join Lenora and Will in this latest project."

"Thank you for stopping in. Welcome back to D. C., Presley. I look forward to working with you again," the General bade them goodbye.

"Alright, Son, let's me and you get on back to the farm. You've got a house to build."

***

Back at the house, the Rolen brothers were hard at work. Seeing the headway, they had made in one day, Will was pleased with what they had done.

"Looks like you boys have been hard at it while we were gone. Maybe I'll leave again tomorrow and stay outta your way some more," Will grinned. "You know I'm only teasing. We got to have a little fun, boys."

"That's OK, Mister Will, we can handle this job," Henry smiled.

"Yes Sir, Mister Will, we done this before for Mister Harry," Marvin chimed in.

"I believe at this rate the three of us can finish this house in about a month. What do you think, Henry?" Will wondered.

"That sounds about right to me, Sir," Rolen assented.

***

As they were washing up for dinner, Parker spoke to his son-in-law. "Son, I noticed you are speaking differently than when you were last home. What happened?"

"Well, Sir, I remembered the first time I came to D.C. and tried to find a job. People knew from my mountain accent that I wasn't from around here. Everybody assumed that I was a Reb. Couldn't find a job anywhere.

"I decided, I could talk like Lenora and Colonel Runkle. I just need to think about it before I speak.

"It's amazing how people judge you by little things like that," he shook his head.

"Alice and I both noticed it immediately. We both are pleased that you've made the effort. It will be helpful for you in the future."

Chapter Thirty

POLITICIANS

O n Saturday morning at breakfast, the conversation turned to the visit to General Howard. Harry said, "General Howard was delighted to know that the Presleys, both of you, are passionate about the Fourteenth Amendment. Alice and I talked last night, and we believe you need to meet John Hall.

"John is a member of our church who serves as the Senior Warden. Because he's a cattle farmer with a large herd, he is well-known in this area, and an influential man.

"Also, he is an abolitionist and proponent of the Fourteenth and Fifteenth. The organization he heads is called The Anti-Slavery Society of Virginia, a branch of the national association."

"Oh, that's the group Mary Agnes belongs to," Lenora exclaimed. "We met her on the train, and she helped me with the boys. She's a sweet lady."

"Great," Alice added. "You need to know the people here who are as passionate about your cause as you are.

"But if you're going to attend church with us, you must have clothes. Can we go Monday to the tailor shop in D.C., Harry?"

"I think that can be arranged,Will. You make certain that Henry and Marvin know that you'll be away on Monday. All the farm crews know what I expect of them, but I'll make sure they know we'll be away from the farm on Monday, too."

***

When Monday morning dawned, the Presleys arose at 5:00 A.M. While Will washed and got dressed, Lenora dressed the babies, they switched roles as Lenora prepared herself for the shopping excursion.

"I never realized how much two babies would change our lives," Will mused.

Chuckling, Lenora spoke loudly, "You're just *now* finding out about that? Well, welcome to reality, Poppa."

Will carried both boys as Lenora toted a large cloth bag containing the supplies she would need for Ronnie and Randy on this day trip.

Harry drove the carriage to the front of the house, and Alice and Lenora climbed into the back seat. When they were comfortable, Will handed the boys to them. Alice held Ronnie while Lenora held Randy.

***

Driving into downtown Washington, Will related that his grandparents operated a tailor and dressmaking shop in Graham. "Patrick O'Conner, my grandfather and Eunice, my grandmother kept us Presley kids in clothes while we were growing up. Some of them were samples from last year or the year before, but all were well made. I like nice clothes."

Alice spoke, "Lenora has been wearing clothes made by the dress-maker in the shop next door to the tailor. Their shops are just one block from the Ford Theater.

"Both shops make costumes for the actors who work there. Sometimes they have samples for sale at reduced prices. I like bargains, don't you?"

"Yeah, I think it was Ben Franklin who said a dollar saved is a dollar earned," Will interjected.

"Actually, he said a penny saved is a penny earned," Lenora corrected him.

"It's going to take more than pennies to pay for what we're buying, Sweet Lady," he grinned.

"Harry and I discussed it last night, and we are paying for your church clothes this time," Alice informed them. "When you get on a regular salary at the farm, you can pay for them."

"That's a mighty nice gesture," Will was grateful.

***

Ralph Pendleton's Tailor Shop was located just one block from the Ford Theater. When the Parker entourage entered the shop, Pendleton immediately spoke to Harry. "Hello Parker. You have a nice-looking group with you today."

Pendleton was a slender, balding man in his fifties with long, full sideburns but no beard or mustache. He wore glasses perched on the end of his nose.

"What brings you to town?"

"My son-in-law needs some Sunday-go-to-meeting clothes. What can you offer him today?"

"Well, of course, I can make something for him, but we might have a sample or two in his size. And here's an entire rack of costumes used by Ford Theater actors. There's one that was worn by John Wilkes Booth."

Will looked at Lenora and winked. "We saw him in a show there once," Lenora remarked.

"Don't want no clothes worn by Booth," Presley declared. "Not at any price."

"Oh, look here, Will," Lenora's face lit up. "This black suit looks very distinguished."

"That is a nice suit, Mr. Presley. Let's try it on for size."

"That's not too bad. We'll need to shorten the sleeve, but that's minor. Step into the dressing room and try the pants."

"The cuffs need to be shortened. Let me mark them."

"Ralph, how long will it take for the alterations?"

"Probably about an hour, I have nothing in front of you."

"OK, we're going next door to get Lenora a dress. Be back in an hour. I'll pay you then.

"Hey, do you know John Hall who heads the Anti-Slavery Association?" Harry asked.

"Sure do, I'm a member myself. John is a good man and passionate about his cause. Now that the war's over, he wants to work on the Fourteenth and Fifteenth Amendments."

"Yes, Will and Lenora have spent the last year in Memphis working for the Freedmen's Bureau. Now they're interested in the amendments."

Pendleton said, "There are many of us who want to see Virginia re-join the Union. Passing the Fourteenth is going to be the most challenging and controversial requirement for us to, once again, be part of the United States of America.

"The election for Delegates to the State Constitutional Convention will be a crucial element in achieving our goal. We are going to need some outstanding candidates for office. Getting the right people elected to office is critical," he informed them." The election won't be held until November of '67, so we've got more than a year to find candidates."

Alice whispered to Lenora, "Do you think Will would be interested in running to be a Delegate?"

"I don't know, but I do find the idea intriguing. It certainly would position him to do something about righting the wrongs that have been done to our black neighbors," she answered.

***

While riding back to the farm, Lenora decided to broach the subject with Will about the Constitutional Convention. "Will, would you consider running for an opportunity to be a Delegate from our district?"

Harry spoke before Will had a chance, "I've been thinking the same thing, Presley. You are a decorated veteran with a year's experience in the Freedman's Bureau. Your wife is also passionate about the cause of civil rights for freedmen.

"Action must be taken at the state level to ratify and bring Virginia back into the Union. If we can elect enough good people, it can be accomplished."

"Whoa, slow down for a minute. I've never been involved in politics in my life. I know nothing about how to do that."

"There are plenty of other people who do, and it's my guess, they'll help you and provide some money to make it happen. You just think about it for a few days before you decide," Harry added.

This was a momentous day in Will Presley's life.

Chapter Thirty-One

CONNECTIONS

"Let's drive the carriage to church this morning, Harry," Alice suggested. "Walking that far carrying those babies will be difficult."

"OK, I'll get the horses hitched up and have them ready when the Presleys come down for breakfast."

Cradling a baby in each arm, Will walked into the dining room. "Me and the babies are ready. It'll take Lenora a little longer," he grinned.

"I heard that snide remark, Will Presley." She entered the room. "I had to get the boys ready before I could get dressed myself."

"Oh, the joys of motherhood," Alice smiled.

***

As they arrived at the church with the large entourage, the Parkers attracted a lot of attention from the other parishioners. Women remarked about the babies, and men sized up the young man accompanying their daughter.

John Hall approached and spoke to Harry. "Hello Parker, I see you brought your daughter and son-in-law with you, and it looks like two additions to the family."

"Yes, John, I want you to meet Will Presley, Lenora's husband."

"I met Mr. Presley last year at their wedding. Pleased to see you again, Presley. I've heard many good things about you and the work you and Lenora have been doing.

"Things got a little rough down in Memphis, recently didn't they?"

"Yes, Sir they did. And in New Orleans too," Will shook his head.

Lenora joined the conversation, "That's why we came home. We are eager to assist in any way we can to end the *black codes* and pass the amendments."

Hall smiled and replied, "I'm delighted to hear that Lenora. In case you had not heard, the Anti-Slavery Society has moved on to champion the ideas encapsulated in the Fourteenth and Fifteenth Amendments. We are looking for people to help us. Are you interested?"

"I was hoping you'd say that, John," Harry spoke. "Alice and I will help too, but we don't have the energy level of these young folks.

"Our children will help on the farm, but I'm certain they can find time to meet with your organization and carry out some assignments."

Hall looked at Will and said, "We'll be meeting on Saturday morning at 10:00 A.M. in the Masonic Lodge here in Falls Church. I'll look for you then."

"We saw Ralph Pendleton on Monday, and he said he was a member of your group. Do you know him?" Harry asked.

"Of course I know him. He's been with us almost from the beginning. Ralph's a good man."

***

On Monday morning, work continued on the new house. The Rolen boys proved excellent workers and well-skilled at building. Will was a decent carpenter himself and worked well with the farmhands. At the end of two weeks, walls were erected, and the roof was on the house.

Friday evening after dinner, the Parkers and Presleys walked over to survey the progress of the new residence. "Oh, look Lenora, here are the rooms for the twins. And your kitchen is going to be large enough for you to do some entertaining."

"Entertaining? I'm going to be entertaining?" She was surprised.

"Yes, young lady, you will be entertaining politicians and activists working with you and Will on your new project. That's what you came here to do."

"I didn't realize that would be expected of me."

"But I'm here to help you," Alice replied. "I love hosting a crowd of prominent people. That's one action Harry, and I can take to contribute to the cause.

"Of course, I'll be available for babysitting when you have to attend other functions away from here.

"Oh Lenora, I'm so excited to have you and Will and the twins back home."

***

Saturday morning dawned with a cloudy sky and high humidity in the air; it would be a typical late-summer day in the Chesapeake Bay area. Will and Harry ate breakfast, then prepared themselves for the meeting.

"How many people do you think you will know, Harry," he asked.

"Well, Ralph and John for sure. Other than those two, I can't think of anyone else in the group, but you never know who will show up," he answered.

When they arrived at the Masonic Lodge Hall, Will saw John standing at the front door. The woman he was talking with looked vaguely familiar. As they neared the entrance, he recognized Mary Agnes Weadon, the lady they met on the train.

He whispered to Harry, "That lady talking to John is Mary Agnes, who was on the train with us from Memphis. She was awfully helpful to Lenora with the twins. She said she'd be here.

"Mary Agnes, so nice to see you again. I'd like for you to meet my father-in-law, Harry Parker," Will greeted her.

"Harry this is Mary Agnes Weadon. She's been working for the Fourteenth and is eager to pass some legislation pertaining to suffrage."

"Suffrage for blacks *and* for women, too," she said emphatically. "I believe that women should receive *equal treatment*. The Constitution doesn't exclude us.

"The phrase, all men are created equal, includes women."

Hall joined the conversation. "Mary Agnes will be speaking to us today. I hope you'll listen with open minds to her ideas. Susan B Anthony, Elizabeth Cady Stanton, and Mary Agnes Weadon all worked fervently for the Thirteenth, and now for the passage of the Fourteenth and Fifteenth Amendments. The least we can do is listen to them."

***

Riding back to the farm after the meeting, Will spoke to Harry. "I think Miss Mary Agnes done a good job. But I wonder if it'll be harder to pass the Fifteenth if we include women. It might be easier if we just try to get black men the right-to-vote."

"You could be right, Presley. We'll see what happens."

THE WAR DEPARTMENT

"Miss Parker, please take this note to Sargent Moody at the loading dock. I want to see Harry Parker and his son-in-law when they arrive Friday. Rep. Stevens and Sen. Sumner will be here in my office, and I want to introduce them."

***

Precisely at 9:00 A.M. on Friday, the Parker wagon pulled up to the loading dock at the War Department. Moody smiled his greeting, and said, "General Howard wants to see you two in his office at 10:00. Representative Stevens and Senator Sumner will be here, and he wants to introduce you. We'll get this load checked in quickly so y'all can get there on time."

"Thanks. Bill. I appreciate it. Much obliged to you." Parker nodded.

Rising from their chairs when the Congressmen entered the office, Parker and Presley smiled broadly. Oliver Howard also stood to greet them.

"Good morning Gentlemen. I'm happy you could take the time to stop in today. Harry Parker, Will Presley, meet Thaddeus Stevens and Charles Sumner from Capitol Hill."

Howard looked at the elected officials and said, "These two citizens are eager to assist you in passing the Amendments. I wanted all of you to meet so your efforts can be coordinated."

Stevens spoke first. "Happy to meet you, gentlemen. I've heard a lot of good things about both of you, but especially Presley. I'm always eager to meet the heroes of our army. From what I heard, you are a two-time medal winner, including the Medal of Honor."

"I certainly concur with those words," Sumner added. "As you gentlemen are well-aware, only three states have ratified the Fourteenth so far. We must get Virginia as soon as possible.

"There are still many of these Virginians mourning their *lost cause*, but that's true in fourteen of the fifteen Confederate states who haven't ratified. That's the biggest hurdle to their re-joining the Union.

"Can you help us with that task?"

"Yes, Sir, I think we can get that done. We certainly can contact our assemblyman in the 53rd district where we live," Harry replied.

"We need to elect some Delegates to the Virginia Constitutional Convention who are supportive of *our* cause. Presley, would you be open to that?" Sumner inquired. "There will be an election in November of '67."

"Gosh, I've never thought about that. Don't know much about it either," Will smiled. "If I can help there, I'm willing to try."

Stevens nodded in assent and added, "It's just a few quick steps from the Constitutional Convention to the national House of Representatives. We need some fresh blood there, too."

"Thank you, Sir. I'll discuss it with my wife and mother-in-law. We'll give it some consideration." Will was thoughtful.

***

Sitting down at the dinner table when they returned home, Harry broke the news to Alice and Lenora. "They want Presley to run for political office. Maybe even the United States Congress," Harry blurted.

"Wow, just wow." Alice was impressed.

Lenora looked at Will, "This is our opportunity. Just what we've been waiting for."

"It would be a big chance to accomplish some of what we've wanted to see. Let's see what happens."

Chapter Thirty-Two

NEW HOME

A t breakfast the next morning, Harry spoke, "When you get this house finished, we need to talk with John Hall again. He has that big cattle farm with almost one thousand acres and more than five hundred head of beef cattle.

"His group, the Anti-Slavery Society, is composed of a lot of other wealthy land-owners, too. It'll take some money and campaign workers to get you elected to state office, and these folks are like-minded and have the same goals we do."

"Mr. Parker, I know almost nothing about being a politician, and I've never in my whole life made a speech in front of many people. I don't want to be an embarrassment to the Parker family."

Alice looked him straight in the eye and said, "You'll never embarrass us, Will. We're proud of you and what you stand for."

Lenora spoke, "Just say what you so passionately believe about the issues. You have some definite ideas, and you can express them with passion and ardor. People will respond to that.

"You will be a great candidate."

"OK, but I've gotta get this house built first. These twins are gonna drive Miss Alice crazy," he grinned.

"Oh, shut your mouth, boy. I love my grandbabies," Alice insisted.

***

When the finishing touches had been completed on the house, the Parkers and Presleys walked over to inspect.

"Oh look, Will," Lenora exclaimed, "The leaves are already beginning to turn, it will be beautiful here in a couple of more weeks."

"All we need now is some furniture, I reckon," Will smiled. "I'm leaving that up to you, Lenora."

Alice replied, "We have a few things we're not using in our house, but there is a furniture and cabinet maker here in Falls Church. Lenora and I can visit him next week. We'll have you living in this house before Thanksgiving."

"Presley, after the women, purchase the furnishings for the house, you and I will visit John Hall. Planning for your election will need to begin after Christmas. The election will be held in November of '67, so we'll have plenty of time to get the word out about you."

***

Charles Rose's furniture shop was buzzing with activity when Alice and her daughter entered the front door.

"Hello Charles," she spoke to the owner. "Lenora and I are looking for some things to furnish her new house. Do you have anything we can look at.?"

"Why certainly Alice. Come into the showroom. What do you need.?"

"Just about everything, we have a parlor, a gathering room, three bedrooms, and a kitchen."

"I think we can fix you up with all of that, Alice. How quickly do you need it?"

"Well, it's October now. We want to be in the house before Thanksgiving."

"We can get that done. Now just show me what you like. Many of the standard beds and tables are already in our warehouse. We can custom-build anything you don't like in our stock."

"Now Mama, we don't have to furnish every room right now. The boys are still sleeping in cribs, so the two extra bedrooms can sit empty for a while. The gathering room and the parlor furniture we'll need right away. We can get along without the kitchen for a spell if we eat at your house. I don't want to spend too much of Daddy's money," she grinned.

"That is smart thinking, young lady. I'm proud of you for being so thoughtful."

"Well Mama, you raised me right," she hugged her.

***

After choosing the things they wanted, the two women returned to the farm. "You would have been proud of your daughter, Harry. She saved you a lot of money today," Alice spoke with tongue-in-cheek.

"I am truly grateful that you had mercy on me Princess," Harry remarked.

"There are many things we can wait to acquire, Daddy. Thank you for being so generous with us."

Will walked in the front door with a question. "Did you get everything we're gonna need, Sweet Lady?"

"We're going to wait on a few things, Will, but we ordered the things we must have to move in. They will deliver them next week."

Alice added, "The ladies at our church will want to gift things like bed linens, towels, curtains, and decorative vases and figurines. If we throw a party, people will have fun, and it will be a great chance to show off the twins."

Alice looked at the calendar and continued, "The party can be organized for Saturday, October 27, and you can be ready to move in on Monday, the 29th. You'll be all set before Thanksgiving."

Will was listening intently, then said, "Thank you Alice, we are much obliged."

"President Johnson has declared that we celebrate Thanksgiving Day on November 29," Harry informed them. "We have some turkeys here on the farm, and Alice will be happy to cook a few for all of us."

Smiling broadly, Alice replied, "It will be my pleasure to prepare a feast on that day, but Lenora will have to assist me."

She looked at Lenora and said, "We'll need to be cooking for two or three days to get everything Harry wants for that party."

"We usually invite our unmarried employees to have dinner with us," Harry reported, "Those who don't have families.

"Presley, you and I will have to set up our temporary table and benches. We keep it for the gathering room on these special occasions," Harry remarked.

***

When the furnishings from Rose Cabinet Shop were delivered, moving in was a relatively simple chore. Alice tended to the babies while Lenora, Will, and Harry sorted and placed things in their proper locations.

"That's another thing we can check off our list of things to do, Sweet Lady." Will hugged his wife. "Now, we can move on to Thanksgiving and Christmas."

Chapter Thirty-Three

CAMPAIGNING

"Let's go see John Hall this Saturday, Presley," Harry Parker suggested. "We should get started with your campaign for the Constitutional Convention."

"OK Sir. It is only about eleven more months until the November election. Better get started on it, I reckon."

John Hall's Estate

Even at first glance, the Hall manor was impressive. A two-story brick with four Corinthian columns extending to the second story covered veranda; it looked like a plantation house, although John called it a cattle farm.

The sitting area on the lower level was furnished with four oak rocking chairs painted white. A wrought iron black fence guarded the roses, which lined the path leading to the house.

"Wow, I ain't never seen such a grand house as this. Since Paw had to share half of what he made with Mr. Graham, we couldn't afford nuthin' like this," Will thought to himself.

"Hello John," Parker spoke to his friend. "Presley and I would like to talk to you for a few minutes."

"Sure Harry, Come on in the house. Marian, Harry Parker, and his son-in-law are here. We'll be in the parlor," he said to his wife.

"What's happening with you gentlemen today?" Hall asked.

"Thaddeus Stevens and Charles Sumner suggested that Will would be an excellent candidate for a Delegate to the State Constitutional Convention, and we would appreciate your endorsement and any financial contributions you can make."

Hall looked at Will and asked, "What do you hope to accomplish in the Constitutional Convention, Presley?"

"Well, the first thing is, I want to help pass the Fourteenth Amendment. That is a requirement before Virginia can re-join the Union. A new state Constitution is required. I believe I could help with that process.

"The Reconstruction Act that Congress has just passed will install military governors all over the South.

"If Virginians want to govern themselves and rid us of martial law, we must get these things done as soon as possible," he said and nodded his head for emphasis.

"The Act provides that freed black men will be full citizens of the United States, with all the rights of other citizens-including the right to vote.

"I am well-aware that your organization is committed to these same ideals. I want to join with you to make this happen."

With a smile, Hall stood and approached Will. "Presley, that's a damn good stump speech, and I think voters will readily accept your ideas and support you whole-heartedly. Count me in on your campaign.

"I'm sure Harry has made you aware that the current Assemblyman from your district who has been in his position for several terms plans to run to be a Delegate. John Madison Eubank is a descendent of one of Virginia's early settlers.

"His great-grandfather was an early landowner in the Gordonsville area. *Glenmore Plantation* comprised more than 1000 acres and had almost a dozen slaves."

Hall continued, "John M. did not inherit the plantation; however, he was left with enough money to buy a sizable farm just south of ours. He likes to play up his middle name and state that he comes from an FFV."

"What's that?" Will was puzzled.

"*First Families of Virginia,*" Hall laughed. "As if that made him any better than the rest of us."

"Let's get back to you, Will. I'd like to have you come and speak to our group. You might find some more financial contributors there.

"We'll be meeting Thursday evening at 7:00 P.M. in the small chapel at Falls Church. I'll look for you then."

THURSDAY EVENING

After calling the meeting to order, and tending to mundane business matters, John Hall introduced Will to the crowd.

"Ladies and Gentlemen, it is my honor and privilege to introduce our special guest speaker this evening.

"He is a decorated Union soldier-receiving the Medal of Honor at Gettysburg. Along with his wife, he served a year with the Freedmen's Bureau in Memphis, Tennessee.

"Building schools, dealing with riots in Memphis and New Orleans, then rebuilding the burned-out schools there, he's been on the battlefield for our country and our cause.

"Recently, he moved his family back to the Falls Church area and has built a home on Parker's Farm with his in-laws.

"With the encouragement of two prominent abolitionist politicians in D.C., he decided to put his *hat in the ring* to become our representative to the State Constitutional Convention from here in Fairfax county.

"Ladies and Gentlemen, please make welcome to our meeting, *Mister Will Presley.*"

Standing to acknowledge the applause of the assembly, Will spotted Ralph Pendleton and Mary Agnes Weadon. Seeing familiar faces, he took a deep breath and began to speak.

"Thank you, thank you very, very much. I am delighted to have this opportunity to address this august body of like-minded friends.

"Lenora and I promised our Memphis co-workers that we would continue the work we started when we arrived here. Ratifying the Fourteenth Amendment must be the top priority for our great Commonwealth of Virginia.

"Re-joining the Union must immediately follow that Ratification. Until we once again become part of the United States of America, Virginia will be governed by an appointed military governor. We, in this great state, have prided ourselves on the ability to manage our own affairs.

"Do you want to continue under *Martial Law?*" he shouted.

Thunderous applause drowned out his next words as the crowd stood to show their approval. Shouts were heard.

"No Martial Law."

"Re-join the Union."

"Repeal the black codes."

"I pledge to you my undying support for the Fourteenth and Fifteenth Amendments, and I humbly ask for your vote in the upcoming race in November.

"Thank you for being such an attentive audience. And thank you, John Hall, for inviting me to speak here."

Rushing to speak to him after the speech, Ralph Pendleton said, "Come by my shop next week, I have a gray suit and a brown one that will fit you nicely. As you campaign, you must look presentable. That's my contribution to your campaign."

"Thank you, Mr. Pendleton. I sure appreciate it. I'll ask Harry to come with me."

Smiling broadly, Mary Agnes shook his hand and said, "Give my regards to Lenora and Ronnie and Randy. I'm confident I'll see them during this campaign.

"Here's a small check as my contribution to the cause. I have several friends who will, also, want to give a donation."

John Hall approached to shake his hand. "Great job, Presley. You and Harry come to see me next week. I'll introduce you to some of my associates who are interested in re-joining the Union. There might be some more contributions to help finance your campaign."

"Will do, Mr. Hall, and thanks again for inviting me to speak. See you next week."

***

As they rode back to the farm, Harry said, "That was a wonderful speech and a great kick-off to the run for office. For a beginner, you were *magnificent.*"

Will told him of the offers from Pendleton, Mary Agnes, and Hall. With an incredulous tone in his voice, he said, "Wow, what a *terrific* response we got, Harry. I'm *overwhelmed.*"

"We're gonna win this thing, Presley. Then it's on to Washington. Congressman, Senator, maybe even *President of the United States,*" he exulted.

"You had better let me ask Lenora about that President business," he grinned with his tongue in cheek.

There is always a danger with overnight success, and Will was about to learn the realities of politics.

John Madison Eubank was a rather lazy politician; however, he was not going to lie down and concede his influence to an unknown newcomer.

John's wife, Katherine Beckham Eubank, also claimed to be from a First Family. She warned her husband not to be complacent. "Everything's different since the *War of Northern Aggression*, John. We must do whatever is necessary to protect our way of life."

Within their social circle, they began to plant rumors about this out-of-state competitor. "Why this Presley boy's not even from Virginia," Katherine told the ladies in her garden club.

"Looks like Parker is desperate to drum up work for his new son-in-law," John M. said to the guys at the men's club. "I feel sorry for Harry having his only daughter go off and marry a scalawag who fought against his own kind with the Damn Yankees."

***

Harry began to hear rumblings in early Spring and set up a meeting with Hall to update the campaign strategies.

Gathered again in the Falls Church's small chapel area, Will's initial supporters discussed the opposition. They began to formulate plans to dramatize the choice facing the voters in November.

"Eubank is going to play up two things. Presley being a new resident of the state and their perception that he committed an act of treason by joining the opposite side in the *Lost Cause*," Hall predicted.

Pendleton added, "He may also try to appeal to their fears of more change, bringing additional unwanted disruption into their lives just as they are trying to recover from the war."

"So, what we have to do is get Will in front of more people," Parker concluded.

"If they can see him in person and hear him talk, they will realize that he is not a person to fear. They will see that he actually has the interest of ordinary Virginians at heart, not just the landed elite."

What would you think about a picnic at the Fairfax Courthouse to Meet the Candidates?" Lenora proposed.

Everyone turned to look at Mrs. Presley, having forgotten she was even there. Harry had asked her to accompany Will to the meeting to show that the Presley team would offer two intelligent, politically involved, and caring people as their representatives.

Lenora took the silence as an opening and added, "We would, of course, invite Mr. Eubank to be there. We would give the two candidates an opportunity to answer several pre-designed questions before opening the floor."

"That's a great idea, Mrs. Presley," Hall responded. "I'm thinking the 4th of July would be the perfect time to celebrate becoming one country again. It would give Will an opportunity to clearly show that he is the choice of the future."

***

Back at home, Alice gave her blessing to the picnic idea. "It'll be such fun. We'll have some of Harry's famous Virginia Ham on biscuits, lemonade, and watermelon.

"We will wear red, white, and blue scarves around our necks, and we'll get the Hale family to play background music, then their cousin, Sam, can gather the crowd to the podium with a few blasts from his trumpet."

"Slow down, Alice, people will think you've never been to a party before," Harry chuckled with his arm around his wife.

***

The upcoming celebration was advertised widely in churches, in the local newspaper, on posters, and through the grapevine. By late-morning on July 4th, residents of the area had gathered on the lawn of the Fairfax County Courthouse.

The Parkers and Presleys arrived by ten to ensure that make-shift tables had been set up in a buffet line and that the refreshments were ready to be set out before noon. Some of their farmworkers had accompanied them to help with the physical labor.

Most of Will's donors were present to give him support. Lenora's Uncle Ernest and her cousin, Judy, rounded out the family team. "I will help you with the boys today, Lenora," Judy offered.

"Thank you so much, Judy," Lenora replied. "They are just beginning to test their legs, so I can't let them out of sight."

Making a grand entrance shortly before twelve when the crowd was at its peak, a carriage carrying John Madison Eubank and his wife, Elizabeth Beckham, pulled up close to the courthouse.

Both the Eubanks wore expertly tailored outfits, which seemed to many observers to be more than needed for a picnic. John M. sported a country gentleman's bow tie under his French serge jacket with silk lapels. Elizabeth was adorned in a lace-trimmed floral gown and carried a matching parasol.

John M. Eubank spotted John Hall standing next to Harry Parker and pushed his way through the crowd, avoiding speaking to anyone, to shake hands with Hall. "Thank you for including us," he said, looking at Hall.

"You are welcome, Eubank, but Harry Parker is actually your host, and it was his son-in-law's idea to invite you to be part of the celebration."

Redirecting the focus and going for a laugh, Eubank said, "Could someone get a chair on the covered porch for Elizabeth? She tries to expose her face to the sun as little as possible. I guess that's why she looks younger than I do."

No one laughed, but Harry said, "Certainly, I will have one of our helpers take care of that, Eubank. I guess an FFV cannot take any risks." Then they all laughed.

By the time the Eubanks arrived, Will and Lenora had met and talked with each family in attendance.

As Alice had suggested, both Presleys chose to wear suitable picnic clothing and tie patriotic scarves around their necks. The twin boys had little matching scarves and were a big hit with the ladies in the crowd.

Comments such as "How precious."

"How do you manage two at a time?"

"What a lovely family," were heard filtering through the group of approximately 150 local folks.

At Harry Parker's request, John Hall stepped to the podium to call the gathering to attention.

"Ladies and Gentlemen, thank you for coming out on this historic day to celebrate our nation's birth and to talk about Virginia's part in that history as we go forth.

"We want to thank the Parker family for providing refreshments for us today, and they hope you will all enjoy their famous Virginia Ham after the formalities.

"This may be the first time you have met Will Presley, but I am betting it won't be the last." Loud applause arose.

"Presley will talk with you about why he is asking for your vote in November, but because he is very polite, he has asked our guest, his opponent, to speak first.

"Please welcome John Madison Eubank to the podium." A more modest level of applause was offered.

"My fellow Virginians of the 53rd district, you already know me and my family. I have served in the Assembly since before the War of Aggression and I now ask for your vote as a Delegate to the Constitutional Convention. Not that we really need to change anything," he smirked.

"I am proud to be descended from one of the first settlers in this area. I have lived here all my life. I have always stood up for Virginia's values and fought to save what is best for our state.

"Virginians are proud of our history. We don't need Yankee Do-Gooders telling us to rewrite our Constitution, but they're holding that over our heads if we want to re-join the Union.

"So, you need someone representing you at that unnecessary Convention. Someone who will look after the interests of Virginia's fine traditions. Someone who's not going to take away any more than was already taken by the *damn war.*"

A few men shouted, "That's right, we don't need no Carpet Baggers or Scalawags."

To gracefully end Eubank's diatribe, John Hall walked to the podium and thanked him for sharing his position.

"Now I am pleased to turn over the program to our other choice in the upcoming election, Mr. Will Presley."

As Will walked forward, he stopped to shake hands with Eubank and thank him again for attending.

Elizabeth had exited her perch on the covered porch and was now by her husband's side. She did not make eye contact with Will nor offer her hand. She looked at her husband and said, "We need to get going. There are more important things on our agenda for the day."

Will stood at the raised podium silently for a few moments, looking into the faces of the people he had only met a few hours ago. Then he decided to step down onto the ground level.

"My name is Will Presley and I am not a member of the First Families of Virginia." Laughter and applause followed.

"In fact, I am just a son of an indentured worker who came to this country in search of opportunity. I grew up on a small farm in North Carolina, working tobacco and logging. It took my paw twenty-seven years to pay off his indenture.

"I am the third born of nine children. My maw taught all of us, including paw, to read and write.

"When the war came, our town leaders decided we had to join the Confederate Army. My two older brothers did as they were told. In good conscience, I could not take up arms to protect wealthy landowners' rights to own other people. I had learned from our pastor that the Bible says we are all God's children.

"So, I left home heading North, not knowing what I was going to do. I had no intention of joining any Army, but because of my mountain accent, no one would give me a job. They all assumed I was a Reb and maybe a spy.

"After trying everything else, I signed on for one tour with the Union Army. It is a part of my life that I would like to forget but can never put behind me.

"War is a horrible way for people to solve disagreements. When influential people decide that fighting is their last resort, they do not go into battle themselves. They send the poor, the working class, the disposable people.

"I saw the bodies of hundreds of those disposable people lying in the mud at Gettysburg. *A Rich Man's War is a Poor Man's Fight.*

"My maw lost two of her nine children in the war. For what? Our family was just hard-working average folks trying to make a good life and do the right thing.

"After my tour of duty, I felt I could not return home; so, I looked for a job that would allow me to help repair some of the damages.

"My wife, Lenora, and I spent a year working for the Freedman's Bureau stationed in Memphis, Tennessee. There we worked on building schools for the newly freed people. It was rewarding work, and we were proud to see how eager people were to better themselves.

"Then, the riots happened. The schools were all burned, as well as churches and some homes. Many died.

"We stayed in Memphis long enough to get the schools rebuilt, and then we decided to come back to Lenora's home where we thought we might continue our involvement with repairing the nation.

"Now, I am asking for your vote to become a Delegate to the Constitutional Convention. Hopefully, I can help write the new document with the welfare of all Virginians in mind.

"My opponent wants you to believe that the way to improve your lives is to ignore the facts and hang on to the old ways, which mostly benefit people of wealth.

"When I was logging, I learned that once you cut down a tree, you can't put it back up. What you can do is nurture the new saplings that, given the right environment, may become even stronger than the dead tree.

"Think of your future and the future of your children. Do you want to go backwards or work to build a better tomorrow? I want my little boys to grow up in a better world than the one that tried to destroy itself in a useless war. Will you give me the chance to help make that happen?"

Ladies were crying, and men were shouting, "Yes!"

On November 5, 1867, George Wilhelm Presley was elected as a Delegate to the Virginia State Constitutional Convention by a landslide vote.

Chapter Thirty-Four

RECONSTRUCTION ACT

T he year-of-our-Lord 1867 brought many changes to every-day life in the United States of America-especially in the South.

Under the tenure of President Andrew Johnson, *black codes* were enacted in all eleven of the former Confederate states. These codes should reverse the results of the Union victory in the war.

The entrenched state and local governments which remained in power continued their domination of the freed slaves.

Black people were forbidden to marry. Land ownership, or rental, was not allowed. Therefore, the only employment option open to the freedmen was to return to the plantations as hired labor ($10 per month) or as indentured servants or sharecroppers - not much different from being slaves.

Black children were forbidden to learn to read or write, limiting their opportunity to escape from the plantations' low-wage jobs

Black people could not sue in court nor appear as a witness in court. Also forbidden were black churches and denominations.

Notwithstanding the Freedmen's Bureau and other pro-civil rights groups' efforts, it was business as usual in all the former Confederate states.

The President signed an executive order returning plantation land to its original owners.

This was Johnson's appeasement plan to re-unite the seceded states into the mainstream of American life.

Congressman Thaddeus Stevens, from Pennsylvania and Senator Charles Sumner from Massachusetts, led the effort to pass a Civil Rights Act early in 1866. Johnson quickly vetoed it. Then Congress, in a historic act voted to over-ride the veto. This was the first time such an action had taken place.

The Civil Rights Act stated that before a state could be re-admitted to the Union, a new State Constitution must be written, secession must be renounced, and the Fourteenth Amendment must be ratified.

Tennessee became the first secessionist state to do so in July 1866.

In May 1866, the Memphis Massacre occurred, resulting in fifty black lives lost. Many of these unarmed people were shot by policemen. All the Freedmen's Bureau schools and local black churches were damaged by the fires- many of them burned to the ground.

On July 30, 1866, a riot occurred in New Orleans, resulting in thirty-four blacks being massacred by policemen and firemen.

These events aroused the ire of the Radical Republicans (Progressives) and stirred them to action. People were outraged in every state of the Union.

When Congress reconvened in December 1866, a consensus emerged that meaningful changes needed to be made to Johnson's Presidential Reconstruction. The Reconstruction Act, a result of Congressional opposition, was overwhelmingly passed in February 1867.

All the black codes which had handicapped the freedmen were replaced by national laws that eliminated the discrimination. Adulthood suffrage was incorporated, and anyone born in the United States was declared a citizen with all the rights and privileges so entitled.

Ten secessionist states (Tennessee had already been re-admitted) were divided into five military districts, with an appointed governor who ruled under martial law. Those heretofore in power were removed from office.

A requirement that all secessionist states enact a new state constitution was included. This Constitution must contain a loyalty oath to the United States, male suffrage, a renouncement of secession, and ratification of the Fourteenth Amendment.

All these requirements must be met before re-admittance to the Union.

Blacks were empowered in many unprecedented ways and flourished for a season. By gaining financial credit to buy land, the right to vote, legalized marriage, and to form their own churches and denominations, black lives were changed.

Additionally, a new concept was established. Now, the federal government could and would exercise control over states. States' Rights was dead.

To prevent the President from removing Edgar Stanton as

Secretary of War, the *Tenure of Office Act* was instituted. Johnson had planned to place Ulysses S. Grant in the Secretary of War position. He would reduce the Military Governors' power in the South.

The Tenure of Office Act prevented a President from removing a cabinet member approved by the Senate. Stanton refused to vacate the office when Johnson fired him, then the House voted to impeach the President.

When the Senate voted to remove Johnson from office, the tally was one vote short for removal. Senator Lyman Turnbull of Illinois, a Republican, believed that the system of checks and balances would be negated-thus destroying the Constitution.

Although the Civil Rights Act had mandated reforms, it was believed that an amendment was necessary to Constitutionalize it.

The Fourteenth, then later the Fifteenth, Amendments were passed by Congress and ratified by the states. The Fifteenth gave black men the right to vote. (Women were still denied the vote.)

Tennessee was the first Confederate state to be re-admitted, Georgia was the last, in July 1870.

***

On July 2nd, Lenora received a letter from Charlotte Peterson. It read:

June 25, 1867

Dear Lenora,

I have some fantastic news to share with you. Norville and I married soon after you and Will left Memphis. He, along with Willie and Li'l Georgie Johnson, built houses in South Memphis for black families to rent. As you know, many of the black homes were burned in the massacre in May.

Now the Freedmen's Bureau is ready to open their office in Knoxville. Norville's family is all there, and he is eager to return home to continue our work. He will build schools and houses, and I'll teach.

Hope you and Will are well and busy with the mission we are all dedicated to accomplishing. When we get settled into our home in Knoxville, we will try to visit you in Washington.

Keep us informed of your plans and the work you are doing. Write to me when you can. We are eager to hear from you.

Regards,

Charlotte Peterson Hill

Lenora read the letter to Will, Harry, and Alice. Recounting their collaboration with the couple in Memphis, she was elated to hear of their wedding and move to Knoxville.

All Will could think of was, "Norville is the only other living person who knows what really happened in Gettysburg."

Chapter Thirty-Five

RETURN TO ROARING FORK

A fter services on Sunday, May 17, 1868, Reverend Henderson sat with Sally Presley, her four remaining children, two daughters-in-law, and six grandchildren outside the two-story Presley home and offered a blessing before their meal.

This tradition of gathering for the Third Sunday meal began in 1840, shortly after a new church was built in Roaring Fork to serve the growing families who found it stressful to make the trip to First Methodist in town with their small children.

Everyone in Roaring Fork looked forward to this day. It was a welcome break from their daily labors, a chance to socialize, and a leisurely opportunity to catch up on local gossip and news from town and the wider world.

Neighbors from adjoining farms shared in the preparations, each providing their specialties. Vernon, his wife Savannah, and their children were always part of the group.

Since losing Jay, Sally cherished her friendship with Savannah. They had shared all the joys and sorrows of motherhood.

When their stomachs were full, and the ladies had cleared the tables, neighbors sat in small groups to chat, while the younger children romped through the yard making up games.

Preacher Henderson spotted Sally sitting alone, looking wistfully toward the old cabin.

"May I join you, Sally?" he asked softly.

"Most certainly Reverend. I'm pleased to have your company," she replied.

"May I be so bold as to ask your thoughts, Sally?"

"I was just remembering it has been almost five years since two of my boys died on the same day fighting for a lost cause, and just over three years since my two youngest babies died for no reason, because of misinformation," she said. He detected a tone that combined grief and rage.

"Tell me, Reverend, where is the sense in all that has happened to my family, our friends, our town, and this country?"

He thought it best to continue listening instead of commenting as she obviously had more to say; therefore, he gently touched her hand and looked into her eyes.

Sally swallowed hard, trying to control her emotions, and continued, "All of us honest, hard-working, God-fearing folks had dreams of building a better life for our children. We just tried to do the right thing.

"It wasn't the folks like us who started the fight. We were too busy with the everyday work of raising our families to get involved in politics."

Sally's voice became louder, and a few tears escaped as she continued. "It was those people who never get their hands dirty and have the leisure to sit around thinking how to make sure they are always on top of the heap.

"Then, when they work themselves up to a fever pitch, who do they send to fight their futile battles? Why it's always the working folks, of course."

John broke his silence, said, "The rich man's war is the poor man's fight."

He put his arm around Sally's shoulders to comfort her, and she did not protest this sudden show of affection.

"If you will allow me to speak for a moment, Sally, I would like to summarize your remarkable life as I have witnessed it."

She gazed at him in utter surprise, and said, "There's nothing remarkable about me, Reverend. I'm a shopkeeper's daughter who married a tenant farmer, had a passel of young'ins and did the best I could with what we had."

"Sally, I must disagree with you. I watched you grow into an intelligent and compassionate young woman. I saw how you honored your parents, how you respected people of every kind. I heard from others how you helped them make the most of their resources when working at the General Store.

"I saw you turn a young, almost illiterate stranger into a man of confidence and determination. I watched with some envy as you built a family with him overcoming many hardships, while always keeping a loving presence and an optimistic attitude toward what the future could hold.

"I marveled as you taught not only your own children, but your neighbor's children to read, write, think, and to believe they were worthy of an ever-improving future if they worked for it.

"I sadly watched you grieve for losing your beloved husband, and still hold the family together, always pursuing his original dream.

"In the horror of this war, I saw you lose four children in violence, and one who disappeared to an unknown destiny."

With her jaw-dropping a bit, Sally said, "I don't know who that gal is you are talking about, but I would sure like to know her."

They both laughed, hugged, and the dark cloud that had hovered over the day of remembrance seemed to be replaced by filtered rays of light seeping through the trees on the ridge behind the big house.

"Sally, I have something else to discuss with you if you will give me a few more moments of your time," Henderson said. Then he took her hand in his.

"Would you like something else to eat or drink first?" she asked.

"No, thank you, Sally, I just want your attention."

"This sounds serious, Reverend, should I be worried?"

"No, but I would like you to stop calling me Reverend; my name is John. We have known each other for more than thirty years. I have shared most of your life's crucial moments with you, and you were there for me when I lost my Nellie. We are certainly more than friends.

"Sally, you and I are now facing the latter years of life without the partners we thought we would always have. If you are worried about disloyalty, I believe that both J.W. and Nellie would want us to be happy and would be glad for us.

"Billy Bob, Pete, and Andy are strong young men who can carry on the work at the farm, they will look after Martha, Willadeen and the children. Maggie has married and moved to town."

Sally was listening intently with puzzlement. "All that is true, John, but I feel there is something more on your mind."

John replied in a soft voice, "Sally, I would like you to consider becoming my wife and moving back to town.

"You don't need the heavy labor of farm life at this stage, and you could teach full-time more children in a larger school in town. With the recent loss of your Father, you would also be close enough to care for your Mother in her golden years."

"I don't know what to say to all of that. Those ideas never even entered my head."

"Don't worry, Sally, you can take all the time you need to think about the possibility. Just know that I have always loved and respected you at a distance. I also feel that we would increase our community efforts as partners.

"You and I share many concerns about what has happened in the recent past and what may happen in the future. It would be rather presumptuous of us to believe that we could change the world.

"However, as a team, we could use our remaining years to act as a positive influence on our community. As a teacher, you can inspire the next generation to strive to become their best selves.

"Hopefully, I can continue to provide pastoral care and to challenge our friends to listen to their better angels.

"It only takes one or two people in a group to steer people toward the light instead of the darkness. I want us to be those two people for the community of Graham, Sally."

"I am honored, John, but I do need a little time to absorb all that you have said," Sally answered, touching his hand gently.

Suddenly, her attention was shifted to a carriage's sound, pulling up the road and into the lane past the cabin. "Who could that possibly be?" Sally thought.

As the carriage neared the gathering site, she spotted a young couple, and the woman was holding two small children.

The man stopped the horses and stepped down. He walked to the carriage's passenger side and lifted two toddlers to the ground, and then took the woman's hand to help her down.

Sally and John approached the carriage as other people formed a line in the same direction to see what was happening.

As Sally neared the man, he smiled at her with an awfully familiar curled lip crooked grin.

"Oh, I cannot believe it, but that is my long-lost boy, Will," she said. Then she ran and cried at the same time.

Will grabbed his mother in a tight embrace, "I've missed you so much Mama."

John came closer and said, "We have all missed you, Will. Now, who are these beautiful folks with you?"

"Mama, this is my wife, Lenora, and these little tykes are your grandsons, Ronnie and Randy."

Sally bent down to hug the little boys and then took Lenora by the hand.

"Let's all go inside and sit down. You must be hungry.

"After I fill you up, we'll be having a long talk, because you've got a lot of questions to answer, young man."

***

Lenora offered her apology to her Mother-in-law for not sending notice of their visit. Still, Sally embraced her and responded, "My goodness, Lenora, the surprise was worth everything to me.

"It has been seven years of not knowing what became of my third-born son and now he returns, bringing me a beautiful new daughter and two adorable grandsons. You have made me a happy woman."

Willadeen ran to pick up Ronnie, Maggie scooped up little Randy, while Martha busied herself preparing plates for Will and Lenora on the dining table inside the big house.

As promised, Sally allowed Will's new family to eat before engulfing him with questions. She then stood up and insisted Will should greet all the neighbors who had assembled for the traditional Sunday meal and who were straining their necks for a look at the newcomers.

"We'll have plenty of time to talk with just the family when everyone goes home," she explained with a smile.

Lenora watched every move Sally made, marveling at this woman's calm composure who had borne so much and lost so much.

Lenora thought, " *At fifty-four, she is still beautiful with her auburn hair beginning to show streaks of silver. I can see strength in those green eyes. I can never compete with her, but I can thank her for raising such a wonderful son who chose me as his bride.*"

Billy Bob, Pete, and Andy slapped Will on his back, congratulating him on his fine-looking boys. Sally chuckled to Lenora, "Just like men taking all the credit."

Lenora laughed and said, "We have to allow them to boast about some things. That way, they don't have to face the fact that we are the smartest members of the team."

"You and I are going to get on very well, Lenora."

***

Back inside the big house with the immediate family and John Henderson, the questions began.

"Where have you been, Will?" Billy Bob started.

"How did you and Lenora meet?" Maggie asked.

"Why didn't you let us know you were alive, Son?" Sally posed in a solemn tone.

Will's head was spinning. *Where to begin? How much could he share?*

Lenora spoke up, trying to give Will more time. "We met when we were both living in a boarding house in Washington, D.C.. Will was stationed at Fort Whipple, and I was working at the War Department.

"I am sure you are proud of your son, Mrs. Presley. He is a decorated war hero."

Will decided he should stop her before she went further. "The answer to your question, Maw, is that I was not sure you or my family wanted to hear from me after the way I left. I am also fairly sure that the war is the last thing you want to discuss now.

"What I can tell you is that in my travels north, I found it impossible to find work, mostly because my accent made everyone believe I was a Rebel spying agent.

"In desperation, I signed on for a tour of duty with the Union Army. At the end of that tour, I did not reenlist but was fortunate to find a job at the Fort. The medals were just for doing my job, nothing special." He gave Lenora a look that told her not to add anything.

"When the war ended, I wanted to find a way to help repair some of the damage. I signed on to work with the Freedmen's Bureau, and my first assignment was at Fort Pickering in Memphis.

"Lenora and I had married in August 1865 at her home church in Falls Church, Virginia. After the wedding, she joined me in Memphis, where we worked together in developing schools for newly freed people. Maw, you would have loved to see how eager both the black children and adults were to get the chance to learn to read and write.

"After the riots and the birth of our boys, Lenora and I completed our one-year obligation and decided to move closer to the center of government where we could continue to help with passing laws to ensure all people have a chance at being really free.

"For the past two years, I have been helping Lenora's parents with their farming operations, building a home for us, and becoming involved in local politics.

"That's about enough detail for now. What I want to say is I have missed all of you and I am so happy to see you again."

Maggie clapped her hands, "Golly, Will, that was quite a speech. With that gift of gab and Paw's crooked smile, you should have a future in politics."

Lenora could not contain herself from adding, "Will left out the most exciting part. He was elected in November as the Representative from district 53 as a Delegate to the Virginia State Constitutional Convention. That means he has a seat at the table in decision making, can influence votes on the 14th Amendment, and can help get our state back into the Union."

Billy Bob rolled his eyes as he looked at Pete and Andy. "Guess ye've got too important fer yer old fam'ly. Did ye jist come home ta show off?"

"Don't be so rude," Sally interrupted. Sh3 stared angrily at Billy Bob. "Will is your older brother. He will always be your brother and my third-born son. Let's just be happy for a while and celebrate the fact he is alive and doing well."

"But, Maw, he's the one that left us here ta do all tha work ta keep Paw's homeplace goin'," Pete said. And he spoke a little too loudly.

"Even our poor slaughtered brothers, Buck and Johnny, found a way to come home and help with the harvest," Andy added. A tear ran down his face. "Where were you when Maw needed ye?"

Lenora sat silently, feeling the uncomfortable atmosphere that had erupted. She looked with empathy at the sadness in her husband's eyes.

"Perhaps I should not have returned," Will said. He bowed his head. "I certainly did not want to revive the old disputes that caused me to leave in the first place or create any new problems for my family.

"During the past seven years, I have thought many times about coming home or sending a message, but did not know what to say about where I had been."

"You will stay for a while, won't you?" Sally asked. "We don't need to talk about everything tonight. We are all tired and have said some things we might regret in the morning. Tonight, I just want to enjoy having my lost boy back."

John Henderson decided to end the evening with a Benediction of sorts. "There is a well-known story in the book of Luke, Chapter 15, about the Prodigal Son who returns home after being assumed gone forever. He is greeted with joy and a feast. Some resent the way he is received, but the message is that one who was lost is now found.

"That is the way God feels about us. If we lose our way for a time but come back, he welcomes us with open arms. With that, my good friends, I bid you good night."

Will and Lenora decided they could stay for the week, but would need to start the trip home the following Sunday. Will would not want to miss the next state meeting later in May.

***

On Monday morning, the family enjoyed breakfast together despite tension still hanging in the air from last night's confrontation.

When his brothers went out to begin the day's work, Will followed them. He had changed into his work clothes in anticipation of helping with either the tobacco or the logging. "Where can I help?" he asked.

"Didn't know big city politicians could git their hands dirty," Billy Bob said. He only half chuckled.

"Come on boys, I grew up here. I was helping Paw before you could walk. I've done every job on this farm. While I'm here, you might as well use the extra hands, unless you'd just rather keep givin' me the business."

"Alrite, Mr. State Delegate, go on over thar 'n' git yerself a axe," Pete smiled.

"Yeah, cain't wait ta see how hard ye kin swing it," Andy chimed in.

Will decided to let them have their fun at his expense, but he was determined to show them he had not forgotten his roots. Being so long out of practice, the first day of logging took its toll on him, but the payoff was they had exceeded their usual one-day volume of lumber.

***

"I sure miss Matt," Will said as they were beginning work on Tuesday. "Maw told me what happened to him and little Lizzie. To think they were taken for no reason after the damn war was over, is a hard thing to accept."

"Maw's had more than her share of misery 'cause of tha damn war." Pete shook his head. "We've all tried our best ta make sure she's got what she needs, and she's never lonely."

"Maw, don't even know where Buck and Johnny are buried," Billy Bob solemnly whispered. "They jist tole us they wuz killed in Gettysburg."

As he felt the pain in his heart, Will knew precisely where they were buried because he buried them himself in the new cemetery-at Gettysburg.

He knew he should give them some closure by telling them Buck and Johnny had been honorably laid to rest, but this was the burden he could never share.

"It looks as if you did a wonderful job of keeping everything going." Will complimented his brothers. "Paw would have been proud of you."

"Do you still deliver lumber every week to Henderson's mill?" he asked. He felt the need to change the subject.

"Like clockwork. We finally paid off the rest of the debt on the extra land and materials Paw had bought before he died," Billy Bob told Will. There was an unmistakable sense of accomplishment pn his fade. "Now, we still work on both Mr. Graham's land and Presley's land."

"Could I go with you on Saturday?" Will asked. "I would like to see the town for at least one more time."

"Course you kin go wit us," Pete responded. "Thars some folks in town tha'd like ta see ye."

***

On Wednesday, Will decided to take Lenora to the Roaring Fork Church, where his mother would be teaching school. He explained how his mother had first taught his father to read and write before they were married. Willadeen offered to keep Ronnie and Randy while they were gone.

"Teaching was always her dream, so she began with her own family. As soon as her children were old enough to hold a book, she had daily lessons in our small cabin. She was determined all of us would have a basic education and be able to make choices about our adult lives."

"When I was born, Paw built the big house and Maw turned the cabin into a regular school. She began teaching other children in the Roaring Fork community. When Buck and Johnny got married, she moved the school to the church so Johnny and Willadeen could have a place of their own."

"No wonder you have put her on a pedestal," Lenora responded. "She did all that while raising nine children and helping your father on the farm. She is remarkable."

"Maw is the main reason I needed to make this trip, Lenora. It was not right for me to never let her know I survived the war and that she had two grandsons named in honor of two of her lost sons.

"I knew my remaining brothers might not welcome me. They all disagreed with my decision not to join the Confederate army," Will sighed. "In their minds, they were protecting everything Paw had worked for over twenty-seven years until his death.

"I tried to explain to them why I could not go to war to protect slave owners, that people should not own other people. Only Preacher Henderson agreed with me."

Lenora took all this in quietly, feeling the need to console her husband. "Will, you know you did the *right thing*. You stood up for what you believed, which is courageous to do when everyone around you thinks another way.

"I am so proud of you. I think your father would be proud of you. I know your mother is proud of you, although she says nothing to create more friction in the family."

"Thank you, Sweet Lady, it helps to have you by my side. This will probably be my last trip to Roaring Fork. A man really cannot go home again after he has burned his bridges, but I *needed to do this* one time."

When they arrived at the Church, Sally gladly welcomed them to sit with the students and observe how eager her neighbors were to learn.

To Will's surprise, Preacher Henderson was in the building, apparently attending to some church business. After a few minutes, Will approached John Henderson, "Can we take a walk by the creek, Preacher?"

"Certainly, Will, I am glad to have a chance to talk with you privately. I noticed some unpleasant reactions from your brothers on Sunday, and I'm sorry for that."

"Well, I'm not really surprised," Will admitted. "I left with a cloud over my head seven years ago, and they heard nothing from me in all that time. They suffered along with Maw the loss of Buck and Johnny in the war, and then Matt and Lizzie because of misinformation. They held the homeplace together with no help from me.

"Then here I show up unannounced with a new family and talking about war medals and elected office. How could they not be resentful? I get it, but there is not much I can do about it now. I resisted coming back or even sending word for all this time because I expected this reaction.

"I really only came home for Maw. I wanted her to know she had not lost a fifth child to the damn war. I also wanted her to meet my wife and her grandchildren. Lenora encouraged me to make the trip, and that is why we are here this week."

Henderson put his arm around Will's shoulders and said, "I am proud of you, boy. You did the right thing in 1861 and you did the right thing by coming back even if it will only be once.

"There is always a price to pay for letting your voice be heard. Sometimes that price is losing friends or even relatives. But there is also a price for not speaking out. That price can be losing your soul."

Henderson continued, "When people spend their entire lives in one small town, their world view is naturally limited.

"Unless they continue their personal education through reading and through talking with people who have different world views, it is unlikely they will be open to change even if the difference is for a better world.

"It is common for people to hold tightly to what they know because the familiar is always more comfortable than the unknown.

"Circumstances placed you in a position to witness many horrors and to do things you will continue to mourn and hold silently in your heart.

"You now have a much broader view of life. You have lived in several places. You have had different jobs. You have had responsibilities of managing important programs. You have made your way on your own and now you are in a station to have influence. I am proud of you."

Will felt tears streaming down his face as Henderson added, "If you ever need a shoulder or a non-judgmental ear, I will be here for you."

"Thank you, thank you very, very, much, Pastor."

"Please call me John. I feel like we have been family for many years, Will. I need to tell you about something I discussed with your mother on Sunday before you and your family arrived.

"I asked her to consider becoming my wife and setting up a larger school in town. I have always loved and respected her and think it would make for an easier life as she ages. We would make a good team for the town of Graham, a Teacher and a Preacher," he laughed at his joke.

"Your brothers are all doing a competent job taking care of the farming and logging business. Maggie is living in town with her husband, Dr. Mahan. Sally would also be close to your Grandmother, who is living alone since Patrick passed.

"Nothing has been decided. Sally needs time to think about it, but I hope we will have your blessing if she accepts my proposal."

"I think it would be a wonderful arrangement for the next phase of her life. Please let me know when she decides, John."

***

Saturday morning, the Presley boys loaded their weekly lumber harvest, preparing for the trip to town. This tradition began when their Father, J.W. Presley, first set up in Roaring Fork as an indentured worker. All the surviving sons, except Will, had made the trip every week even during the war.

As they entered Graham, Will noticed a few changes. "Did the Graham Gazette expand?" he asked.

"Not really. Sum of tha buildin's got messed up durin' tha war and had ta git fixed back," Pete answered. "But G.W.'s got himself a new young reporter who's always stirring sumthin' up."

Pulling up to the loading platform at Henderson's Sawmill, Will saw something that he wished he had not seen. "Hey, Billy Bob, who's tha stranga ye got wit ye," a man on a wooden leg yelled out.

"Our long-lost brother's blessed us with his presence fer one whole week," Billy Bob sneered.

"Let me have a look at the coward," a man walking on crutches joined in the conversation with an awkward laugh.

After the initial shock, Will realized he was looking at Vic with the wooden leg and Andrew with crutches.

"Well, I'll be damned, it's Will Presley," Vic said.

Andrew scoffed, "The Preacher tells us yer sum kinda war hero and, now a fancy elected official. Well, yer wuzn't fightin' on our side when I got crippled by a cannonball in Gettysburg."

"Where were you hurt, Vic?" Will asked, trying to ignore the insults.

"Yer two brothers, Buck and Johnny disappeared at Antietam. We got blindsided and attacked by Yankees on the left flank. I got shot twice in my right leg. The doctors in the field hospital decided they had no choice but to take it off. Steve made me this new leg."

"I'm simply happy to see you both alive. I saw more death than I ever want to see again," Will sadly shared.

Walking to Graham's General Store, Will looked at his three brothers and said, "I know you will never understand why I left. I hope that you will be spared any additional impact of war. There are really no winners in a war, at least not among those who must fight it.

"You know who ends up fighting, don't you? A rich man's war is a poor man's fight."

Charles Graham greeted the Presleys as he did every week, but this week was different. "Your fame precedes you, Presley," Graham smiled and stuck out his hand to Will.

"We will not talk about the war because there are hard feelings on both sides. I am pleased that you came home to see your family and I applaud your new political success," Graham said.

Will could see his brothers rolling their eyes behind Graham and most likely resenting his attention.

"Thank you, Sir." Will said modestly. "I am only trying to help put things back together in any way I can. I think it is important for all the states to rejoin the Union so we can be one country."

"It just so happens, Presley, that my brother, Thomas Graham, has a farm in south east Virginia. He has been an Assemblyman for several terms. I'll write to him about you. Perhaps you can become friends when you meet up in Richmond."

On the way back to Roaring Fork, everyone was reasonably quiet until Pete spoke up. "Will, I don't want to hate you. You are my brother and it's not right for me to feel that way about my kin. I just cain't git over tha way ye left. It hurt Maw so much."

"It's alright, Pete. I understand how you feel, and I don't hold it against any of you. The damn war killed more than just people. It destroyed many relationships.

"The best we can all do now is work hard to make the rest of our lives and the lives of those we love mean something. I plan to do that and my hope for you is the same. Even if I never see you again, I will carry you in my heart and in my prayers."

The wagon remained quiet, but a few tears could be seen on every cheek.

The next morning, Will, Lenora, and the boys loaded themselves on the carriage to begin their trip to Asheville, where they would catch the train home.

Sally was crying and smiling as she waved goodbye to her Prodigal son.

Chapter Thirty-Six

CONVENTION

Returning to the Parker Farm after they visited Roaring Fork, the Presley family was greeted by Alice Parker.

"Oh, lookee who's here. Grandmother is so happy to see her two boys get back home. Come and give me a big hug, both of you boys."

Will, whispering to Lenora, said, "I reckon she's happy to see us, too." He winked.

Running to Alice, Ronnie blurted, "Gran, Gran, guess what?" I got 'nuther Gran in Nor' Ca'lina."

"Nor it's Ca ro li na," she corrected him.

"Did you have fun, Randy?" she asked.

"Yes Gran, we rode on a choo choo train and it had a loud whistle. It went Whoo, Whoo."

"Come on into the house and tell me all about your trip to North Carolina. Harry is down at the orchard, but I'll send somebody to tell him you're home."

"Oh, Mama, the mountains are so beautiful. Flowers of every kind just grow wild in those hills. Roaring Fork is a big farm with all types of trees growing on the hillsides. Will's brothers harvest trees to make building lumber.

"His mother is so sweet and loving. She leads a school for mountain children. That is one reason Will was so eager for us to start schools in Memphis.

"Maggie, his sister, is married to a doctor. Two sisters-in-law live on the farm with their children. Three brothers do the farm work.

"They raise tobacco as well as the timber. An extensive garden provides the family with vegetables, and pigs and chickens are raised for meat.

"They just grow what they need for their own use, but there are nearly two hundred acres with the timberland.

"Reverend Henderson is their minister-a Methodist. But they are not much different from us as far as religion. John Wesley was an Anglican minister, before he started the Methodist Church."

"Well, it looks like you learned a lot of things on your trip. I'm thrilled you got to meet Will's family.

"Will, you come here and give me a hug. I've missed you too."

"Gladly, Alice, I'm happy to be back home again. Parker Farm *is* my home now. It's hard to go back where you were born when you've been away for a long time. But it was good to see my family, and my Pastor, Reverend Henderson. He was an enormous influence on me after my paw died."

***

Harry entered the front door and hugged his daughter and grandsons. As he shook hands with Will, he said, "Good to have you back home where you belong, Son. We missed every one of you. I didn't realize how much I depend on your help here on the farm."

"It's good to be back home, Sir. I was happy to see my family again, but Parker Farm is *our* home now. Thanks for welcoming us back."

"You will need to go to Richmond next week for the Constitutional Convention meeting. Some controversial issues have arisen. It will be interesting to see what happens with it," Harry informed him.

"What are they fighting about now?" Lenora wondered.

"Several things, but the big problem is whether or not to allow former confederate soldiers or officials to serve in the new government. Most of the previous officeholders were in one way or another associated with them.

"Another major issue is whether to allow male suffrage. The Conservatives (that's what they call themselves now) are strongly opposed to voting rights for blacks," Harry explained.

"I heard something about a group calling its self the *Committee of Nine.* Who are they?" Will asked

"They're a group of men who are former Whigs. Alexander Stuart and John Baldwin from Staunton are the leaders.

"Their proposed compromise is called *universal suffrage and universal amnesty.* It would allow freedmen and free blacks to vote if former Confederates are permitted to serve in the new government."

"Do they have the authority to do that?" Lenora asked.

"No. It can be done only if the convention approves it. Working this out will take a long time, I'm afraid," Parker shook his head.

"There are twenty-four blacks who have aligned themselves with the Radical Republicans, and together, they outnumber the Conservative Democrats and Moderate Republicans in the delegation," Parker related.

"How long do you think it will take?" Lenora questioned.

"I don't know, but John Hall is hopeful we can get it done before the November election for President this year. It's not yet June, so we have more than five months."

"Is Ulysses Grant going to be the Republican nominee, Daddy?" Lenora was hopeful.

"Hall thinks so, and he is pretty knowledgeable about the inner workings of the party. John is a vigorous supporter of Grant," Parker told them.

"I like the general, too, Harry. When he took over as General-in-Chief of the Union army, the tide of the war shifted in favor of the Union. I'd sure like to vote for him." Alice joined the conversation.

"Daddy, do you think women will be included in the suffrage vote. Will and I met Susan B. Anthony and Elizabeth Cady Stanton in '64. They worked for the Thirteenth Amendment and for Lincoln's re-election, but they are pushing for women's suffrage," Lenora reminded them.

***

A surprise letter addressed to Mr. Will Presley arrived at the Parker Farm in the first week of June.

May 25, 1868

My Dear Will,
What a happy day it was for me when I saw my long-lost son arriving at Roaring Fork. I was even more delighted to meet Lenora, and my two precious grandsons, Ronnie and Randy, and celebrate their second birthday. John told me he spoke with you about his proposal and I want to let you know that I have accepted. We will be married on June 21st with Bishop Cooper presiding. I will move into town to set up the first

school for all the children who live in Graham. I know that your additional responsibilities make it impossible for you and Lenora to be here, but John has promised me a wedding gift of a future trip to the Nation's Capital.
Love, Mama

With a tear in his eye, Will shared the news with Lenora. "I am happy for both of them," she responded, kissing Will tenderly. "Your mother deserves to be close to someone who loves and appreciates her."

RICHMOND, VIRGINIA

When he walked into the Capitol building in Richmond, Will noticed three men chatting. Two were black, and one was white. He approached the group, extended his hand, and spoke.

"Good morning gentlemen, I'm Will Presley from Falls Church in Fairfax county."

"Presley, the war hero and former Freedmen's Bureau agent," the white man acknowledged him. "I'm Caleb Wilson from here in Richmond. I've heard a lot of good things about you."

One of the black guys, smiling from ear to ear, spoke. "My name is Jeremiah Jones, and I live over in Hampton. Happy to meet up with a Freedmen's Bureau worker. Did you build any schools for them?"

"Sure did. Down in Memphis, Tennessee."

"Didn't they burn them all down?" Jones asked.

"Yep, they did. But we built them all back before we left. My wife Lenora was with me, and our two sons were born there."

"We need to have public schools here in Virginia. Black kids and poor white kids need to be educated too. Lots of folks can't afford to send their children to private school. We been working on that in Hampton, but it needs to be done state wide. Hope we can put something like that in the new constitution," Jones was fervent.

The other black man smiled and extended his hand, "I'm Rufus Brown from Gordonsville. I lived on Glenmore Plantation. Raised tobacco.

"Confederate army was around there a couple of times, but we didn't see any fighting. The town survived very well."

"Rufus, I was raised on a farm in North Carolina. We raised tobacco, too - burley and bull head. What did y'all raise?"

"Mainly burley. The Boss Man exported most of it to England and

France. We had about twenty acres of it.

"Boss Man wanted us to plant it in a different field every year. He had plenty of ground, so twar'nt no trouble. Said it preserved the ground and wouldn't wear it out. Guess it worked, because we raised thousands of pounds every year."

"We didn't raise that much, but we cut timber, too. Our Boss Man owned a sawmill. Sold his timber to himself."

"Was you on a plantation? Never heard of no white man working one."

"No, we were sharecroppers. My paw started out as an indentured servant. Took him over twenty years to pay off his contract.

"What do you do for a living, Wilson?" Presley asked.

"I'm in the export business. Export cotton and tobacco to England and France. Seems like we all are in interrelated enterprises. Maybe we can work together to get some things accomplished.

"We've gotta get rid of this military governor and start governing ourselves again. The Committee of Nine have a good compromise plan. Maybe it'll work."

"I ain't gonna be for no Confederates in the government," Jones spoke boldly. "Stuart and Baldwin can't convince me to go for that."

Brown nodded his assent. "Not me neither. Them Rebs is traitors."

"This convention is going to be about give and take, gentlemen," Wilson was adamant. "If you get the right to vote, concede having some Rebs in the government."

Will asked, "Were you a Reb, Wilson?"

Wilson raised his voice. "Hell, no, but I did business with some of them. Most of the landowners in these parts, worked with them. My customers were all planters and farmers. We must get business going again. This economy needs statehood before it can thrive like the old days."

"Harry, my father-in-law, said this was going to be hard. I reckon he was right. I don't believe we're going to get it done before the election. I was hoping to vote for Grant."

***

"Delegates, let me have your attention, please," a loud voice boomed from the front of the room. "We have a speaker for you.

"All the way from Staunton, Virginia. Please make welcome Mister John Brown Baldwin."

"Thank you, Mister Chairman and delegates. I appreciate the

opportunity to speak to you today.

"As a member of the Committee of Nine, it is my honor to share with you some ideas we have planned for your consideration. The imperative to create a passable constitution in this great Commonwealth has been laid on our shoulders.

"Many diverse thoughts and ideas have been bandied about with a large controversy. The compromise we have crafted is fair, and, most importantly, passable.

"We propose that universal male suffrage be included in our draft."

Thunderous applause broke out on the floor among the delegates.

"We are, also proposing universal amnesty for the former confederate soldiers and officers."

Once again, polite applause was heard but mixed with a few boos and scattered shouts of, "Hell no, no way, Shut your mouth, man."

Week after week passed without a solution. The convention was adjourned just before the November election. Plans were made to re-convene after the first of the year in 1869.

Grant was elected President of the United States, but Virginia was prohibited from voting in that election.

"Well, gentlemen, I'll see you all again after New Year's Day. Maybe we can get it done next year." Will bade his three friends goodbye.

Chapter Thirty-Seven

RECONVENE

"Hey Will, let's me and you go visit John Hall next Thursday. It's Election Day, but we can't vote because your convention didn't get the State Constitution finished."

"Your mother-in-law, nor your wife can vote for Grant. But neither can John, nor you and I. Maybe John will have some ideas about how to get this thing done so we can re-join the Union. Virginia is just going to sit here and stagnate if we don't get the job accomplished."

"Yep, John is a pretty astute politician. I respect his opinion, and I need to talk to him before we go back to Richmond after New Year's Day. Working out a compromise is a hard task.

"Universal male suffrage will be easier than universal amnesty, I think. Freedman, free blacks, and Radical Republicans have a lot of resentment toward Confederates. I heard them called traitors, and murderers," Will said.

"Yes, that is true, but Alexander Stuart and John Brown Baldwin say that there are not enough reliable, competent men to operate this Commonwealth if the Rebs are excluded," Harry replied.

***

As their carriage pulled onto his property, John Hall walked out to meet them. "Saw your carriage coming down the road and wondered what you fellows had on your minds," he greeted them.

"Good afternoon, John. Figured you wouldn't be too busy since this is election day and we can't vote," Harry said.

"Hi John," Will spoke. "Hope you got some time to chat with us today."

"Sure Presley. What's the topic today?"

"This situation we're in on this constitution has me baffled. I do not know which way to go. The Fourteenth must be approved, but if we exclude Confederates, I'm uncertain it will get done. Harry and I both value your advice. Can you help us?"

"Thank you for asking me, Presley. I'm flattered that you would seek my advice. I am a firm believer that compromise is both necessary and advisable in politics and business. It is a matter of give and take. One-sided deals rarely last. Somebody always has regrets.

"Is there another issue the freedmen are passionate about?"

"Well, now that you mentioned it, there is one thing that might motivate them. Jeremiah Jones, from Hampton, Virginia, was talking about public schools for poor white and poor black children. Said that most people can't afford private school.

"I helped build some Freedmen's Bureau schools in Memphis, and there are many of these all over the South, but the Bureau doesn't have the funds to continue doing this.

"Jones said that the people of Hampton will probably do it there, but some things are better done at the state and national level where funding is more adequate."

"That just might be the tool we need to get this constitution approved," Hall thought.

RICHMOND, VIRGINIA

As he returned to Richmond for the continuation of the convention, Will spotted Alexander Stuart.

"Hello, Mister Stuart, I'm Will Presley from Falls Church. I'd like to chat with you for a few minutes."

"Greetings, Mister Presley, I've heard your name often repeated in this great hall. What's on your mind?"

"Well, Sir, I know you are the chair of the Committee of Nine and that you have a lot of experience in the State Assembly of Virginia. I'm still new at this, so I have a lot of questions."

"Go right ahead, Presley. I'll try to answer any question you have."

"You are adamant that universal amnesty must be a part of the new Constitution. Why do you feel so strongly about that?"

"Good question, Presley. Almost all the business and professional men in Virginia associated themselves with the Confederacy.

"Although I voted against secession as a member of the Assembly, I am a lawyer, and many of my clients were officers and soldiers in the Confederacy. Virtually every member of the assembly had some association with them.

"If these people are excluded, those who are available to serve will be inexperienced in the workings of government. I believe you will be a good assemblyman from the 53rd District, but *your lack of* experience will handicap you.

"We need fresh voices in the Assembly, but that should be tempered with some people who have been there before.

"My Committee of Nine traveled to Washington during the recess here. We talked with President Johnson, President-elect Grant, and many other Representatives and Senators. The consensus is that we definitely need some knowledgeable folks in the Assembly."

"Alright, I'll take that. Now, how do you feel about free public schools for poor black and poor white children?"

"It's never been done like that before, but I'm willing to listen. Go on."

"My mother started a school in the small town where I grew up. Most of the folks in our town could not afford to send their children to private schools in the big cities.

"Maw started teaching us to read and write in the church building in our community. All the kids in our family and most of the neighbor's young'uns too.

"Then, when my wife and I moved to Memphis with the Freedmen's Bureau, we built several schools for black children. It was paid for with funds from the War Department's budget, but federal and state money could fund a state-wide system.

"A delegate from Hampton, told me they are planning a local system, but state schools would be better. We would have the first free public schools in the Confederate states. I believe a proposal to proceed on that front will be a *deal maker* for universal amnesty."

"By golly, Presley, I think you are on to something here. I will discuss this with my Committee of Nine to get their reaction. I'll get back with you on this."

***

Will sought his three friends from the previous session and told them of his conversation with Alexander Stuart. Rufus Brown strongly opposed the idea of compromising with Confederates. His life as a slave was still very much on his mind.

Jeremiah Jones warmed to the idea when he heard the plan for free public schools. "If we can get a state-wide school system started, we can work around these Rebs. I'll vote for that idea."

Caleb Wilson wanted very much to re-join the Union for economic reasons. "Our economy has been stagnant, there are no new investments from the North, nor from Europe. If public schools will get us a Constitution, I'll vote for it."

"Alright, that's three votes. Now, let's talk to delegates about our idea."

Jeremiah spoke, "I think you should make a speech on the floor, Presley. You convinced us. If Stuart and Baldwin's group endorses it, it will pass."

Rufus Brown still was not convinced. "I ain't gonna vote for no Rebels to be in the government. Ther' traitors to the United States of America."

"Brown, there is no perfect plan. We just must find one that most folks will vote for. I fought with my family because I believed that slavery was wrong. I fought with police in Memphis because they were abusing their authority so they could dominate freedmen. Now, I'll fight with anybody who wants to prevent the reunification of this great country of ours."

"I don' wanna fight with you, Presley, but it really irks my soul to concede to these *muggings.*"

"I'm going to suggest to the chair that you make a speech, Will," Caleb Wilson said. "Next week will give you enough time to prepare. You *already know* what you are going to say. Knock 'em out, boy."

***

Rising to speak, Will looked up into the balcony and saw Lenora standing and waving to him. She and Harry had ridden down with him when he returned to Richmond.

On the ride to Richmond, Will had rehearsed his speech several times. Lenora had memorized most of it. As he began to speak, she mouthed the words with him.

"My fellow delegates, it is my distinct honor and privilege to stand before you today. In consultation with many of our delegates, I offer a plan that will be palatable to the diversity of this body.

"Universal male suffrage, and universal amnesty for former Confederates are the two issues which have prevented the ratification of the new constitution. Both concepts have merits and demerits, but a perfect solution which satisfies everyone is never possible.

"I have discovered an idea which makes sense to me. My good friend Jeremiah Jones, from Hampton, suggested a state-wide free public-school system.

"It would be the first one in the seceded states. Poor black and poor white children should learn. *Universal education* will revolutionize our great Commonwealth.

(Polite applause was heard.)

"Many folks have said if former Confederates are excluded from serving in the government, we will not have qualified people serving. This idea has merit, because our former Assembly members were white, educated men."

(Applause burst forth from the audience.)

"If blacks were educated, they would be enabled to make greater contributions to the good people of Virginia."

(Loud applause greeted this sentiment.)

"I am proposing a compromise solution. In exchange for a yes vote on universal amnesty, a provision to establish the first state-wide, *free* public-school system in the former Confederate states be incorporated into the new Constitution."

(Thunderous applause erupted and as he looked to the balcony, Will saw Lenora rise to stand in applause. Soon all attendees followed her, in giving him a standing ovation.)

When all returned to their seats, he spoke softly but intently. "Thank you for listening so attentively. I appreciate your kind consideration of this proposal. Thank you, thank you very, very much."

15th Amendment

***

The New Constitution was completed (with mandatory funding and attendance for the schools) and submitted to the voters of Virginia (including freedmen and free blacks). When the Constitution, and Fourteenth and Fifteenth Amendments were approved, Virginia was re-admitted to the Union early in 1870.

"Presley, you made a remarkable speech at the convention. You have a career in politics. I sincerely hope you and the Missus will give it some consideration," John Hall opined.

"Virginia needs you in the State Assembly, and, maybe later, in the United States Congress."

"Will, I'm so proud of you," Lenora beamed.

Chapter Thirty-Eight

VIRGINIA POLITICS

T he apple orchard on the Parker Farm was at its peak as Will walked with Harry to evaluate the harvesting process. "It's been a good year, Son. You have made our family proud."

"Thank you, Sir. It was my privilege to serve as a delegate to the Constitutional Convention. You were certainly telling the truth when you warned me the process would be difficult," Will replied. He dropped his head.

"I learned that doing the *right thing* is always hard. It is guaranteed, there will be people who see the situation differently."

Harry nodded his head in agreement. "But the struggle is worth the effort. You played a part in getting our new State Constitution written and in getting the 14th and 15th Amendments ratified. That was a major accomplishment."

"Now we need to get Virginia officially readmitted to the Union," Will sighed.

"What you need to do immediately, Son, is announce your candidacy for the State Assembly." Harry slapped Will on his back. "You made a name for yourself around here, and you need to keep going."

"How do I start?" Will asked.

"You will need to align yourself with one party. We'll talk with John Hall, but I'm thinking the safest bet would be the Moderate Republicans," Harry said.

***

John Hall agreed with Harry. "There's no way Virginia voters are going to elect a Radical Republican, especially with a black man on the ticket for lieutenant governor. There is only so much change people can stand at one time."

Will met with the Moderate Republican group and received their endorsement to represent District 53. He received monetary support for his campaign from Hall and other previous donors.

Moderate Republicans formed a coalition with some former Confederates to oppose the Radical candidate for Governor.

Even though the Party's candidate for Governor was a carpetbagger from New York, he had promised a moderate return to governing. Most voters liked the message of reconciliation and promise of moving into a calmer, more stable decade.

Gilbert Walker became the Governor of Virginia in 1870, Will Presley was elected as a State Assemblyman, eighteen black men were chosen to the Assembly, and Virginia was readmitted to the Union.

As promised, Governor Walker did not propose any radical changes during his term.

***

The year of 1870 was one of dramatic change in the Presley family's routine. Will's newly elected position required frequent trips to Richmond, some of several days at a time.

Lenora was happy for and proud of Will; however, she was not sure she liked the sacrifices that came with his triumphant entry into the political world. She and her husband had not been separated since their marriage in August 1865.

The twins, Ronnie and Randy, had never spent a night without their father. Now going on four years of age, the boys would cry on nights when Daddy wasn't there to kiss them goodnight.

***

Although the Virginia State Assembly was usually in session from December through February, 1870 would be different. While under Federal control, the Assembly had not met; therefore, there were re-organizational tasks to be handled before the annual legislative session.

New members came to Richmond for a week of orientation in February. All members were officially installed after taking their oaths. Votes were taken to elect leadership positions, and committee assignments were made.

During those Richmond trips, Will renewed relationships made during the convention and established additional ones with several newly elected Assemblymen.

Caleb Wilson, from Richmond, and Will had formed a strong bond during completion of the new constitution. Will's speech supporting the universal suffrage/universal amnesty compromise impressed Wilson, whose economic interest was positively affected by Virginia being readmitted into the Union.

Learning on the job, Will began to formulate his own political philosophy and strategies. "*It seems you have to find out what is important to each person and offer them something related to their issues if you want to get anything important accomplished,*" he told himself.

"*I wish you could just count on people doing the right thing with no self-interest involved,*" he lamented. "*This isn't the first time I've been disappointed expecting people to be better than they are.*

"*I have to learn how to make my case in a way that has a chance of being accepted. I have to stop getting mad when people act selfishly and don't want to do what is best for the common good.*"

As Lenora had coached him, Will gradually developed the skill of *disagreeing without being disagreeable*. "It was usually a trial-and-error process." Will told Lenora, "My paw always said there're some things you just got to learn by living."

When talking with Rufus Brown, Will was fully aware that he would not change his friend's mind about forming a coalition with former Confederates. He mostly listened as Rufus shared what his life had been like as a slave.

"People tells me I otta be glad I had me a good owner who let me keep my wife 'n' chil'ren. That's like tellin' a drownin' man, at least he ain't thirsty."

"Now ya wants me to play nice and trust these traitors to do tha rite thang? I say Hell **No** ta that, my brotha."

Will spoke in a soft voice, "I hear you, Rufus, and wish we could have gotten the new constitution approved without the amnesty clause, but the reality was we did not have the votes.

"The choices we had were to either wait until we had different delegates or to push ahead with what was possible. There is much more work to do to get to a time when everyone will have their rights protected by law.

"Without the new constitution, we would not have been readmitted to the Union, and we would have dreadfully little voice in what happens in the future.

"I don't like it any more than you do. People tell me I am an idealist and that I am naïve to think we can change everything that needs changing all at once.

"The hard lessons I am learning is that people will try to stop change as long as they can get away with it. If I believe that something needs to change, I need to have a place at the table and so do you. Otherwise, we will just be giving up. Rufus, you don't strike me as a quitter."

"I sho' ain't no quitter, Will. I'm just mad as hell and tired of being looked at as less than human."

"Then you have to stick with me and try to convince enough people to do the right thing, even if it's only a bit of the right thing at a time."

"I'm with you, Will. You are a good man."

***

In conversations with Jeremiah Jones, Will encouraged his idea of free public school. "If we are successful in making your dream come true, Jeremiah, it will be a proud moment for the State of Virginia. We will most likely have some opposition along the way, but if we don't lose sight of the goal, we will eventually win. I'm counting on you, my friend."

"Will, it's always good to talk with you. You give me hope when I'm just about to give up the fight."

Since racial segregation was still the norm, Will could only meet with Rufus and Jeremiah while in the State House. He could, however, go out to dinner or meet with Caleb in his Richmond home. In fact, Caleb invited Will to spend the night frequently.

"You made quite an impression on my wife, Will. She thinks you have a brilliant future in politics, and I think I agree with her," Caleb said. With a smile and a handshake, they parted and Will left Richmond to return home.

***

Immersion in the culture of politics opened Will's eyes to the give and take necessary to reach any goal. Like most young people who pursue their ideals, he held an image in his mind of what that goal looked like. Like many crusaders, he had difficulty remaining positive when his efforts were curtailed continuously by compromise.

One of the hardest blows came from his wife. Lenora had remained in contact with Mary Agnes Weadon and her organization's efforts to secure voting rights for women. When the new Virginia Constitution was finally approved, Lenora was not happy.

"What about women, Will? What is your definition of universal suffrage? Are we not human beings with minds and ideas? I read that Utah gave women the right to vote in February."

Will was taken by surprise and stumbled into his answer. "When it takes a consensus, it is not always possible to get all that you wanted to accomplish in a timely manner. If we had not made certain concessions, Virginia would still not be a part of the Union."

"I don't think you even tried to include us. From what I heard, no one even brought up women's suffrage in the debates."

"Mary Agnes asked me to tell you that you have a lot more work to do and that you should remember the Ladies," Lenora said. She shook her head and walked away.

"This only gets more complicated," Will thought. *"Now, even my wife is mad at me. Do I really want to stay in the middle of all this?"*

Virginia holds elections for State positions in odd-numbered years. Because of that, Will would need to run for re-election in the fall of 1871 if he desired a second term 1872–1873.

Chapter Thirty-Nine

VISITED BY THE KLAN

On Monday morning, Will packed his bag, kissed Lenora and the twins goodbye, and left for the train station.

Making his weekly trip to Richmond was not a duty he looked forward to, but this morning he felt unusually uneasy. He could think of no logical reason for his feelings, just that it was there.

"I sure hope nothing strange happens in our meetings this week, but the conservatives still don't accept that the war is over. I reckon they never will," he thought to himself.

"If people would just follow what Jesus and the church teach us, do unto others, and love everybody like we love ourselves, this would be a different one.

"But Paw used to say, just do the best you can with what you got. I can't make folks do right. Just have to hope they will."

His thoughts troubled him all the way to Richmond.

The week was filled with mundane matters, so his mind drifted back to his thoughts, *"Maw used to say sometimes things don't feel right. That's all I can think of,"* he worried.

Finally, the week was finished, and he could think of riding back home on the train. *"This politics is not what I was thinking it was gonna be. I sure miss my family."*

When he arrived at the Parker farm, he noticed something unusual. A strange smell filled the air, and a cross's charred remains could still be seen standing in front of the Parker house.

He looked toward his own house and saw the same thing. *"Oh my God, the Klan has been here. I knew something bad was gonna happen."*

As he hurried into the house, Ronnie met him. "Daddy, Daddy, some ghosts came here and started a big fire in our yard. They had fire sticks in their hands, big pointed heads with eyes but no mouth, and they were talkin' real loud to Papaw Parker."

Randy ran to his father and cried, "I was scared, Daddy. Mommy was too. She cried. I saw her."

Ronnie spoke up, "She said she didn't cry, but she did, Daddy."

Hearing the twins talking, Lenora entered the room. Will grabbed her in a bear hug, and she began to cry again. "Oh Will, it was so awful and scary. I wish you had been here."

"I do too Darling. I had a bad feeling when I left here on Monday. Maybe I'll just quit politics."

"No, you can't quit. The job is not yet finished. There is more you need to do for all of us especially if we add a daughter to our family," she smiled.

"What are you talking about, Lenora?" Will looked confused.

"I believe we will have another blessed event in January. This time I'm hoping for a girl and I want her to vote when she grows up. I want this to be a better world for all our children."

"Oh, my Sweet Lady, you have turned a *bad* day into a *great* one. You have made me so happy." Will kissed her gently on the lips.

"Let's go talk to Daddy and see what he says. By the way, I haven't told Mama and Daddy yet because I wanted you to be the first to hear."

Lenora looked at the twins and said, "Come on boys, we're going over to Papaw and Mamaw Parker's house."

When they walked up to the front porch, Alice opened the door and greeted them. "Come in children, Harry wants to talk to Will."

Harry rose to greet their arrival and spoke, "Happy you're home, Son. We had a little excitement last night."

"Yeah, I noticed that right off, Sir. Guess they wanted to leave us a message. What'd they say?"

"Aw, they said we were Nigger-loving scalawags and a disgrace to the white race-their usual wild rhetoric. But we need to protect ourselves and our family and property.

"In the morning, you and I will go downtown. There's a shop across the street from Ralph Pendleton's Tailor Shop. They sell army surplus equipment. We can get a couple of Burnside's lever-action carbines, and a couple of six shooter pistols."

"Don't you think we need some sentry guards? In the army, we always had night-time security."

"Yeah, I thought about that, too. We have some men on our crew here at the farm. Since it's winter, they are not terribly busy. I'll ask for volunteers to work at night. We can provide them with weapons. I'm certain a couple of our freedman employees will be interested."

"Before we make any more plans, Lenora has something to tell you and Alice."

"Will and I are going to add another baby to our family after the first of the year." Lenora held Will's hand and smiled at her parents. "I sure hope we can count on you for help."

With a twinkle in her eyes, Alice said, "How exciting! I suspected this was coming based on my observations."

"Will is considering backing out of the political arena, but I told him he needed to stay involved. There are too many issues that affect all of us for any good men to drop out of the conversation."

Will looked with amazement at his remarkable wife. He had always felt Lenora would make him a better man just by being at his side. She had encouraged his work from the beginning. His loving wife had traveled far from her home to assist him. She was the backbone of their family, and he felt truly blessed to have found her.

"Will, are you day-dreaming?" Harry noticed the far-away look in his son-in-law's eyes.

Snapping back into the conversation, Will questioned Harry. "What do you know about the Ku Klux Klan? We had a run-in or two while we were in Memphis, but I learned little about them."

"They're mostly former confederate soldiers and planters who are still fighting the Civil War. They believe their cause was just, but they're calling it a *lost cause.*

"The group was officially organized in '66 down in Pulaski, Tennessee by a former Confederate Cavalry General named Nathan Bedford Forrest. Some called him the *Wizard of the Saddle.*

"Terrorism is their weapon, and those white sheets and conical hats identify the group yet protect their personal identity.

"They have carried out lynching of freedmen and of some white men. Beatings, robberies, rapes of women, and general terrorism are all tools of their trade. They called the whites, carpetbaggers or scalawags."

"I reckon we are scalawags since we're from south of the Mason-Dixon line. Carpetbaggers are from north of the line, or so I'm told," Will replied.

"Yeah, that's right." Harry answered.

Continuing, he said. "We should talk to John Hall and see if anybody else has received a visit from these scoundrels. It's possible we can organize some sort of security system for our area. Many folks in Northern Virginia who weren't Confederates could be a target of their vitriol. We'll go visit him on Sunday."

***

Preparing to leave on Saturday morning for the Surplus Store in D.C., Harry gave instructions to Alice. "Get word to Alvin, Simon, Raymond, and Elijah, that I want to talk to them this afternoon. Oh, and Henry and Marvin Rolen, too. Since they work in the orchard, maybe they'll want to guard it. Orchards take a long time to mature if we are forced to start over.

"I'll offer them the security jobs we talked about. We must have guards here before Will leaves on Monday to return to Richmond.

"They will be needed for security until this session of the Assembly ends in March."

Precisely finding the weapons and ammo they needed in the gun shop, Parker and Presley returned home.

***

On Sunday, when they drove the carriage up to the hitching post at Hall's farmhouse, John quickly walked out to greet them. "To what do I owe the pleasure of this visit gentlemen?" he smiled.

"Hello, John. We need to tell you about a visit we had from the Klan on Thursday night. Damaged nothing, but they threatened us for the next time."

"Yeah, there's a group that's been working around these parts. They've visited other farms.

"I don't think they've damaged property yet, but you can never be certain what they will do."

"I'm not nearly as worried about property as I am about my family. From what I read in the newspaper, there have been some hangings, and rapes," Harry said.

"Yeah that's true, but the lynching and rapes have been just freedmen and blacks - no whites."

"John, I don't care if it is just blacks, as you said. *Right is right and wrong is wrong.* It must be stopped now," Will declared.

"I am placing some of my men in security positions to guard us at night. They will be armed, and I want the word to spread that my men are armed. We will defend ourselves.

"To deter these scoundrels, it would be helpful if other folks would do the same thing. We bought weapons downtown at the army Surplus Store. I would appreciate it if you will tell people around here of our plans," Harry informed him.

"Will do Harry," Hall assured Parker.

"Presley, run again for your Assembly seat in November of this year for the '72-'73 session. But in November of '72, the United States Congressional election will be held.

"As soon as you finish the '72 session in March, you need to campaign for the seat in Congress. The district is much bigger than the state district. There's a lot more travel than your other campaign. There are only eleven districts across the state, so you've got a lot of work ahead."

"Mister Hall, I'm gonna talk to my wife and my father-in-law about that. I'm uncertain, that's what we want to do for our family."

"Well, I hope you will consider it very strongly. There are many Confederate sympathizers still in Congress. Freedmen must have as many Congressmen as we can muster working for their cause," John urged.

"There is much time left to make that decision, John," Harry offered his opinion. "Lenora and Alice will give us their thoughts on this subject as well."

Chapter Forty

WOMEN'S SUFFRAGE REDUX

"Will, I think you should make a concerted effort in this next session, for Women's Suffrage," Lenora told him. "We were involved with Susan B Anthony and Elizabeth Cady Stanton way back in '64 in the Lincoln re-election campaign.

"Except for American Indians, everybody but women can vote now, and the idea of equal rights for women has not been established. Owning property, suing for divorce, inheriting assets from a deceased relative, nor voting rights have been guaranteed.

"Half the population of this country has no freedom nor rights."

Alice, joining the conversation, added, " We must depend on our husbands to assure we have what we need to survive. When a woman becomes a widow, she is without an advocate. *That's not right*."

"I'm not certain that's a winning strategy, Sweet Lady," Will replied, "You've gotta win re-election first. Once you're seated in office, proposals can be offered without regard to viability."

"I agree with Presley," Harry said. "But John Hall's advice is needed at this point in time. He's the expert politician.

"Will and I will pay him another visit on Sunday."

"Please understand, Lenora and Mrs. Parker, I'm not opposed to equal rights for women, I'm just concerned about voter's reactions.

"Hall says the first rule is get re-elected, then tackle the issues you wish to pursue," Will explained.

***

On Sunday, after church, Will and Harry drove the carriage to Hall's farm. As they approached the house, Harry remarked on the landscape, "Beautiful rolling hills filled with grassy bottoms, this place is perfect for raising cattle. And being less labor-intensive, I understand why Hall chose to raise cattle.

"He has much more time for his favorite thing - politics."

"Yeah, it's a pretty place right along the Potomac. It is very desirable property," Will observed.

Hall was sitting on the front porch in a rocking-chair and rose to greet their arrival. "Well, here's the candidate for the State Assembly coming to visit. Welcome, gentlemen. Come in and sit a spell."

"Hope we're not intruding, John," Parker spoke. "Are you up for a political strategy session?"

"Now Harry, you know I'm always up for politics. What's on your mind?"

"We want to pick your brain about Will's upcoming campaign. Our wives have some ideas, but I thought it best to seek your advice first," Parker told him.

"Alright, what did the ladies say?"

Will then spoke, "Lenora thinks I should be talking about Women's Suffrage," he replied. "Almost everybody else can vote, but women."

"And that's the biggest reason you had better back off from that issue," Hall quickly replied. "Women are interested in that issue, but they won't be voting in this election.

"Change usually comes incrementally. Folks need time to adjust to the idea of black suffrage. There is plenty of time to work for Women's Suffrage.

"Susan B. Anthony and Mrs. Stanton are the best ones to preach that sermon. Support them, but lay off for right now, is what I would advise," he said. His lips were taut..

"Keep this campaign one that emphasizes your background and record as a soldier and freedmen's advocate. Even the Radical Republicans will love that.

"Try this slogan- *A man of the people, for the people*," he smiled. "Stay away from controversy for now.

"After this state session is finished in March, your campaign for United States Congress will need to start," Hall concluded.

"Alright, John, we appreciate your advice. May we count on you for some financial contributions?" Harry asked.

"Of course, and I will solicit my friends and former contributors to join us in the state race, then later in the Congressional race," he smiled.

"I'm with you all the way to the United States' Congress."

"Thank you, thank you very, very much," Will was grateful.

FAIRFAX COUNTY COURT HOUSE

Standing on the courthouse steps, Will spoke to a crowd of over one hundred people:

"It is my honor and privilege to announce today my intention to seek re-election to the state assembly's 53rd district.

"Many of you are aware that I worked in the Constitutional Convention, then was elected to the Assembly. In the past, I served in the Union army and spent a year in Memphis, Tennessee, working for the Freedmen's Bureau, where we built schools for black children.

"Serving the good citizens of Fairfax County is my sole purpose for seeking re-election.

"Raised as the third-born son of sharecroppers, I have always championed the rights of working people. Those who are oppressed and abused are my major concern. My paw used to say *God musta liked common people, 'cause He made so many of us.*"

Laughter and applause greeted this last remark.

"I will always look out for your interests in every issue that arises in the Virginia Assembly."

Once again, he was interrupted by applause.

"I ask for your vote and support in the upcoming election in November.

"Thank you, thank you very, very much."

"I'm votin' fer Presley."

"He's got my vote."

"I like that Presley boy."

***

"Obviously, this crowd loved you, Will," Lenora said as they returned home. She, along with their two boys, and the Parkers had accompanied him to his announcement speech.

"Well, that's a great start, Son." Harry nodded and grinned at Will.

"I am so proud of you, Will," Alice said. She smiled her approval.

"I do hope that you can get something done to allow women the right to vote. The Wyoming Territory and the Utah Territory already have laws for women's suffrage."

"I will promise you I will introduce a bill to that effect. What I can't promise is that it will pass, Mrs. Parker." He shook his head.

"That's all we can ask of you, Son," Harry said.

***

In the November election, Will easily won re-election and made preparation to attend the legislative session of '71-'72.

When he left for the first official State Assembly session in December 1871, Lenora was less than two months from her expected delivery date.

It's understandable that she was super nervous about him not being around.

Following many discussions, Harry and Will had made plans to increase security after the Klan visit. They decided to hire eight night watchmen as sentries armed with rifles for the three-month legislative session.

Two would be stationed at the Parker house, two at the Presley house, and four would patrol the remainder of the farm.

Harry agreed that fewer men would be necessary when Will was home between sessions.

Lenora resigned herself to the reality that Will would only be home on weekends during the legislative sessions. He would take the train from Richmond each Friday evening and return on Monday morning.

Against her natural tendencies, but at Will's insistence, she had learned to use a shotgun if necessary.

"Your mama and daddy are right next door and Dr. Brewer is just a quick ride away." Will reminded her and kissed her goodbye the first morning.

"Make Ronnie and Randy help you as much as they can and have them run next door if you need help." He turned to look at his sons.

Chapter Forty-One

THE KLAN RETURNS

"When he returned to Richmond for the opening session of the Assembly in December 1871, Will sought his friends from the Constitutional Convention who were now serving in the Assembly-Rufus Brown, Jeremiah Jones, and Caleb Wilson.

"Gentlemen, I have been bombarded by requests that we tackle women's suffrage. Wyoming and Utah have already passed local laws which allow women to vote. It is a big stretch getting a national law or an Amendment, I know. But maybe we can start at the state level here in Virginia and lay the groundwork for national action."

"I'm gonna pass on that, Presley. I have some issues relating to trade which are more important to me," Wilson told him.

"I'm wit ye Presley. I know what it's like not havin' no rights." Brown smiled and nodded.

"Yeah, I owe ye, Will. Ye helped me git my school bill passed," Jones said. "I'll co-sponsor any bill you propose." Jones nodded and smiled.

"Me too, count me in as a co-sponsor," Brown answered.

Wilson conceded."I know Miss Lucy Stone, who's been working with Anthony and Stanton. I'll see if I can get her to speak here, and I'll vote for your bill. That's all I can do."

The bill was introduced, but never came up for a vote on the Assembly floor. Will had to return empty-handed to Parker's Farm when the session ended in early March of '72.

Although disappointed that his efforts had not paid off, he was still thrilled to be coming home to his wife and three children.

***

On Sunday, January 21st, Lenora had presented Will with a seven-pound bundle of joy. "I have a daughter," Will said with tears in his eyes. "You timed it just right so that I could be home to welcome her," he said, kissing his wife. "She is so beautiful, Lenora. Look at those soft yellow curls. What should we name her?"

"I had a name in mind if we had a girl." Lenora smiled, gazing into her baby's eyes. "How do you feel about Mary Amelia Presley?" she asked.

"I think that is a noble name, Lenora, but what made you choose that?" Will asked.

"Mary is in honor of Mary Agnes Weadon. She opened my eyes to the importance of giving full civil rights to women," Lenora said.

"Amelia was Daddy's mother who died when I was young. I remember her as the most loving grandmother who made everyone feel good just being around her. She was lots of fun and everyone called her Mimi. I would like to call our little girl, Mimi, if you agree."

"Mimi, it shall be," Will said. He held his daughter's tiny hand. "Mimi will be my little Princess, a Presley Princess," he laughed.

***

"I did the best I could, Alice." Will had apologized upon his return from Richmond without bringing home a win for Women's Suffrage.

"Maybe you can make some progress in the House of Representatives, Presley," Harry said. "John Hall says there is some sentiment for that in D.C.

"Will, there's a meeting of the Fairfax County Republican's Club on Thursday night. You and I should attend," Parker said.

"Daddy, do you think it's safe for you and Will both to be away at the same time?" Lenora asked. "The Klan has been active again here in Fairfax County."

As they were leaving for the Thursday night meeting, Harry tried to assure her.

"Now Princess, our security guards will be here protecting you. They have weapons and aren't afraid to use them."

Will spoke to the guards. "Lenora and the children will be with Alice in the Parker house. You two can help Alvin and Simon over there. Henry and Marvin will be down at the orchard. So the six of you can coordinate your efforts, fire a shot in the air if you need help."

"Yas Suh, Mista Will," Raymond answered. "We sho' will do dat."

***

When they arrived at the Republican Club meeting, Will and Harry were warmly greeted. "Happy to have you with us tonight Presley, and you too, Parker," the Chairman, David Alger, smiled. "Would you like to say a few words to the group, Presley?"

Alger was a mild-mannered man, forty-seen-year-old, with gray-tinged hair and a ready smile.

"Well, yes, I suppose I could say something. I don't have a prepared speech, but I can speak, off-the-cuff, I reckon."

"I've heard rumors you are considering a run for the House of Representatives," Alger grinned. "Any comments on that?"

Dropping his head modestly, he answered, *"Maybe."*

When he stood to call the meeting to order, Alger announced, "We have the State Assemblyman for the 53rd district with us tonight, Let's make him feel welcome, then maybe he'll say a few words. Could be that he'll have a special announcement for us," he smiled and said.

"Thank you, Chairman Alger, I'm happy to be with you tonight, and I sincerely appreciate the opportunity to speak to this assembly. We have tentatively decided to make a run for the House from this district. Your endorsement and support would cement our decision."

Arising from a seat in the back of the room, John Hall announced, "Presley has my support and the support of many of my friends. I will write a check tonight as evidence of that support. Are there others in attendance here who will follow my endorsement?"

Alger spoke, "I can't speak for this body, but Presley has my personal endorsement and a donation."

A voice from the audience was heard. "I move that we officially endorse Presley now. We know him-where he came from and where he's going. Let's do it, Gentlemen."

"You heard the motion; is there a second?"

"Second the motion."

"Any further discussion? Hearing none, the Chair calls for the question. Those in favor vote Aye."

Ayes were heard all over the room.

"Those opposed vote Nay."

"The Ayes have it. Congratulations Presley, and good luck in your campaign," Alger smiled.

***

When they started the return trip home, Harry said, "Well I suppose that settles it. Your campaign is off to a running start."

"Yeah, I reckon. Hope Lenora and Alice are OK with it," he replied.

***

As they approached the house, Will grew alarmed. The house was all lit up, and people were milling about in small groups on the lawn.

"Wonder what in the Hell is going on, Harry. I don't like the looks of this."

"Nor do I Will. Something bad has happened."

"Oh, Daddy and Will, I'm so glad you're home," Lenora sobbed, "Marvin has been shot dead, and Henry is gravely wounded.

"The orchard is completely burned to the ground, and some pigs were shot."

"Are you alright?" Will yelled, "What about my boys, my baby girl, and Alice?"

"Marvin and Henry are the only casualties. All of us survived, thanks to the Rolen brothers. They saved our lives," she wailed.

Alice ran to Harry and clung to him tightly while panting. "Oh, Harry, it was awful. They rode in on the backside of the property, so we didn't see them. The first sign we had was when the shots rang out. Raymond and Elijah ran toward the orchard when they heard gunfire.

"Raymond saw a large group of Klansmen in white robes with hoods on their heads. As they rode away, he stopped and fired his rifle three or four times. He thinks he hit somebody because a shriek was heard just after he fired.

"By the time Alvin and Simon got there the orchard was totally ablaze. It was too late to save it." She was hysterical. "Oh, Harry, I am so afraid to be here without you."

"I'm here now, Darling. Just relax and, we'll talk about it. Will, Lenora, and the children will spend the night with us."

"Of course we will, Daddy. I will be more comfortable myself knowing we're all together." Lenora comforted her mother.

***

On Friday morning, as they sat at the breakfast table, Alice was upset and crying. "I was just thinking about Mrs. Rolen. Marvin is dead and Henry's life is precarious. I know her heart is breaking. A mother's heart is so full of love for her children. Later today I want to visit her," she sobbed.

"I'll go with you Mama," Lenora volunteered. "Will can sit with the boys and Mimi."

"Yeah, it is a difficult thing to lose your children," Will noted. "My mother has lost four of her nine children, and her husband. Life goes on, and we have to keep on living, despite our sorrow."

"Harry, we have to take care of Mrs. Rolen; she has lost one of her sons, and the surviving son may not work for some time. I think we owe it to them to see that they have what they need. After all, the boys risked their lives to protect our lives." Alice was sobbing again.

"Of course, we will do whatever is necessary, Alice." Harry placed his arm around his wife. "I think it is a good thing for you and Lenora to visit her today."

***

After breakfast, Alice and Lenora dressed and drove the carriage to the Rolen home. Will and Harry entertained the twins and kept watch over a sleeping Mimi.

"Harry, I've got something on my mind that I need to discuss with you." Will stroked his chin.

"Spit it out, Son, I'm ready."

"When you and I are away, bad things happen. This politics venture can be dangerous. I'm having second thoughts about running for Congress."

"I hear what you're saying, Son, but we can't let a group of militant thugs deter us from doing the *right thing* for the good of our society.

"That seat in Congress will put you in a position to accomplish valuable improvements for the country. The Speaker, James G. Blaine, needs more progressive people to help bring about the changes this country desperately needs. These conservative Democrats will fight every change and return us to a slave-owning culture like we had before the war.

"The war will have been for naught. " Harry's face turned red, and he wrinkled his brow.

"Hall tells me that Grant is running far ahead of his opponent Horace Greeley. He's a Liberal Republican who wants to end Reconstruction. This split in the party could prove detrimental to Grant's re-election.

"Down-ballot Republicans can assist Grant in his campaign by endorsing his agenda. Our Fairfax County Republicans believe that you can help to elect Grant. The future of Reconstruction and of this nation depends on the November 5th election of Grant and Will Presley," Parker proclaimed.

"Yeah, I heard some talk about Greeley while I was in Richmond. He's the publisher of the New York Tribune newspaper, and was a Congressman from New York for one term."

"He could siphon off enough Republican votes to give the majority to the Democrats." Harry was worried.

"There were rumors abounding in Richmond that the conservative Democrats might nominate him. Wouldn't *that* be an ironic turn of events?" Will observed.

***

Lenora and Alice returned from their visit with Mrs. Rolen with a report on Marvin's funeral plans. "The service will be held on Sunday afternoon at Falls Church. Burial will be in the church cemetery.

"Mrs. Rolen was relieved to learn that we will continue to pay his salary to her. The family depends on that money for their survival," Alice reported.

"I took the liberty to, also, commit us to continue Henry's salary while he recovers from his wounds." Alice looked tentatively at Harry and Will.

"Absolutely, we'll do that," Harry proclaimed. "After *all* that's happened to these men while they were protecting you,. We should do it."

"And it's just the right thing to do," Will added.

***

Speaking later, when he and Will were alone, Harry shared a conversation he had with John Hall. "Members of Congress are now being paid $7,500.00 per year ($141,000 in 2020 equivalency). We have never made that much money on the farm. We could easily afford to pay the salaries of the Rolen brothers. That's another reason for you to win that congressional seat, Presley."

"Wow, I didn't know that. On my first job, when I joined

Burnside's volunteers in the Union army, I was paid $13.00 per month. That is an enormous increase from where I started." He was surprised.

"We will discuss it with Alice and Lenora, but I'm convinced that you should seek the position," Harry said.

***

On Saturday morning, when they finished breakfast, Lenora picked up her copy of the Fairfax News, the local newspaper.

"Here's a story about the Klan raid on our place last Thursday night. Oh, and it says they raided John Hall's farm the same night. Killed 37 head of cattle, but nobody was shot and killed like they did here.

"A sheriff's deputy, Bobby Chambers, was shot in the back as he was patrolling Thursday. Will, you don't think...?"

"Lenora, Raymond said he shot one of the Klansmen in the back as they were leaving. He was probably with that bunch of thugs. The sheriff was a Confederate sympathizer. Most of his deputies were too," Will said.

"The Klan is heavily populated with local officials."

Chapter Forty-Two

U. S. CONGRESS

O n Friday morning, November 8, 1872, the headlines in the Fairfax
News read:

GRANT WINS BY A LANDSLIDE

and

Local Assemblyman Elected to Congress

President Ulysses S. Grant has been re-elected to the Presidency of the
United States by a wide majority.

Grant easily wins the contest with an 11.6 percent margin of the
popular vote. Winning 286 electoral votes to Greeley's 66. Our extremely
popular President will serve for four more years.

Grant's victory also swept many other Republicans into seats in
the House of Representatives and the Senate. Republicans now control
both branches of Congress.

Will Presley, our State Assemblyman, easily won his bid to take a
seat in the House. Presley, who was elected in '71 to his second term in the
Assembly, will forego the second year of his term.

When asked for a sta*tement, he said, "I am happy for this glorious
victory, and I will serve the people of my district to the best of my ability.
Thanks to all* of you who voted for me, and to those who voted for my
opponent. I will represent *all* of you."

Presley and his wife, Lenora Parker Presley, live on Parker's Farm in
Falls Church. The farm is owned by Harry and Alice Parker, Mrs. Presley's
parents. The establishment has been a major supplier of produce and meat

to the War Department for many years.

As he read the announcement Will was pensive. *"Well, we've got a big job ahead of us now."*

"Women's Suffrage and federal funding for free public schools for poor white and poor black children, should keep me busy for the next two years."

"What do you mean by *we*?" Lenora shot back. Did you forget that you have a wife and three small children who are depending on you for more than your new federal salary?

"Did you take into consideration that we are living in terror when you are gone, that we have already had one death and a serious injury during your absence? Did you stop to ask how I felt about your new adventure?" She was sobbing.

Taken aback and shocked, Will didn't immediately know how to respond. He just knew she needed reassurance. He put his arms around her and brushed away her tears.

"My darling, of course I have considered all those things. This opportunity will provide us with much needed resources to keep the farm running, to assist the Rolen family, and to ensure that we have all the necessary security during my absence.

"The good thing is that I will rarely be gone overnight as I had to be in the Assembly. Our location here just outside of the city allows a daily commute. You, the boys, and my Princess, Mimi, are always on my mind."

***

As they left church services on Sunday after the election, John Hall was waiting for them to exit. "Hello, Presley, can you and Harry come over to my place this afternoon after dinner? I want to talk to the two of you about politics."

"Hey Harry, Mr. Hall wants to talk to us this afternoon. Can we ride over to his place after dinner?"

"Sure, we can. Hi John, what's going on with you?"

"I just want to congratulate Presley on his election, and I want you to meet my son, Jim. He's interested in politics and wants to meet Will."

***

On the ride home, Will questioned, "What do you think Hall has on his mind, Harry?"

"Uncertain, but it must be a big deal to him for us to meet his son," Harry said.

When they arrived at the Hall Farm after dinner, John met them at the door. "It's a little cool this afternoon, but I thought we might sit on the porch and have a cigar. My wife hates the smell, so I usually smoke outdoors.

"Hey Jim, come on out and meet our new Congressman, Will Presley, and his father-in-law, Harry Parker."

"Hello, Representative Presley, and Mr. Parker. Pleased to meet you."

The younger Hall was a tall, broad-chested man with a small moustache and close-cropped hair. Well dressed and confident of himself with an air of sophistication, he smiled and offered his handshake.

"Jim has just graduated from Yale Law School and has passed the bar exam. He's been offered a job with a big law firm in D.C., but his actual interest is politics.

"I guess that's one thing he gets from his daddy." John smiled smugly.

"I'll get right to the point, Gentlemen. Jim wants to finish the last year of Presley's term in the State Assembly. The Governor is a political ally of mine and he will appoint Will's successor.

"Later Jim wants to move into the U.S. Congress,"

Harry Parker spoke, "Does that mean that Jim will contest the seat Will now holds, John?"

"That's the other thing I want to mention, Gentlemen. As you know, U.S. Senators are appointed by the State Assembly. Presley has friends there and Jim would be another one. A Senate seat will be available in '74.

"Will, can then move to the Senate and make room for Jim in the House. Another Senate seat will become available in '76. We could have two Senators!"

"Wow, my head is spinning. I can't process all this so quickly," Will marveled. "We'll have to discuss this with Lenora and Alice."

"How do you want us to be involved with all these transactions," Harry quizzed.

"First, we want you to be aware of where we are going on behalf of Jim. Additionally, if our plans come to fruition, Will's support and cooperation are desirable to us, especially in the upcoming U.S. races." John smiled.

Jim once again extended his hand to Will and smiled broadly, "I look forward to working with you Presley. You and I will work together very well.

"Mr. Parker, it's a pleasure to meet you. I look forward to meeting your wives and the rest of your family." Jim was gracious.

"Be sure to meet my good friends Rufus Brown, Jeremiah Jones, and Caleb Wilson. They are good people with the needs of their constituents always in mind. Tell them I told you to look them up when you get there." Will shared with Jim.

***

The 43rd Congress convened on March 4, 1873, and Will Presley took his seat representing the 8th district of Virginia. He represented a high-income area which encompassed all of Arlington County and much of Fairfax county, including the Independent towns of Arlington and Falls Church.

John Hall's plan worked to perfection.

***

The trajectory of Will Pressley's life had remained on an upward arc from 1866 to 1873. The same could be said for the railroad industry until September.

Railroad construction had been booming with 35,000 miles of new track being laid across the country. Investment in railroads by banks and other industries met an all-time high, and railroads employed more people than any sector of the economy other than agriculture.

Jay Cooke and Company, the largest financier of the Union military effort during the Civil War, became the principal agent in railroad construction's government financing. Because of massive over investment, the Cooke bank closed its doors on that September day, it set off a major economic panic.

When the Cooke bank failed, a domino effect was activated, and other banks and railroads that were bank-financed failed as well.

The Panic of 1873 would become the longest-running, and most economically devastating recession the young nation had ever encountered. Everything that happened in the next seven years was adversely affected by this downturn in the economy.

Hard times were ahead for almost everyone in the nation.

Chapter Forty-Three

A HOLIDAY REUNION

S hortly after Mimi was born, Lenora drafted a letter to Sally Presley Henderson on behalf of Will. He wanted his mother to know that there was another Presley girl in the world.

In the letter, she invited Sally and her new husband, John Henderson, to come for a visit. She also updated Sally on Will, her third-born son's success as a politician, that he was now serving in the United States Congress and might move to the Senate in a few years.

Sally had responded, congratulating Will and Lenora on the addition to their family and on the amazing path of his career. She said that John had suggested a trip to the Nation's Capital; however, they had not planned a time. She was hopeful that it might happen within a few years.

Lenora read Sally's response to Will, who was excited to think that he could look forward to a visit with his Mother. "I would be so happy to have her here with us. We could talk more openly without all the other members of the family present," he said.

"I would also like to have another opportunity to talk with John, or Preacher Henderson as we called him back in the day. He was a dominant influence on my thinking, and he shares many of my views. I could talk freely with him without fear of ridicule."

"You can always talk with me," Lenora said softly. "However, it is alright with me if you have the chance to talk with a man you respect who is also one who knows your entire background."

"I don't think anyone knows everything I have been through, Lenora. There are some things a man just cannot discuss but unfortunately, cannot forget."

"Will, you and I have been together now for almost ten years. Don't you think I know you are haunted by something? I have seen you *wake up sweating and crying out from a nightmare which you refuse to share with me.*

I have watched you lost in your own thoughts with a look of despair. I wish I could be the one to help you shed your demons, but if it has to be someone else, I will welcome his assistance."

"Lenora, I do not intentionally hide anything from you, but there are some memories that I simply do not have the words to express." Will mumbled, holding his head in his hands.

"War is a horrible experience for anyone who has the misfortune to be involved on a face-to-face level," Will told Lenora. "Those of us who survive, try our best to put it all behind us by not talking about it, by keeping busy with every-day duties, by finding someone to love, and by committing lives to an idea or cause bigger than ourselves. We hope, in some small way, to make up for our sins.

"Whatever we do, it is never enough. We cannot escape the wrath of God."

"But Will, you are a good man. Since I first met you, you have been trying to make a difference in the world. You have treated everyone with dignity and respect. You have put yourself on the line for others. You are a wonderful husband and father. You are a kind neighbor. You are a trustworthy public servant. *Isn't all that enough?"*

"I don't know what I would do without you, Lenora. You have given me a second chance at life. You and the children are my life and everything I do as work is an attempt to give back to you." Will embraced Lenora and kissed her deeply.

Will's campaign to represent the 8th District of Virginia was successful, and life for the Presley household changed again. While the U.S. House was in session, Will mostly commuted daily to his Washington office. He only had to spend occasional nights away from home, which thrilled Lenora .

Being thrust so suddenly into the limelight on the national stage, Will had much more to learn about how politics works. Because he realized that he was limited in both experience and knowledge, he listened closely to the more seasoned heads and tried to understand the various philosophies held by men in both parties.

Will's natural charm and aw-shucks attitude disguised his passion for advancing politically controversial policies; consequently, he was not seen as a threat by any of his new colleagues.

When Lenora and Alice questioned him about what he was doing in Congress, Will would often respond, "Keeping my eyes and ears open and my mouth shut."

"How is that going to get us closer to Women's Suffrage?" Lenora asked one evening. "Every time I ask about this issue, I'm told to be patient."

"Trust me, my darling, I'm as impatient as you, but I have

learned that I cannot do anything if I am not at the table. I am making friends across parties. I am learning how things get done. Whenever the opportunity arises, I ask probing questions that hopefully make people rethink their positions."

"I do trust you, Will. It's just that being confined to the farm with the children, I feel so out of touch with what is happening. I look forward to *hearing vicariously from you.*"

"Lenora, I have learned that politics is the art of the possible. That means there is always compromise involved . That is a hard pill to swallow when you are consumed with the desire to make things right that have been wrong for a long time."

***

According to John Hall's plan, Will won his second term in the House in the November '73 election. By this time, he had gained the respect of his colleagues and the voters of the 8th District.

The Virginia Assembly named Will Presley to fill a Senate vacancy in the fall of 1874. "Lenora, I can't rightly believe that a sharecropper's son is headed for the U.S. Senate," Will said . He felt humble, but he still grinned his contagious crooked smile.

John's son, Jim Hall, was then appointed by the Governor of Virginia to fill Will's unexpired House term.

***

Lenora wrote to Sally to tell her that Will would be sworn in as a Senator when the 43rd Congress of the United States came back into session in January 1875.

She suggested that this might be the perfect time for a visit. "We will meet you at the train station in Washington and my parents Harry and Alice Parker invite you to stay with them during your visit. We are right next door with a houseful of noisy children, so you will be more comfortable at Mama and Daddy's place. If you can come before Christmas, we can spend the holidays together."

Sally and John Henderson made plans for their holiday visit, despite some concern expressed by Maggie and the Presley boys. "Mama, that's a long trip to be making at your age," Maggie said one Sunday after church. "You've never even been out of North Carolina since you were ten years old, and that was fifty years ago."

"Maggie, John and I may not be young, but we can still take care of ourselves. We only need to get to Asheville where we will spend the night with Bishop Cooper, John's uncle. The next morning, it will be a six or seven-hour train ride to Washington where we will be picked up and taken to the Parker Farm. There is no way that I am going to miss watching my son sworn in as a United States Senator. Why are you so worried?"

"I don't want to lose you, too. So many of our family is gone: Paw, Buck, Johnny, Matt, Lizzie, and most recently Grandma O'Conner," Maggie said. Tears slowly fell from her eyes. "I don't want to be the last Presley in Graham."

"You still have Billy Bob, Pete, Andy, Martha, Willadeen, and your nieces and nephews. They are all Presleys," Sally said. She grabbed her *daughter in a tight embrace.*

"Yes, but they still live in Roaring Fork. I don't see them very often, and when I do, it seems we don't have the same interests anymore. In fact, they act like they think I've forgotten where I came from. Just because I married a Doctor, I don't think I'm any better than they are."

Sally thought a minute and then remembered what J.W. used to say, "You ain't better than nobody, and nobody's better than you." They laughed and hugged thinking of J.W. Presley.

Sally remembered the love of her life and how they had struggled in the beginning to build a future for themselves and their children. "He always made me laugh, and he always made me feel loved."

Maggie was thinking of how her paw had held her when she cried and how he always told her how much he loved her. "He made me feel special and smart and gave me the confidence to try new things."

"Tell me what I can do to help you prepare for your trip, Maw. Is there anything that needs to be done at the school while you are away?" Maggie asked.

"Thank you, Maggie, but our trip will be mostly during the winter break at school, so I won't be missed. John has scheduled a seminary student to hold church services in our absence."

***

Will and Lenora were excited when they received the word that Sally and John would be arriving by train in Washington on December 21st and would be able to stay for the swearing-in ceremony.

"We have to make this an especially memorable Christmas for

them," Lenora told Will. "Mama and I will decorate both houses with greens, pinecones, berries, apples, candles, and ribbons. There will be wreaths on the doors and over the fireplaces. We will treat them to all of Mama's best recipes and Daddy's special cider."

"Hold on, Lenora, you are turning this into a *major* event. There's no sense in you putting so much work on your mama or on yourself. They're going to be happy just to see us and to hold the children," Will cautioned.

"Nonsense, Will, this may be the last time you see either of them. Why not make it special?"

"I guess you are right, as usual, and I will help in any way I can," Will said. He felt chastised.

"Maybe we can also give them a tour of the Nation's Capital. Neither of them has been here before. They will love talking about it to the family and other folks in Graham."

"You will probably be busy as soon as Congress reconvenes, but it might be nice to show them around between Christmas and New Year's Day. Daddy will help with that," Lenora promised.

***

Harry and Will arrived at the D.C. train depot before 2:00 on Monday afternoon to meet Sally and John, scheduled to arrive at 2:30 P.M. Fortunately, the train was very prompt. Following introductions, Will gathered the luggage and began loading the carriage.

Sally embraced her son and began telling him about their trip. "I had never met John's Uncle Robert, so it was wonderful to spend an evening with him and his wife in Asheville. This morning, we boarded the train at 7:00 for a very pleasant trip. There was even a dining car where we had a enjoyable lunch. This was my first train ride and the first time to leave the state of North Carolina."

John added, "And in a fortnight, you will be watching your son become an official United States Senator as he is sworn in at the Capitol building. What a Merry Christmas and Happy New Year this will be."

"Alice and I are so pleased to have you stay with us during your visit," Harry said. "We will want to hear all the news about your family, your school, and the town of Graham."

"It may sound boring to big city folks like you, not as exciting as the goings on in the Federal Government, but I know Will must be interested in an update. I can't wait to see my new granddaughter and hug my little grandsons again," Sally said gleefully.

***

The porch of the Parker house was adorned with holiday greens and berries and the front door welcomed visitors with a large wreath decorated with more greens, red apples, and a large red bow. As the carriage pulled up, the door opened and Alice, Lenora, and the boys ran out with big smiles.

Alice offered her hand to John and gave Sally a gentle hug. "I am Lenora's mother, please call me Alice. Let's get you settled in so we can visit awhile before dinner. You must be tired."

"You will be staying in my old room," Lenora said. "We, of course, want you to spend time in our house too, but you will sleep better here with no eight-year-old boys jumping on your bed first thing each morning, nor a babbling almost three-year-old girl."

"Where is that girl? I want to see her," Sally insisted.

"She was taking an afternoon nap in Mama and Daddy's room, but she should be waking up by now. I'll get her," Lenora replied.

When Sally saw the little girl with soft blond curls and a mouth shaped like a heart, she began to sob softly. "What's wrong, Maw," Will asked.

"Nothing, Son. She just looks so much like Lizzie; I couldn't help myself. May I hold her?"

"Certainly," Lenora said. "She doesn't meet many new people, so don't be insulted if she takes a few minutes to warm up."

Sally pulled a skein of yarn from her travel bag and cut a yard's length. She tied the yarn into a loop and began weaving it around her fingers without saying a word. The boys were coming closer and little Mimi was curious. Slowly, the little girl moved closer to Sally to see what she was doing with that yarn.

In an incredibly quiet voice, without direct eye contact, Sally said, "Have you ever seen a cat's cradle?"

"Ca-Cad?" Mimi muttered as she climbed up next to Sally.

Ronnie and Randy were excited. "Let's see it. Let's see it," they insisted impatiently.

Sally gave each child a turn at transferring the yarn figures from her hands to theirs and back. Lenora was amazed at how Sally had captured the children's attention. They listened to each instruction and giggled gleefully when a new form emerged in the center of the yarn puzzle.

"I have never seen all three of them so quiet and so attentive for so long," Lenora told Sally. "You have some kind of magic."

"No, I have spent the last forty years working with children. Sometimes you have to pull out a few tricks to get their attention before you can begin teaching your prepared lesson."

Alice called out from the kitchen, "Is anybody hungry?"

Ronnie and Randy responded in unis*on, "Me, me."*

Will smiled as he watched Mimi take Sally's hand and walk with her grandmother to the dining table.

"After breakfast tomorrow, Will and I will give you and Sally the grand tour of our capital city," Harry said. He patted John on the shoulder. "It is typical December weather in Washington, so be sure to wear some warm layers. There will be considerable walking involved."

***

Gathered in front of a roaring fire after a tasty and filling dinner, conversation began with what had been going on since Will and Lenora's visit to Roaring Fork six years ago.

"During your tour tomorrow, Will can fill you in on all the politics," Lenora began. "Below, I summarize what has affected the home front. As you know, we moved in with Mama and Daddy for a short time in 1868 while we were building our house.

"Will served as a Delegate to the Constitutional Convention in '68 and '69. Virginia was readmitted to the Union in '70, and I think Will can take some credit for that," she smiled at her husband.

"Then your son was elected twice as a Virginia State Assemblyman from our District, serving in '71–'72. Since there is no stopping him, he then ran for and was elected to the U.S. House of Representatives in November '72.

"I am not going to give you all the gory details of our visits from the Ku Klux Klan. Will can share that horror story.

"Of course, we had a minor event at home in January of '72. Little Mimi joined our family. It was a busy year."

"Will, I am so proud of you and happy for your family," John said. Sally beamed.

"That was only the beginning," Lenora added, almost out of breath. "Before he finishes his second term in the house, the State Assembly appoints Will to fill an open Senate seat, and that is why we are all here together."

"I didn't know my wife could talk that long and fast. Maybe she should be running for office," Will joked.

"That's another important story that I can tell you later in the week. We met a wonderful woman on the train who is part of a group promoting Women's Suffrage," Lenora said. "Now I promise to let someone else talk," she blushed.

"We might need some of Harry's cider to keep us going," Alice laughed. She headed to the kitchen for the jug and some cups.

"Maw, let's hear from you and John." Will opened the floor. "What's new in Graham and Roaring Fork since our visit?"

Sally took his hand and said, "As I told Lenora in my letter, we lost your grandmother O'Conner the next spring after you were there. She didn't have any ailment, but she seemed to wither away."

"Eunice would have been seventy-four her next birthday, John added. "I believe she never got over losing Patrick. She and your grandfather were an especially close couple."

"After Mama passed, I got permission from Charles Graham to build a two-room schoolhouse next to the church and to offer both elementary and more advanced classes.

"Maggie began assisting me and she now handles the class for children from six to nine years old including her son, Elijah. She is expecting another little one in the spring. I teach those ten years and older."

"Graham has continued to grow over the last decade," John added. "We have a dressmaker and tailor living in the Tailor Shop who were recruited from Boston, a nice young Irish couple, Christopher and Bonnie Riley.

"New homes have been financed by the bank, which are attracting young people who would prefer being closer to town. That growth in population has helped every business in Graham to prosper."

"Your brother, Andy, married Grace Wills in '70, and they have a son, Dennis. We call him Dennie. They built another house near the upper part of the creek.

"Pete is still living in the two-story with Martha and her kids, but I think he is seeing her sister, Lillian." Sally looked pleased. *"He has always been shy around the ladies, but a good wife would help him come into his own self.*

"Billy Bob and Willadeen added a daughter to their brood. Abbie is a real sweetheart and all three children fit together as if it were planned that way."

"I believe the ladies of our group have got us beat as orators, Will." John laughed and was joined by all the others.

***

In the night, Lenora was startled by her husband's cries. "Will, you're having a nightmare, wake up before you scare the children to death."

Sweat was dripping from Will's back as he tried to rouse himself and sit up on the bed. Lenora observed that his hands were trembling. She put one arm around his shoulder and wiped his damp brow and cheeks. "Can you tell me about it, Will?" she pleaded.

For more than a few moments, Will remained silent with a terrified expression indelibly printed on his face. "How can I help you, if you will not talk to me?"

"No one can help me." Will mumbled with his head in his hands.

"I was back on that ridge in Gettysburg, covered with mud and out of ammunition. The valley below me was strewn with the lifeless bodies of young men in gray uniforms. Blank eyes starred up at me. I could hear voices asking, 'weren't you one of us, Will Presley? Why are you trying *to kill your own kind?' I tried to run away from the sounds, but my feet were stuck in the mud. I could hear myself shouting, NO, NO, this was not what I wanted.* Then you woke me."

***

Lenora sat by her husband's side until she could see the sun peaking its head above the trees. "I'll be right back, Will," she told him as she put on a cape and walked over to her parent's house.

"Good morning, Mama, I need to speak with John."

John Henderson appeared in the kitchen fully dressed and ready for the promised tour of the city. "Good morning, Lenora, what brings you out so early?"

"I really need you to speak with Will at our house before breakfast, if possible." She asked as she wrung her hands with some urgency.

"Just go over, the door is open. You will find him in the bedroom. I'll stay here and help Mama prepare breakfast for all of us."

***

Not knowing what to expect, John opened the front door of the Presley house and called out for Will. Hearing no response, he walked down the hall toward the largest bedroom. Still sitting on the side of the bed, Will did not immediately acknowledge John.

"Will, Lenora asked me to speak with you, and you have had an awful night. Would you like to tell me about it?"

"John, can you talk to me as a Pastor instead of a step-father for a few minutes?"

"Of course, Son. I told you when we last met that I would always be available if you needed someone to listen, and here I am."

"Pastor, is there any way to be forgiven or to rid yourself of a mortal sin? Since I left the army, I have been trying to find a way to make up for all the pain I caused, to give back, to help put *right* the wrongs I have seen.

"No matter what I do, no matter where I move, the past is always there just waiting to be revived in my dreams. As Maw was talking about the Presley family, Graham, and Roaring Fork, all I could think about was those who were lost or permanently damaged by a senseless war in which I was awarded medals.

"Why should I receive medals for killing people? Why should I get the chance to live a better life while so many lost theirs? Why should I be elected to high office? Where is the fairness?"

"Son, your questions are the same ones that have been asked since time began. I cannot give you any answers, but I can tell you that there is always a place to go for comfort. I remember that you took the teachings of Jesus seriously as a younger man, and I suspect you still believe.

"I know your decision not to support the rebellion was right. Your decision to work in Reconstruction was right. Your decision to make a difference through political involvement was right. Your decision to let your mother know you were still alive and contributing to a better future for our country was right.

"I don't know and will not ask what you have done that is haunting you, but forgiveness is yours for the asking. Kneel with me, Son, as we say together the prayer our Lord taught us.

"Our Father, who art in heaven, hallowed be thy Name, thy kingdom come, thy will be done, on earth as it is in heaven. Give us this day our daily bread. And forgive us our trespasses, as we forgive those who trespass against us. And lead us not into temptation, but to deliver us from evil. For thine is the kingdom and the power, and the glory, for ever and ever. Amen."

Chapter Forty-Four

A SHARECROPPER'S
SON IN THE SENATE

L enora was relieved to see John, Will, and the children walk into the Parker kitchen ready for breakfast. "Mama has made a hearty morning repast that should keep you going on your tour. Feast your eyes on all the eggs, ham, bacon, grits, and biscuits-and-gravy. She has also made you some sandwiches to have in the carriage for lunch. Daddy always takes a jug of his cider along, just in case," she laughed.

Harry, Will, Sally, and John boarded the carriage for their trip into the city. Sally was so excited; she squeezed John's hand and began to giggle a little. "I can hardly believe that I am going to be in our Nation's Capital in less than an hour. Since Mama and Daddy brought me from London to Graham when I was only ten, I have been nowhere else, unless you count Roaring Fork," she laughed.

"Between the two of us," Harry explained, "We will share what we know of the history of this city that was carved out of two states to create the center of our government.

"I have read, President Washington fired his city planner, Pierre Charles L'Enfant, and then appointed commissioners in 1791 to supervise the planning, design, and construction of the new capital city and surrounding federal district. They oversaw the survey and land acquisition of the district, and approved a changed version of L'Enfant's city plan."

"Why did the President fire the planner?" Sally asked.

"It seems that L'Enfant was a genius at design, but he was a failure at negotiating the deals to acquire the land. Families had been living and farming on portions of the target land for generations. It took people skills to convince landowners to sell all or part of their land or sometimes donate it to the Federal Government.

"The approved plan established the placement of the Capitol and President's House, and recommended the creation of the public promenade from the Capitol to the Potomac.

"That plan, which shows avenues named for the states coming out like spokes in a wheel, is still in process, so you have to use your imagination to see what it will become by the time our grandchildren and great grandchildren visit.

"We will visit the Smithsonian Institution. It is the first museum to be built along the promenade space. Eventually, there will be many monuments and museums."

Will shared something he was told, "An Englishman with no family willed a large endowment to the United States to build a museum for the continued education of the people. The building looks like an old castle and people are calling it, The Castle."

"Sadly, a fire destroyed the museum's lecture hall and many historical relics and works of art," Harry remembered. "Rebuilding began in 1867."

"You saw the outside of the Capitol Building when you arrived at the train station yesterday, but today, you will see it up close and even be able to tour parts of the interior," he promised, parking his carriage at the depot.

The massive white majesty of the Capitol rising on a hill above the rest of the city was awe-inspiring to two people who rarely saw a building of more than three or four floors. Standing inside the rotunda and looking up 180 feet inside the dome, John and Sally dropped their jaws like children on Christmas.

United States Capitol

Harry explained that the hallway to the south led to the House of Representatives and the one to the north to the Senate Chamber. "That's where you will watch your son take the oath of office on the first day Congress resumes after the New Year."

"By the way, the train station opened in '72, but the depot buildings only opened this year. There has been some controversy about all the noise and dirt being on a place that is a spot of beauty and tranquility," Harry added. He made everyone aware that he kept up on the latest news.

"We can ride the streetcar down Pennsylvania Avenue from the Capitol to the President's House. If we are lucky, we might enter the tourist portion and see the holiday decorations," Harry said. He parked the carriage at the streetcar depot.

"Both the Capitol and the President's House were burned by the British in 1814. It just shows you, we Americans don't give up," Will said proudly. "We keep going 'til we get it right."

"I understand that Will's father was born in Ireland, so you might be interested to know that it was an Irish architect, James Hoban, who designed the President's House," Harry told Sally.

"The official title for the house is the Executive Mansion, but people have called it by several names: President's Palace, Presidential Mansion, or the White House because of the white paint used to cover the fire damage.

"John Adams was the first President to live in the President's House because the decision to build it in the Federal City was not made until the Residence Act of 1790, and then there was much time involved in design and construction."

"One block from the President's House, you might like to visit St. John's Episcopal Church built in 1816. Many refer to it as the Church of the Presidents."

"Harry, Sally and I feel honored to be chauffeured around with folks as knowledgeable as you and Will. Hearing some of the history makes the trip more memorable."

"John, neither Will nor I are experts; however, you can't live and work around a town for any length of time without absorbing some interesting tidbits," Harry replied. "Of course, I do a lot of reading in my spare time."

***

"It's all so beautiful," Sally said to Will while they waited for the streetcar to return them to the depot. I am so happy that that the events of your life have brought you here."

"If she only knew the grievous reality of those events, she would not be happy," Will thought. A pang filled his bosom, and John looked at him with empathy.

FIRST PHASE
WASHINGTON
MONUMENT

Harry continued, "You might be interested in seeing the beginning of the monument honoring George Washington." Harry pointed to the first phase of a building a considerable distance from the Capitol.

"It was included in the original design of the city, and the cornerstone was laid in 1848. But construction ceased during the war. When a request for funding to complete construction is introduced in Congress, Will can help get that accomplished.

"We can show you a sketch of the design. It is to be an Egyptian style *obelisk* eventually towering over 500 feet and will be the tallest building in the city. I hope I live to see it."

***

"I have two other landmarks to show you," Will interjected. "We may need to take our carriage to visit them, but it's worth it."

"What could those be?" Sally was curious.

As the carriage approached the corner of 10th and H streets, Will pointed to a three and a half-story house. "That is where I met Lenora. I had a room on the top floor while I was working at Fort Whipple. Lenora worked at the War Department with her cousin, Judy. She stayed at the boarding house during the week and often went home on Saturday.

"A few blocks south on 10th we will see the Ford Theater, the terrible site of Lincoln's murder. Losing our President made me even more determined to find a way to help bind up the wounds of the war and help rebuild our country.

"The boarding house was owned by a widow, Mary Surratt. After Lincoln's assignation, she was included in a group accused of plotting conspiracy and treason. She was tried, found guilty, and hanged, the first woman to be executed in the United States."

"Did you suspect anything while you lived there?" John asked.

"Not anything specific; however, we heard some mumbled conversations that showed they were Confederate sympathizers. Lenora and I decided to remain distant and not to reveal any information that could be helpful to them," Will replied.

***

The foursome continued the tourist routine for several hours before stopping near the Smithsonian to eat the sandwiches Alice had made for them. They spent two more hours walking through the historical displays inside the castle, then decided their legs would not carry them further.

"You'll have another chance on January 4th to see anything you may have missed," Harry said. Then they boarded their carriage for the return to Parker's Farm.

***

"How has this recession affected life in Graham, John?" Harry asked. "Our local papers paint a dismal picture with little hope for early recovery."

"Because Graham is still mostly an agricultural area, we may not have experienced the same level of devastation as more industrialized areas; however, all of our small businesses have suffered the downturn of the economy," John said.

"Even the *Graham Gazette* reports that the failure of other banks has tightened the availability of loans for new construction," Sally added. "That translates to a reduced need for lumber and a lower price for the logging efforts at Roaring Fork. It is fortunate that my children can grow enough food and produce enough meat to keep all the Presleys fed. I worry about those folks who have moved to town and cannot provide for themselves if they lose their jobs."

"Many factories have been forced to close, resulting in widespread loss of jobs," Harry said with a sad tone. "There are thousands of families who have been left with no resources. Our church has been helping all that we can, but the need is greater than all the churches and charities can handle."

"Will, you are going to be in a position of influence," Sally blurted out. *"Do something!* The government *must* do something. We can't just allow children to starve and people to lose their homes."

"Mama, I wish that I could wave a magic wand and take care of all the needs. I wish I could undo the recession just like I wished I could undo the *damn war*," Will said. He frowned and shook his head.

"All I *can do* and *will do* is make suggestions. It takes a consensus in the Congress to bring a proposal to a vote. Then it takes a majority of both the House and the Senate to pass a bill which must be signed by the President before anything can happen."

"From what I hear inside the Republican Party, Grant is not eager to take sides in the arguments between workers and business leaders. However, he is most likely to adopt the proposals that benefit the business community."

"So, you are telling me that by the time anything official can be done, hundreds of thousands could be dead," Sally cried. "What are people supposed to do in the meantime?"

Taking Sally's hand to calm her, John began to outline his good government concept, which aligned with his theology and political philosophy. "I refer you, Will, to the Preamble to the United States Constitution, which states:

'We the People of the United States, in Order to form a more perfect Union, establish Justice, insure domestic Tranquility, provide for the common defense, promote the general welfare, and secure the Blessings of Liberty to ourselves and our Posterity, do ordain and establish this Constitution for the United States of America.

"If promoting the general welfare was important enough for our founders to include as part of the purpose of our nation, I think there should be some ongoing governmental processes that can handle national problems.

"There will always be economic downturns, natural disasters that affect the life, health, and livelihoods of our people. We should not wait for each additional problem to arise before we devise a plan of action. We should have a department or bureau that can respond with minimal authorization.

"If you want to make a lasting impact, Son, that is where you can start. I am not a politician, but I can imagine creating jobs for the unemployed funded by the government to perform obviously necessary functions that benefit all of us. By creating those jobs, people will have money to purchase food, clothing, housing, and anything else that they need. All the small businesses will prosper from those new customers.

"I am just an old country Preacher remembering the Sermon on the Mount. 'Because ye have done it unto one of the least of these my brethren, ye have done it unto me.' Matthew 25:40

"Will, I know that you have a gift for influencing other people, and I look forward to watching you use that gift to make a permanent difference. The ideals set for our country are challenging, but are certainly worth fighting for."

The heated conversation had morphed into a quiet meditation.

The foursome was mostly silent for the rest of the ride.

***

Alice, Lenora, and the children warmly greeted the returning tourists who could sense the aroma of fresh bread in the Parker kitchen. At the insistence of Alice, they relaxed in the gathering room while Lenora helped her Mother with the evening meal.

Conversation around the table included all that Sally and John had seen in the city and then turned to the approaching holiday.

"Friday will be Christmas," Alice reminded everyone. "We always attend the candle lit Christmas Eve services and want you to join us on Thursday."

"We look forward to attending the historic Falls Church especially as we celebrate the birth of our Lord," John assured her. "Will has shared the fact that some of our Founding Fathers worshipped and served on the vestry."

***

On Christmas Eve, 1874, the Parkers and Presleys climbed into the carriage for the brief trip to Falls Church Episcopal Church.

The red door opened, and John and Sally felt an immediate sense of calm serenity. Something about the ubiquitous fog and shadows wafting from the flickering white tapers numbering at least one hundred, demanded bowed heads and lowered voices.

The liturgy of the service was slightly more formal than what John and Sally were accustomed to hearing in the Methodist Church; however, many sections were familiar, and they did not feel out of place in this welcoming group. The service ended with everyone kneeling as they sang *Silent Night*.

***

Ronnie and Randy were the first to rise on Christmas morning and pulled at Will and Lenora's coverlet to wake them. They had already grabbed Mimi's hand saying, "Get up, Lazy Bones, Christmas is here."

"Slow down, boys, we have a whole day to celebrate," Will laughed. "Give us a chance to open our eyes."

Lenora told them they should put on their clothes and get ready to go to Grandma and Grandpa's house for breakfast. "I'll get Mimi ready."

The breakfast was sumptuous as usual, but the boys were only interested in the tree. There were a few things peeking out from under the decorated limbs that had not been there last night, and some of them were in burlap bags tied with ribbons.

It was a significant display of self-discipline that allowed the three young children to remain at the table until the adults gave a signal that the meal had ended and that it was acceptable to move into the gathering room where the objects of their interest beckoned.

Sally and John had brought partially home-made gifts for the children from Graham. For Ronnie and Randy, there were two rolling hoops, two yo-yos, a whirl-gig, and a game of ninepins. For their sweet granddaughter, there was a set of chalk boards with chalk, building blocks, and a personalized doll on which Sally had embroidered Mimi.

***

The week between Christmas and New Year's Day gave Sally and John an opportunity to talk with Alice and Harry alone. They came to know and understand each other as only people of the same generation can. They talked about Will and Lenora. They talked about their grandchildren. They acknowledged that they might not have another chance to be together because of the distance.

Sally thanked Alice and Harry for embracing her son. "He was so lost when he decided to leave home, to abandon everything and everyone he knew and loved. I worried about him for so many years, not sure what had become of him.

"It was a most blessed day when he arrived in Roaring Fork with Lenora and the boys. I could see that he had found love, that he had a new family. I learned that he had made a new and better life for himself. I am so thankful to you for the way you have made him part of your family. I don't have to worry about him anymore."

"Sally, we love Will as if he were our son and we are very proud of him," Harry replied. "We only have one daughter, so we were protective, but your son won us over in no time. You raised him to be a gentleman and a scholar. He is always ready to learn. And you, John, were a significant influence on his thinking. He looks to you for moral leadership."

"Alice, I have a special favor to ask of you. I may never see my son again. Would you allow me to prepare one meal for him, a meal that will remind him of the old days in Roaring Fork?"

"Why, of course, Sally. I will help you in any way that I can. How about on New Year's Eve?"

"This is what I need, and you may already have most of it. I need cornmeal, beans, side meat, potatoes, mixed greens, apples, flour, and a couple of iron skillets."

"Yes, we have all of that. I'll get it together before Thursday. I will stay in the background and just follow your directions. This should be a great surprise and treat for Will."

***

On New Year's Eve, the family gathered at the Parker house, and Will thought he smelled a familiar aroma. When they sat down at the table, Sally passed bowls of beans, each topped with side meat, small plates piled with fried potatoes and seasoned greens. An enormous platter of skillet cornbread and a fresh apple pie were in the center of the table.

"This is just like Roaring Fork," Will smiled and kissed his mother on the cheek. "These Yankees don't know much about cornbread."

***

After the children fell asleep, the adults rang in the new year of 1875 with a cider toast and wished each other the best possible fortune.

***

On Monday, January 4, 1875, everyone excitedly climbed into the carriage and headed for the United States Capitol. There were assigned seats reserved for the families of Senators in the chamber.

All seventy-six of the new and returning Senators were seated at the front of the room. At exactly 12:00 noon, the Presiding Officer of the Senate rose to the podium and asked the Senators to rise, raise their right hands and repeat after him.

I do solemnly swear (or affirm) that I will support and defend the Constitution of the United States against all enemies, foreign and domestic; that I will bear true faith and allegiance to the same; that I take this obligation freely, with no mental reservation or purpose of evasion; and that I will well and faithfully discharge the duties of the office on which I am about to enter: So help me God.

Harry was holding the hands of both boys while Lenora held Mimi.

John placed his arm around Sally who was smiling with tears streaming down her cheeks.

"If only J.W. could see this. He would be bursting with pride to see a sharecropper's son, his Son, in the United States Senate."

Chapter Forty-Five

RECONSTRUCTION ENDS WITH A WHIMPER

When George Wilhelm Presley took his seat in the United States Senate, it had been almost ten years since he embarked on his mission, which, in his words was "fixing things that were broken."

During that ten years, he had matured exponentially. He had lost most of his rural naivete. He had married. He had become a father.

He had seen his efforts at creating new hope for the hopeless be considered evil acts of oppression by the losers of a war of sedition. He had seen hatred and bigotry result in senseless death and destruction.

He had changed his mountain accent enough to be accepted in polite urban society. He had learned to listen more than he talked and to talk in terms that appealed to his constituency's self-interest. He had made peace with the intricate art of compromise. He had vowed to be patient for the arc of justice to move, but to do everything in his power to push it forward.

The official legislative work of the Congress is usually a slow, plodding exercise composed of research, propositions, committee meetings, arguments, compromise, deal-making, rewriting, and waiting. Occasionally, the monotony is interrupted by a floor fight, or a protestor. Occasionally there will be a commemoration or a celebration blurring the lines between opposing parties.

During his first year as a new Senator, Will was witness to several exciting events.

On March 1, 1875, the United States Congress passed the Civil Rights Act prohibiting racial discrimination in public accommodations and jury duty. Will was proud to cast his vote in favor of this bill.

"Lenora, it seems to be the unfortunate reality that both legislation and enforcement are necessary to ensure any change in behavior." Will reflected with regret. "I may play a small part in the legislative piece, but it takes the executive branch at the State and Federal levels to enforce the laws."

"Don't tell me you are thinking of running for Governor or President." Lenora looked at him frowning. "No, Sweet Lady, I have already bitten off as much as I can chew."

Lenora had her hands full with active twin boys and a slightly clingy three-year-old girl. Ronnie and Randy were now nine years of age and doing well in the fourth grade. Mimi was very curious and enjoyed pretending she was reading from her brothers' textbooks.

In the small amount of time she had remaining, Lenora began to assist Harry with the farm's record keeping functions.

It was a good life with Will earning a Senator's salary and coming home almost every evening. He even had time to shadow his father-in-law in the oversight of farm management. "This will be your farm in the future, Son," Harry said as they walked the grounds. "I want to ensure that you understand what it takes to keep things going."

"Please don't be leaving me in charge anytime soon, Sir. I'm not ready for that, and I know Lenora and your grandchildren are not."

***

On November 22, 1875, Vice President Henry Wilson died from a stroke. The position remained empty until the next election.

The holidays were celebrated as usual, but Will remembered fondly the time spent with his mother and John the past year.

The next year was to be a significant celebration. The country would be celebrating its one-hundredth anniversary.

***

On May 10, 1876, the Parker/Presley family rode the train to Philadelphia, where they were among 186,272 attendees on the opening day of the Centennial International Exposition in Fairmount Park. With over 200 exhibits and countless displays, the Exposition was the first World's Fair to be held in the United States.

The family made reservations to spend two nights in Philadelphia returning by train on the 12th. Except for the trip from Memphis to Falls Church as infants and a trip to Roaring Fork at age two, the boys had never set foot out of northern Virginia. Mimi had even less exposure to the outside world.

Everything was an adventure for Ronnie and Randy. Sleeping in a hotel, eating in a restaurant, running through the elaborate displays, and trying out new products promoted such as popcorn and ketchup.

"Daddy, Daddy, can we have some of that white fluffy stuff? It smells so good." They begged, grabbing both pant legs.

Will agreed. "It does smell good, doesn't it? If it is alright with your mother, we'll get some."

Lenora smiled and nodded her assent. "I would like to know more about that red concoction they are calling ketchup."

"We can ask the man at the booth, I reckon."

"Excuse me, Sir, can you tell us a bit about your product? What is it made from, and what is it used for?"

"Step up folks and taste the novel sensation. People will be using it world-wide before long on almost anything they eat. It makes everything better. Try it on meat, eggs, potatoes, or use your imagination. Here, try this," he said as he handed Lenora a small bite of ham on a wooden toothpick. "Dip it in this cup of *ketchup.*"

"That is delicious, Will, try it," Lenora said. She licked her lips. "I'll have to take some to Mama. I bet she'll be using it on meatloaf or who knows what."

Little Mimi was dazzled by the crowds, colorful displays, sounds, and smells, but she clung tightly to the hand of Lenora or Alice and frequently asked to be held. Tugging on Lenora's skirt, Mimi said with an excited voice, "Mama, look, pretty blue, pretty red, on strings. Can Mimi have one?"

"Those are balloons, Mimi. Yes, you may have one."

Mimi grabbed the blue one and smiled broadly with a grin that resembled her father's.

Right Arm and Torch of
Proposed Statue of Liberty

Although they didn't fully understand the significance of the right arm and torch of the Statue of Liberty, the boys were impressed by the size. Ronnie asked, "Daddy, what is that?"

Lenora picked up a flyer explaining the significance. "It seems there is a plan to erect a colossal statue in the New York Harbor, celebrating Freedom and Liberty offered to all people who come to this country.

"It was a project begun by our friends in France in 1865 and was intended for installation this year. However, funding is still being sought to complete the venture. Look at this drawing of the final statue of Liberty Enlightening the World."

All three generations enjoyed the Exposition, each at their level of understanding. They marveled at Alexander Graham Bell's telephone and wondered when, if ever, they might have such a device.

Lenora was beguiled by the Sholes and Glidden typewriter, daydreaming about its usefulness in record keeping. She giggled when she first felt the bubbles of Hires Root Beer on her lips.

Harry pondered the possibilities of Kudzu being touted as a new miracle for the control of soil erosion.

All four adults had their imagination stimulated by the new mass-produced sewing machines, stoves, lanterns, guns, wagons, carriages, and agricultural equipment.

***

In June, the first transcontinental railroad train made its way from New York to San Francisco in eighty-three hours and thirty-nine minutes.

Also, in June, Rutherford B. Hayes was selected by the Republicans as their Presidential Candidate.

On July 4th, cities nationwide celebrated the country's birthday with a wide variety of festival activities. The Parkers and Presleys decided to spend the day at a picnic with fellow Virginians on the lawn of the Fairfax Courthouse, where Will had made his first significant political speech.

Will and Lenora made efforts to explain to their children in age-appropriate language why this year of 1876 was of particular importance.

They created abbreviated history lessons mixed with parables of their own, hoping that Ronnie, Randy, and Mimi would garner some sense of what their country's promise was all about, and why it was essential the work to achieve that promise continue.

"You can never be certain how much they hear and how much they understand what they hear," Lenora observed. "At the same time, we should never underestimate the depth of what they absorb from our actions as well as our words."

***

On November 7th, 1876, the presidential election ended indecisively with one hundred eighty-four Electoral College votes for Samuel J. Tilden, one hundred sixty-five for Rutherford B. Hayes, and twenty in dispute.

"How can that happen," Lenora asked Will the day after the election.

"It sounds complicated, Lenora, but our Presidential electoral system, as prescribed in the Constitution, is one of representative democracy rather than direct. That means that we elect people who vote for us. Each state has a certain number of electors. Most of their votes determine who wins the Presidency."

"Did our founders think we were not smart enough to vote for ourselves?"

"Good question, Lenora. The founders were mostly aristocrats and, had reservations about the educational level of the populace. So, as I understand it, this was their solution."

"Those representatives as a group are referred to as the Electoral College."

"So, what do you think will happen?"

"There is discussion of a compromise. Democrats will accept Hayes as President in return for the removal of federal troops from the south, granting the states home rule."

"What are you going to do, Will?"

"According to procedures detailed in the Constitution, a disputed Electoral College vote is to be resolved in the House of Representatives. That means I will not vote on that compromise.

"That sounds like another step backward. It means all we struggled for in the war, in Reconstruction, in enacting the 13th and 14th Amendments is being reduced to kind words on paper.

"If the southern states can just decide to ignore everything that has happened, the black folks won't be much better off than they were as slaves. Sure, the whites cannot legally own them, but they can make it impossible for them to live free lives. They will end up even less than my family was as indentured workers. At least we had a chance of buying some land."

"Oh, Will, I hate to see you so disappointed."

"I'm more than disappointed, Lenora. If I speak out and attempt to persuade others to vote against it, I will surely lose most of my friends in the House and the Senate.

"That means that my days may be numbered as a politician. I know what I have to do, and I know what I have to lose, but John reminded me it's better to lose people and position than to lose your soul."

***

On March 2, the Compromise of 1877 was accepted by the Commission's vote of eight to seven.

The U.S. presidential election of 1876 was resolved with the selection of Rutherford B. Hayes as the winner, even though Samuel J. Tilden had won the popular vote on November 7, 1876.

After almost four months, Rutherford B. Hayes was sworn privately as the 19th President of the United States.

Hayes received a public swearing ceremony on March 5.

The removal of federal troops from Louisiana and South Carolina effectively ended the Reconstruction Era and issued in the Jim Crow system.

Epilogue

I n sixteen years, the third son of an Irish immigrant sharecropper, who received only a primary education from his mother, the daughter of a tailor and seamstress, had made his way from a rural community in southwestern North Carolina to a seat in the Senate of the United States of America. The improbable journey began when his conscience would not allow him to join an army of rebellion against his country to preserve the rights of rich men to own poor men.

Because he chose a different path, his future was forever changed.

Those who experience the realities of war from an *up close and personal* point of view, especially in eras of almost hand-to-hand combat, can rarely put their memories behind them. Will Presley was not one of the rare fortunate ones.

The shock of discovering that his two older brothers had perished at his hands would forever remain his secret shame and burden. The rest of his life would be involuntarily dedicated to his atonement.

Will refused to concede defeat despite frequent disappointment and personal danger, always seeking an avenue of private penance through public or political programs.

"What are you going to do now?" Lenora asked Will as he sat pensively in their gathering room on March 2, 1877.

He looked at her without speaking for several minutes. "I reckon I'll continue to serve the remaining four years of my term as a Senator from Virginia. What do you mean, Lenora?"

"I mean that I know you, Will Presley. I know you are not going to give up. What do you think you can do to make a difference under the new circumstances?"

"What does anyone do when faced with defeat? Even in the darkest moments, we all choose how we react to the new reality."

"The new reality? Tell me what you see. Tell me what you are thinking of doing."

"What I see coming is not pretty, Lenora. You and I witnessed what anger and resentment can do to people when we were in Memphis.

"We saw clearly that others viewed the world differently than we did. We were visualizing a better world in the aftermath of a senseless war, including everyone, while others perceived only their potential loss of status and control.

"I am fearful that much of the south will try everything possible to turn back the clock. With the removal of federal troops and the agreement to allow home rule in the states, there is little to stop local officials from setting up roadblocks to prevent freed black people from achieving anything like equality."

"But Will, they cannot take away what people fought and died for, can they? Can they not take away the rights that were earned in the13th, 14th, and 15th Amendments?"

"Not legally, but without enforcement, many people will try to play tricks that effectively render those rights meaningless.

"We must be on guard against believing that progress is permanent; it isn't. It can be reversed if the wrong people are in power.

"I have heard rumors of local rules; that may be enacted to prevent black men from voting. Some white men, right here in the State of Virginia, are terrified that allowing black people to vote will eventually change the power structure.

"These folks have been upset about the election of black men to the State Assembly for some time, and they are thinking of ways to discourage that trend."

"Why are people afraid of other people who look different from them?" Lenora said.

"That, my Sweet Lady, is a profound question. I am not an educated man, I'm not a historian, a theologian, or even a country philosopher, but I can tell you what I believe over my forty, almost forty-one years on this earth.

"We folks of the human variety are not perfect. The good Lord may have intended us to be, but he made the mistake of giving us free will.

"Now some Preachers will tell you that all our problems come from our original sin way back in the Garden. I can't explain that with absolute certainty, but it looks like part of that sin was always wanting more, even when we have what we need.

"Some say that Greed is only one of the deadly sins, but by itself, it creates constant stress and friction among people over property and other resources. Pride is close to the top in the fatal sin category, and we see that every day with people feeling that they are better than someone else.

"Preacher Henderson told me long ago that we are all God's People. I believed that then and could not support slavery. I still believe that now, and I cannot support limiting civil rights to any group of people regardless of their skin color, gender, education, family, or wealth.

"Our Founding Fathers, who were also human, and not perfect, were inspired to write the words:

We hold these truths to be self-evident that all men are created equal, that they are endowed by their Creator with certain unalienable Rights, among these are Life, Liberty, and the Pursuit of Happiness.

"I believe that our country was founded on a dream that we will always fall short of reaching. The United States of America is not only a place, it is a noble idea. It is a cause worth holding in our hearts and worth fighting for if necessary."

"Will, you are a leader even though you came to it reluctantly. I am so proud to be your wife and that you are the father of our children. I want to help you in any way I can as you move forward."

"Thank you, my Darling. I don't know what I would do without having you by my side. To answer your second question, to be honest, I do not know what my next step should be.

"We each have a limited time on this earth, and we have choices how we use that time. I refuse to choose to withdraw from the world or live in constant anger about the state of things.

"I choose instead to use much of my time to help raise our children to be thoughtful, loving, contributing members of society. With you as their mother, they will have a stable foundation.

"I choose to use the rest of my time to, hopefully, influence some people to make the ideals of our founders and the great commandments of our Lord the centerpieces of future social and legal actions.

"If we, as a people, truly believed in the unalienable rights, and if we loved our neighbor as ourselves, our political decisions would lead us in the right direction for our children, grandchildren, and the future of our beloved country.

"I choose to believe both principles and act accordingly."

If you enjoyed reading this book, please write an Amazon review and share your thoughts with others. Click here

https://www.amazon.com/dp/B08M149DWL#customerReviews

Acknowledgments

We are indebted to many organizations and sources for the historical information that provided the background for our story. At a personal level, we have found the process to be both educational and emotional.

Making our way through the Post Civil War period, we discovered, unfortunately, many issues and happenings that could be current day news. The old maxim about what happens if we do not know history, seems truly relevant.

We are grateful to:
Sylvia Sheh for her beautiful cover design and interior formatting
Our Beta readers for their time and feedback
Lucy Maples
Robert and Kay Terrell

The Library of Congress - photos and drawings
National Archives - photos and drawings
Wikipedia and other internet historical information

About The Authors

Ron and Nancy

Ronald E. Pressley, a native of Knoxville, TN, is retired from a bi-vocational career in Sales and Church Music. He and Nancy Holder Preessley have now co-authored three books of historical fiction.

Ron began his retirement writing efforts with his Memoir, Straight Outta Lonsdale—Memoirs of a Working-Class Family, in2017. He produced an anthology of stories at his friends' requests, Straight Outta Lonsdale II - Voices from Lonsdale, in 2018.

In 2019, he and Nancy published the first book in their series, Blood Brothers-A Family Divided.

The sequel, Blood Brothers II-Reconstruction, Racism, Riots, Ratification, was completed during the Pandemic of 2020.

The third book in the series takes the Prodigal Son of the Presley family through the Jim Crow era and the Gilded Age.
Look for the continuing story in 2021.

Nancy P. Holder emigrated from her birthplace of Washington, D.C., to attend college and spend most of her adult life in East Tennessee. She retired from a long career that morphed from social work to human resources consulting.

Like her writing partner, Nancy began with her own story, The Fourth Quarter—Reflections of a Septuagenarian, published in 2018.

While collaborating with Ron, Nancy has continued to write essays and poems, which may be found on her blog, Beltway Baby, hosted on their website at www.1122creations.com.

Together, they found the research required to write a historical novel illuminating and developing characters and placing them in the period fascinating.

They came to think of J.W., Sally, John, Will, Lenora, and others as real people. They laughed and cried with them on their journeys. That is the experience they hope for their readers.

Nancy's book and all the team's books are available on Amazon in both printed and digital form.

You   may   contact   Ronald   and   Nancy   - ronaldpressley12@gmail.com

nancypholder@gmail.com

www.ingramcontent.com/pod-product-compliance
Lightning Source LLC
Chambersburg PA
CBHW020827260626
47169CB00003B/861